Adeline Sergeant

The Lady Charlotte

A novel

Adeline Sergeant

The Lady Charlotte
A novel

ISBN/EAN: 9783337027261

Printed in Europe, USA, Canada, Australia, Japan

Cover: Foto ©Andreas Hilbeck / pixelio.de

More available books at **www.hansebooks.com**

THE

LADY CHARLOTTE

A Novel.

BY

ADELINE SERGEANT,

AUTHOR OF

"Jacobi's Wife," "Deveril's Diamond," "Brooke's Daughter,"
"Winifred's Wooing," "Seventy Times Seven," "No
Saint," "The Mistress of Quest," "The
Story of a Penitent Soul."

———

CHICAGO AND NEW YORK:
RAND, McNALLY & COMPANY,
PUBLISHERS.

THE LADY CHARLOTTE.

CHAPTER I.

COUSINS.

"You seem to have made yourself pretty snug down here!" said Arthur Ellison, stretching his limbs comfortably over the chintz-covered sofa, and settling his fair head into the solitary cushion with which his cousin had provided him.

"Why shouldn't I?" said Esther, a little sharply, as if she discerned a possible reproach in the words.

"No reason in the world. I may smoke, I suppose?"

And without waiting for her consent, he exerted himself so far as to extract a cigarette from a silver case, and to light it with a fusee which diffused a pleasant aromatic odor through the room. Esther watched him silently, with a doubtful look. When the cigarette was well alight between his lips, he laid his left arm behind his head, and surveyed the apartment with an air of quizzical satisfaction.

It was a fair-sized room, but with a low ceiling, across which ran a broad whitewashed beam; the casement windows had diamond panes, and evidently

opened into a garden, for sprays of jessamine and rose
seemed to be trying to force their way across the low
wooden sill.   It had, to some eyes, a rustic, old-fashioned charm, emphasized by the wooden paneling and
rudely carved mantel-piece, now dark with age; by the
red tiles of the floor, where the carpet left them ex-
posed, and the gleaming brass of the high fender.
There were quaint old engravings on the walls, in
black frames, and some curious and rather valuable
china on the mantel-shelf.   Fortunately, the farmer's
wife to whom the room belonged had not modified its
general aspect of old-world simplicity by any attempt
at modern fashions; and the utmost that Miss Ellison,
her lodger, had done by way of alteration was to hide
some faded upholstery with loose chintz covers of
artistic design, and to fill every available jug, vase and
basin with flowers and leaves and grasses of all kinds.
When she had arranged her books on a side-table,
and stacked her papers neatly on each side of the
great inkstand, Esther felt that the room left nothing
to be desired.

Esther Ellison's face and figure were not out of
place, even in this rustic environment, although she
knew less of the country than of the town.   One could
imagine that she would be by nature a lover of out-
door things, of trees and flowers, birds and beasts.
She was not very tall, but she was lithe and strong,
and her movements had the quick alertness of some
wild creature rather than the more languid grace of a
town-bred girl.   She had a grace of her own, but to
the trained eye, it was too unconventional; it had

the swiftness of the swallow's flight, the aloofness of the untamable woodland bird. Her complexion was as brown as a gypsy's, melting into a rich crimson in the cheeks, intensified by the deeper red of her curved mouth with its rather pouting lips; her eyes were dark and brilliant, between two rows of curling black lashes; her hair, cut short and slightly parted on one side, like a boy's, curled all over her small and prettily-shaped head. There were dimples in her cheek and chin which seemed, somehow, to match the sparkle in her eyes; but there was none of the plumpness which one might have expected with the physique that she possessed; indeed, she was quite too thin for beauty, and the little nervous brown hands which were clasped before her on the table, were undeniably claw-like. Her face, her figure, her usual attitude, expressed vivacity and eagerness amounting to passion; she could be brilliantly handsome and attractive at times, but she could also sink into absolute insignificance. When she lost her color and her eyes were dim and her small features at rest, she was merely a little plain brown person with a clever look, a shabby frock, and an appearance of age not justified by her three and twenty years. She depended on her health, her spirits, and her surroundings for her good looks.

Arthur Ellison knew this very well, and commented on it to himself as he lay and looked at her and at the room. The rustic background set her off very well, he thought approvingly. Esther's dark head and vivid coloring were finely relieved against the yellow-brown of the paneled wall. It was a pity that she sometimes

lost her color when she was in London. The country
air suited her better.

He said so aloud.

"Why?" Esther asked immediately.

"Does it need saying? Your eyes are bright and
your color is good: two things which show that you
are happy and prosperous."

"Is it not time that I was prosperous after the years
of hard work I have had?"

Arthur shrugged his shoulders. "Prosperity does
not always follow on toil," he remarked sententiously.
"Look at me."

"I do look at you," said Esther laughing. "And
I observe no special signs of toil about you."

She laughed, though with some reserve of manner,
as though she thought more than she meant to say;
but Arthur remained grave. He altered his position, bringing his feet to the floor and resting his
head on one hand while he kept his eyes on his brown
boots as though in profound meditation concerning
their shape and color. During the short silence that
followed, Esther observed him keenly, and somewhat
furtively. There was a touch of anxiety in the knit
of her eyebrows and the set of her red lips.

He was not in her eyes an unpleasing specimen of
humanity to contemplate, but he could not be called
a handsome man. He was rather under middle-height,
and slightly built; his hair and skin were fair, and
his eyes a brilliant but somewhat chilly blue. The at-
tractiveness of his appearance consisted chiefly in the
refinement and intelligence of his face; his features

were clearly and delicately cut, and denoted intellect
above the average. But it was not a strong face, and
it was undeniably a cold one; thereby differing in es-
sentials from that of Esther which expressed warmth,
perhaps, first of all, and strength next.

Unlike as they might be, they were first cousins
and had been brought up together, until, as their
friends and they themselves averred, they were more
like brother and sister than cousins. At seventeen
and one and twenty respectively, they fell in love with
each other, were engaged, and fell out again with
remarkable rapidity; the engagement was dissolved,
but the habit of comradeship only interrupted and
never broken. For a time, however, they saw little
of each other. They were alone in the world, and
had nobody to interfere with them. Arthur came up
to London and plunged into journalism and desultory,
and rather Bohemian, literary life; Esther, whose passion was for learning, managed to get a scholarship
at a woman's college, and by means of it and by the
expenditure of her very small patrimony, secured four
years of residence at Oxford. She was almost penniless when she left it, but she had secured a first-class
in History, had excellent testimonials, and was con-
fident of her powers of earning her own living. But
she was not quite sure whether she could earn a living
for Arthur as well as for herself; yet it sometimes
seemed to her as if he half expected her to do so.

Well, she was willing to do what she could for him;
a woman is always tender to the man whom she even
fancies that she has loved; and Esther was no excep-

tion to the rule. Only sometimes she thought that
Arthur took her sisterly affection a trifle too much
for granted. And when he began to talk about her
"prosperity," she shrank a little as if she knew that
she was about to be hurt.

"It is strange," he said presently in a reflective tone,
"strange to think how seldom prosperity comes to
men of real genius. Perhaps poverty and ill-success
should be accepted as signs of merit, after all. The
greatest men have lived in a garret."

"A garret isn't a bad place sometimes," said Esther.
"Are you working very hard just now, Arthur?"

"Of course I work hard," he answered, resenting
the question. "But, as you know, the work that the
world might some day value is exactly the work that
doesn't pay. The work that pays is the miserable,
degrading routine of journalism——"

"I think it may be very fine work," said Esther, with
kindling eyes.

"What do you know of it? What do you know of
modern daily life at all?" he said, with weary scorn.
"You have lived like a Sybarite—immersed in luxury
and lapt in dreams—first in academic Oxford"— he
always sneered when he spoke of Oxford —"now, in
the most delightful part of Surrey, with a little easy
coaching to do up at a grand house—oh, yes, my
dear Esther, you have always fallen on your feet."

"Have I, indeed?" said his cousin indignantly. "And
do you remember those three years before I got my
scholarship?—how I drudged as a nursery-governess,
or earned a few shillings a week by addressing en-

velopes, while I was working up for Oxford? Do you
think it was even easy for me at College, when I
couldn't afford to be properly coached, couldn't dress
like other girls, couldn't allow myself one scrap of
rest or recreation? Oh, Arthur, you forget."

"No, I do not forget. But I remember that it was
all done to carry out your pet project, your one idea.
It is always so with you, Esther; you set your heart
upon one object, and I believe you would sacrifice
your dearest friend if he stood in the way."

"I sacrificed no one then," said the girl, her dark
eyes flashing fire.

He moved his hand negligently. "Oh, no," he answered in a half-hearted way. "I don't mean to say
that you did. You worked well for yourself, that was
all. I have often wished I had your chances; the few
hundreds your father left you would have made a
tremendous difference to me."

"I offered to divide them with you, Arthur, and you
refused to take anything."

"Say rather," said the young man coolly, "that you
threw me over and made it impossible for me to take
a gift from you."

It sounded well, but Esther knit her brows over the
remembrance of the many gifts that she could ill afford
which he had taken from her during the last few
years.

"Oh, Arthur, don't let us quarrel!" she said thrust-
ing back the ugly thought. "I was so pleased when
I saw you this morning; I didn't think that we should
begin to discuss unpleasant things so soon."

"We won't, then," said Arthur, starting to his feet, not unmoved by the tears in those brilliant eyes. "I did not mean to be disagreeable either. I was in a bad temper when I started, I suppose; I had a manuscript returned this morning. That's enough to sour any man for the day. Isn't it, little one?"

He put his hand on her shoulder as he spoke, in a caressing, fraternal way. Esther put her fingers over it and held it silently for a minute or two. She had to get rid of the tears on her cheek before she could venture to open her mouth. She was sometimes very meek with this cousin of hers—this man whom she had ceased to love, yet blamed herself for not loving.

"I am so sorry," she said at last in a perfectly natural tone. "What manuscript was it, Arthur? The novel?"

"No; a short story; I counted on it. I thought I was safe to get ten pounds. I'm stone broke now. What a thing it is to be poor!"

"I have got ten that I can spare," said Esther eagerly. "Take it and pay me back when your story is accepted, Arthur. Really, I don't want it."

"No, no; I won't do that. I shall get the money some other way. Never mind about me. You've told me no news of yourself yet, Esther. I scarcely saw you when you passed through London."

"I had no time," said Esther, quite restored to brightness by this time and smiling upon him gayly; "and I wrote you a long letter, but I daresay you never read it. Sit down again comfortably and light another cigarette. We shall be having tea directly and then we can go for a stroll."

He did not move away from her side at once, although he disengaged his hand from hers and began turning over the papers on the table with all the freedom of a brother.

"What are these?" he said. "Exercises?"

"Papers for me to correct. My pupil's papers, you know."

"This isn't a child's writing, is it?"

"My pupil is not a child. Miss Daubeny is twenty-one."

"What does she want a governess for, then?"

"Oh, Arthur, don't be so hopelessly retrograde. She did not want a governess. I am not a governess. I am a coach. I have coached her since Easter."

"I know you are an awful swell at history; but do you know anything else?" said Arthur in a rallying tone.

"I hope I do. But she has a special fancy for history, as it happens, and she means to take it up when she goes to College. She has persuaded her uncle and aunt to let her go to Oxford."

"Ye gods!" ejaculated Mr. Ellison. "Will wonders never end? A wealthy well-born young woman (she is that, isn't she?) with no need to earn a living for herself as teacher or journalist, to throw over a pleasant, easy-going country life in favor of a woman's college. It must be your doing, Esther!"

"So Lady Charlotte says," remarked Esther rather dismally. "But I have done nothing. I talked of my own experiences, that was all. But they seem to have fascinated Lisa."

"Lisa? Is her name Lisa?"

"Yes; do you like the name?"

"It isn't a happy name," said Arthur in a lazy, fantastic way that was peculiar to him at times. "You remember that heart-rending book of Tourgenieff's? 'Lisa' it is called in the French translation. Ever since then, any woman called Lisa is bound to be miserable."

"Oh, don't say so; it sounds like an evil omen."

"Omens hang around the name. Your friend is doomed to an evil fate and a melancholy end."

"Arthur, don't! I am not superstitious, but your prognostications are not pleasant."

Arthur laughed and turned over the papers again. "If you are not superstitious, my dear, you are wonderfully sensitive. What's this flaming circular thing, with Lady Charlotte Byng's name on it in big red letters? Oh, I see, a flower show 'will be opened at three o'clock precisely by the Lady Charlotte Byng.' And who's the Lady Charlotte Byng? I seem to know her name."

"Of course you do. The Byngs are the people who have Westhills, the house that I visit every morning. Miss Daubeny is their niece. And Lady Charlotte is a very well-known woman; she was the daughter of the Marchioness of Muncaster."

"You don't say so!" said Arthur, recalling with interest a name which had once had a European fame

and influence; the name of a woman as beautiful as
she was witty, who had possessed the confidence of
a monarch, the friendship of the greatest men and
women of her day. She was dead now, but her memory survived, and Lady Charlotte, her only surviving
daughter, had inherited a fair share of her mother's
talent, and also the prestige of her mother's name.
To be one of Lady Muncaster's daughters had always
proved an introduction in itself to the greatest of
great worlds.

"Which side is Miss Daubeny on?" he asked with
some curiosity. "If she is Mr. Byng's niece I shall
not be surprised that she should be allowed to make
a New Woman of herself. I can't fancy Lady Muncaster's granddaughter being allowed to go to college."

"You completely mistake the position of women
at our colleges, Arthur," said his cousin with severity.
"There are members of the highest classes——"

"Yes, yes; I know all that! At the same time I
stick to it—Lady Muncaster's granddaughter wouldn't
have gone to college. She would have been a beauty
for one thing, and beauties don't give their mind to
books."

"Lisa Daubeny is very beautiful," said Esther.
"And unfortunately for your theories, she is Lady
Charlotte's own niece."

"I'm more interested in the aunt. What is she
like? Handsome, I suppose, like all the Blundell family," said Arthur, surrendering the question of Miss
Daubeny's position.

"She has been splendidly handsome. She is good-looking now, but of course she must be nearly fifty."

"Has she no children?"

"None. Lisa lives with them and——"

"She'll be the heiress, I suppose. I remember hearing that Byng was a wealthy man."

"Yes." Esther hesitated a little. "They will give her a dowry. But there is a cousin in whose career they are very much interested. I have a fancy that Westhills will go to him."

"By Jove!" said Arthur enviously. "What luck some men have!"

Then after a pause:

"Who is this cousin?"

"A Mr. Thorold—Justin Thorold, member for Plowborough."

"Married?"

"No," said Esther with some reluctance. There was a deeper crimson on her cheeks than usual, and a lowering of her eyelids that might have excited her cousin's interest had his thoughts not been centered elsewhere.

"Then, I suppose," he said, "they mean to marry Miss Daubeny to Thorold. It's a very evident arrangement. The college scheme will fall through, Esther. Make the most of your time."

Esther rose abruptly and began to gather her papers together and file them upon the side table. Thus engaged she turned her back upon Arthur, and he couldn't see the expression of her face. The maid-servant brought in the tea, and conversation was interrupted for a time. But as Arthur drank his third cup—he was an inveterate tea-drinker—he recurred to the subject of the family at Westhills.

"Lady Charlotte's by way of being a literary woman, isn't she?"

"She writes books, yes. She loves literary people and artistic people—clever people of all kinds. She cares for so many things that I never know which she likes best. She paints, carves, writes; she has traveled in all parts of the world, and speaks every language under the sun; she is an admirable landscape gardener and a very successful farmer."

"Spare my feelings!" ejaculated Arthur. "What else?"

"Oh, everything else. I can't enumerate all her capabilities. She is a most remarkable woman. She can ride and row, and I hear she is a first-rate shot."

"I should think she has not much time for family affection," said the young man slowly.

"I have never heard her blamed for want of it."

"What a Jesuitical answer! I say, Esther, don't you think your incomparable Lady Charlotte might give me a helping hand?"

Esther looked up at him quickly, a momentary suspicion in her dark eyes. But Arthur met her glance so frankly that she was disarmed.

"She must know lots of people. Somebody might want a secretary. I should like a secretaryship much better than a berth on an evening paper, which is all I have in prospect at present."

2

"Have you that in prospect? Something permanent? I am very glad."

The young man flushed with vexation.

"You used to be more sympathetic," he said peev-
ishly. "What is the use of me wasting my time as
a sub on a half-penny paper when I might be making
my way in the world elsewhere. As a private secretary I might see something of society; I might make
friends who would be useful to me. You never use
your opportunities in that way."

"I'll mention your name to Lady Charlotte if you
like, Arthur."

"It would be better if I could make her acquaintance myself," said Arthur ungratefully.

There was a little silence, and then he said with a
laugh:

"I've hit it. You shall introduce me to your Lady
Charlotte."

"I would if I could; but I don't see how."

"But I see perfectly well. I'll run up to London for
my traps and stay here with you for a few weeks. I
daresay there's a room to let in the house, isn't there?"

"Yes; but, Arthur—I don't want to seem absurd
and conventional—but—the Byngs are very correct
and particular; and I don't think they would think
it a right thing for you to be here with me. I am
quite sure they wouldn't let Lisa, Miss Daubeny, come
to tea with me without a chaperon if you were on the
premises."

"Ridiculous!" said Arthur; but he paused and considered the matter. "Oh, well, there's one way out

of the difficulty—as regards yourself, I mean. You have only to say that I am your brother, and nobody will make the slightest objection."

Esther laughed at the idea.

CHAPTER II.

MISS ELLISON'S BROTHER.

"May I ask what you are doing in my garden, sir?" said Lady Charlotte, in tones expressive of deep wrath and deeper disdain.

She looked like a Juno, Arthur thought, as he rose from his seat on a low stone parapet, and bowed to the stately figure before him. At a glance he recognized the truth of Esther's description, but he amended it. Not only had Lady Charlotte been "splendidly handsome," but she was splendidly handsome now. After all, she was not yet fifty; and although she looked her age, he could not call her old.

She was a tall woman, with a fine figure, loosely clad in a flowing dark gown—he was not sure at first whether it was purple or black, but he vaguely surmised it to be the royal color—which seemed to fall of itself into folds of antique grace and beauty. It occurred afterwards to Arthur's somewhat sophisticated mind that the folds were due to the art of a first-rate dressmaker, and not attributable to Lady Charlotte; but at the moment he could not help admiring their perfect lines, as if they were part of the wearer's individuality instead of a modiste's triumph. There was a fine old silver clasp at her waist and an antique coin, set as a brooch, at her throat; her rather large but beautifully moulded hands were adorned with three curious and ancient rings; but she wore no other ornaments. Lady Charlotte abhorred modern jewelry.

Her thick, dark hair, with the wide wave in it which suggested the classic heads of antiquity, was parted in the middle, brought down loosely on each side, almost over the ears, and coiled in a big loose knot on the nape of her neck. It was not just then a fashionable way of dressing the hair, but it suited the style of Lady Charlotte's fine head and face. Her complexion was pale, the skin slightly olive in tone. The forehead was low and broad, the beautifully-cut mouth rather too large, the high nose and square chin well-shaped but too salient. It was the look of the eyes—dark, passionate eyes, full of life and vigor—with the beautiful stormy brows above them, that excited Arthur's most ardent admiration. "One could understand the writing of a sonnet to one's mistress's eyebrows, with eyebrows like these," he murmured to himself. And later he found out that he was not the only admirer. A good many rhapsodies had been penned, at one time or another, on the subject of Lady Charlotte's beautiful brows. They had a superb arch, a delicate darkness, an expressiveness, unequaled in the annals of contemporary beauty. They almost deserved a place in history.

Her appearance, taken altogether, was imposing, and her voice added to its awe-inspiring effect. It was a very deep, mellow contralto, not loud, but capable, as one could imagine, of a tremendous volume of sound. If she had taken to singing, it had been said, she would have taken the world by storm. But she was not musical. As she would frankly tell you, she could not sing a note.

But she could, on occasion, thunder forth her wrath or indignation with perfectly appalling force. The magnificent tones, the lightning fire of her eyes, the darkness of her stormy brows, were all concentrated for the moment upon Arthur Ellison, whom she had discovered sitting on the parapet of a grassy terrace overlooking a flower garden of which she was particularly fond. Lady Charlotte hated intruders, and this garden was her own especial private property, planned by herself, in which she grew her favorite flowers and tried experiments with imported plants. From the terrace, or grassy plateau above it, a splendid view of the surrounding country could be obtained, and thence a flight of steps led to the garden, which was situated at a stone's throw from the house and was inclosed by stone walls covered with climbing plants. The garden and the terrace were, in fact, copied from an old Italian model, and Lady Charlotte was justly proud of them. But that a stranger should have penetrated to her pet spot and should, without permission, be making a sketch of Westhills, was an outrage not often perpetrated.

Arthur rose quickly, and took off his hat, bowing with an easy grace which, even in that moment of wrath, Lady Charlotte was quick to appreciate.

"I offer my most humble apologies," he said. "I will go at once. My sister left me in the avenue to await her return from the house, and I must confess

that I caught sight of the terrace and was tempted
to turn aside. My intrusion was quite unpardonable—
but easy to understand." He threw a regretful glance
around him as though the beauty of the spot were
hard indeed to leave.

"Your sister? Who is your sister?" said Lady Charlotte abruptly. "And why didn't you come up to the
house with her?"

"My sister, madam," said Arthur deferentially—his
instinct told him that she would approve of almost any
amount of deference—"my sister is Esther Ellison,
who is, I believe, reading with Miss Daubeny!"

A change came over the dark face—such a change
as is seen when a thunder-cloud breaks to let the sunshine through.

"What, are you Miss Ellison's brother? Why didn't
she introduce you? I am pleased to make your acquaintance, Mr. Ellison," said Lady Charlotte, passing
at once from brusque severity to the dignified courtesy of a *grande dame de par le monde.* "You must
excuse my surprise"—one might have used a harsher
term, thought Arthur, suppressing some amusement—
"but I have been so pestered with tourists and prying
cockneys who wanted to make the park into a picnic
ground, that I have grown suspicious of strangers.
But any relative of Miss Ellison's is welcome. We
are all very fond of Miss Ellison down here."

"You are very kind," said Arthur. "But I must
apologize again for intruding."

"Not at all. You were waiting for your sister in the
avenue? Ah, yes, I know one gets a tempting peep

of the terrace down that side-path. I hardly wonder
you were allured. You see," said Lady Charlotte,
yielding promptly to the opening for pointing out the
beauties of the place, "there is no spot more favorable
than this for a view of the district. Look beyond the
garden—you get the whole sweep of the country,
heath, common, river, wood, and blue hills beyond
that. It was a bit of waste ground when I came here
first. I turned it into a terrace, and laid out the garden on the slope below. If you have ever been in
Italy, you will observe that I have tried to copy the
plan of an old Italian garden—only the cypresses and
lemon-trees have poor substitutes in my yews and
fuchsia plants. There's a real *pergola* on each side
of the garden, however, covered with vines. I don't
see why vines should not flourish in Surrey now as
they used to do."

Arthur's journalistic training came to his aid. A
thorough townsman, he had little practical knowledge
of gardening or fruit-growing, but he suddenly remembered a few facts relating to the bunches of grapes
grown in the garden of the Archbishop of Canterbury
in olden time. He had no hesitation in boldly offering
the information at his command.

"That's very interesting," said Lady Charlotte, fixing her dark eyes upon him with an air of utter ab-
sorption of soul in what he was saying. "I had the
Archbishop himself here the other day; I don't believe
he knew of his predecessor's achievement. I'll ask him
if he grows grapes at Addington."

"They could not be sour, at any rate," said Arthur.
"Those would be left for the inferior clergy."

Lady Charlotte laughed and eyed him narrowly. "You mustn't say that to the Archbishop, you know," she said.

"I won't, if I ever meet him."

"I am sure he would be delighted to know you, if you are so well up in the details of the Middle Ages," said Lady Charlotte. "You are like your sister, perhaps; she has a passion for the Middle Ages."

"I prefer my own," said Arthur.

"Ah, well, I like the last century. It's particularly interesting to me—perhaps because my forefathers were mixed up in the history of it a good deal. We are connected with the Stanhopes, you will remember. I've often wished I had been born a Stanhope instead of a Daubeny. Pitt's my hero, and next to him Napoleon. We have a great many original letters and documents up at the house, relating to people of that time—the end of the eighteenth century, the beginning of the nineteenth. Your sister has been a good deal interested in them; perhaps you would like to look over the collection some day?"

Arthur dropped his eyelids a little, so that she should not see the flash of pleasure in his eyes. He had got what he wanted—an invitation to Westhills.

"Thank you very much, Lady Charlotte, I think?" he said, hesitating a little before the name.

"Lord, what a fool I am!" said Lady Charlotte. "Of course you do not know me. I am Lady Charlotte Byng, if we are to introduce ourselves; and you are—?"

"Arthur Ellison, at your service."

"Arthur Ellison? A pretty name, Arthur; but you're not much like your sister in appearance, are you, Mr. Ellison? I should never have imagined you to be the gypsy's brother. We call her the gypsy among ourselves. She's curiously like the Romany type."

"We are of different mothers," said Arthur, hoping that Esther would bear him out in his statement. It wasn't all a lie, he reflected. Different mothers, certainly; as to fathers, that was another matter.

"Ah, so I should have thought. Are you an artist?"

"No, indeed. I sketch only for my own amusement. I am that miserable object, a literary hack."

"Literature is a fine profession," said Lady Charlotte seriously. "I am not sure that it isn't the finest profession in the world, although my family have gone in rather for statesmanship. And you draw for your own pleasure? I have sketched a good deal myself, especially when I was in the East. Will you allow me to see your sketch?"

The fascination of her manner, when it dropped suddenly from sharpness or brusquerie into consideration and courtesy, was irresistible. Even Arthur Ellison, who, like most young men of the day, thought no woman worth looking at after she was five and twenty, was positively startled by her beauty and her charm. He was almost ashamed of the poor little sketch which he was obliged to submit to her criticism; and he was not easily ashamed of his own productions.

Lady Charlotte looked at it keenly, looked up at the house which it represented, and nodded.

"You don't mind my saying it is amateurish, do you?" she inquired. "The fact is you have chosen a peculiarly difficult point of view, as beginners often do. I pointed it out to the President once when he was down here, and he shrugged his shoulders and said it was too difficult for him. So you see!"

"It is worth nothing—a scribble," said Arthur, somewhat abashed. "Do let me tear it up."

"No, no," said Lady Charlotte, in an encouraging tone. "It isn't so very bad. Here, give me your pencil a minute; I won't spoil it!" And to the young man's amaze, she seated herself calmly on the low stone wall, and began to add emphatic touches to his sketch. "Here you want a dark line—here the perspective is a little odd; that tree doesn't come so far forward—you have missed the architectural effect"— and so on for a few minutes; until she handed him back the sketch-book with the result that his feeble little sketch had by a few masterly strokes been transformed into a charming little drawing of the picturesque old house of Westhills, as seen from the terrace wall.

Arthur took it and thanked the lady profusely, but his countenance, in spite of himself, betrayed so much mortification that Lady Charlotte felt bound to be doubly kind to him. "And now that I've spoiled your sketch, for which you will hate me," she said good-humoredly, "you may as well come up to the house and have a cup of tea. I know my niece wanted to detain your sister this afternoon, and so we can set her mind at ease."

They walked on together, Lady Charlotte's violet

gown rustling in the breeze. "You must have studied
art closely," said Arthur at last, having nothing else
to say.

"No. I only took a few lessons once from Julian in
Paris," said Lady Charlotte carelessly. "But, I've
heard about art all my life, you see. My mother was
fond of artists, and they came about the house a good
deal. I know by this time what a good point of view
is and what is not. Sir Frederick said that the point
you chose was impossible. But, I'll show you what
he did for me instead. I think you'll admit I gained
by the change of subject."

Arthur fell to musing on Lady Charlotte's famili-
arity with the great men of the day, and was recalled
to himself only by her next question, which struck him
with dismay. "Did the old chronicler of whom you
spoke mention any particular dressing for the soil in
which the vines were grown?"

Arthur did not know, but his ignorance did not put
an end to the topic, for Lady Charlotte descanted on the
virtues of liquid manures all the way up the drive and
to the very door. Her listener was conscious of a
mental stupefaction, from which he did not recover
until he stood within the fine old entrance hall of the
house, and began to observe the suits of inlaid armor
on the walls, the statues peeping out from bowers of
palms, the oaken beams of the roof, the painted escut-
cheons in the windows, and the wild beast skins
upon the tesselated floor. Very little of the house was
really old: one tower and a few rooms opening on the
court-yard were of undoubted antiquity; but the rest

of the really magnificent building had been erected by Mr. Byng's wealth from Lady Charlotte's own designs. Arthur had no futile yearnings after antiquity, and said to himself that he infinitely preferred a new and comfortable mansion, with all the recent improvements, to a half-ruined keep or a castle in imperfect repair.

"We have tea in the hall generally," said Lady Charlotte, touching an electric bell with one hand and indicating a chair to her visitor with the other "Sit down, Mr. Ellison—tea, Andrews—I want to show you the President's sketch—and, Andrews, ask Miss Daubeny and Miss Ellison to come down as soon as they are ready. There's the sketch; I daresay you will see it reproduced in the Academy next year."

Lady Charlotte held out a drawing in crayons—roughly done, perhaps, but with the roughness of a master's hand. It was a lovely head in profile, the lips slightly parted, the eyes raised and there was a spiritualized expression upon the features which seemed to Arthur Ellison to be too beautiful to be perfectly natural or true. Underneath it was scored the name—"Lisa," and the great artist's initials and a date were added in the corner.

"How beautiful!"

"Yes. Everyone says so. I think it is flattered, perhaps," said Lady Charlotte, in a tone of secret complacency, "but I am not the best judge, as I know my niece's face so well."

"And are very fond of her," Arthur supplemented silently. He thought Esther had thrown doubt on the strength of Lady Charlotte's affection. In his own

mind, he called Esther a little idiot. It seemed to him
that Lady Charlotte was devoted to her niece. But
she could not be as beautiful as her picture represented
her!

He was still looking, doubting and wondering, when
the door opened and Miss Daubeny herself appeared.
"Did you want us, Aunt Charlotte?" she asked; and
Arthur knew that the original of the picture stood before him.

There had been no exaggeration, no mistake. The
Lisa of reality was quite as beautiful as the Lisa of the
picture; and if she had not the sublimated unearthliness of expression, she had an exquisite coloring which
the drawing did not show. She was very fair, daz-
zlingly fair, with a very little of the sea-shell pink that
Arthur especially admired, in her oval face; she had
hair that could only be described as "bright," hair that
gleamed as it rippled back from her white forehead to
the soft thick twists at the back, but was absolutely
smooth, without a hint of fringe or curl or fuzziness in
its golden waves. Her eyes were of the rarest shade
of dark blue-gray, almost violet in shadow; and the
delicate features were cameo-like in their pale perfection, in the creamy whiteness of the beautiful skin.

Arthur Ellison was keenly alive to every detail of her
appearance; he had never been so much struck with a
girl in his life; and he was delighted to notice that her
dress was as perfect and complete as herself. It was
plain, but indescribably fresh and dainty; there was a
look of elegance about her aspect which gave him intense satisfaction. He himself was poor, and had al-

ways been poor, but no one had a stronger sense than he of the advantages given by riches. It flashed through his mind at that moment that he should not care to have a wife unless she could always look as beautiful and be as beautifully dressed as Lisa Daubeny.

Lady Charlotte introduced the visitor in her off-hand way. "I've brought Miss Ellison's brother in to tea, Lisa—Mr. Ellison, my niece, Miss Daubeny; if you fetch Miss Ellison down, she need not hurry away."

A look of swift astonishment passed over Lisa Daubeny's sweet face. Arthur felt an equally swift thrill of agonizing terror lest she should not believe in the averred relationship. Had Esther told her already that he was her cousin?

Evidently something of the kind had been said. Lisa bowed and looked perplexed. "But—Miss Ellison has left some one else in the avenue," she said. "Her cousin, I believe—"

"Oh, my cousin has gone back to London," said Arthur, with perfect gravity and sang-froid. "He was called away suddenly on business. The telegram reached him after my sister left the house this afternoon."

Lisa appeared perfectly satisfied. But what would Esther say? How would she take it? It occurred to Arthur now that he had been playing a frightfully dangerous game. In two minutes, if Esther did not bear him out, he would probably be dismissed from the house as an impostor, or as a maniac, who had told a ridiculous lie for no apparent reason. He felt himself growing white and sick with sudden apprehension.

Miss Daubeny disappeared, and Lady Charlotte, in a friendly way, began to ask Arthur about his work and his prospects—the very subject on which he had anticipated entering with such zest. But his anxiety spoiled the lucky chance. He did not even know what he said in answer to Lady Charlotte's questions.

The door opened and Esther came in, followed by Lisa. Arthur cast an appealing glance at his cousin; he saw that her color had faded and her eyes were dull, also that her face wore a shocked and startled look. But Lisa's face was gentle and smiling as ever: it was plain, at any rate, that Esther had not betrayed him yet. Arthur's spirits rose to the occasion: he felt a momentary thrill of boyish glee.

"I've brought your brother in with me, Miss Ellison," said Lady Charlotte loudly. "I found him on my terrace, sketching the house, and I nearly slew him on the spot; but when he claimed to be your brother, I forgave him and brought him in to tea."

Esther threw a pained glance at her cousin. Evidently she did not know what to say.

"Your cousin, whom you told me about, has had to go back to London: that is a great pity," said Lisa to her friend.

"Oh, yes," said Arthur, smiling gayly into Esther's face, "he had a telegram from London, and wanted to go off immediately, so I am to make his excuses and say that he hopes to see you in London. Fortunately, I have not to hurry off so soon."

And again Esther did not speak. How could she betray him? She who had thought she loved him once. But she was furiously angry. What reason had Arthur for telling this foolish lie, which might place both herself and him in such an awkward situation if their true relationship were discovered?

"How long are you going to stay with your sister, Mr. Ellison?" said Lady Charlotte.

"I have not much to do in town just now," said Arthur. "I thought of running up to London for some luggage, and coming back for two or three weeks or so. Mrs. Brown has another room to let, and it will be pleasant to stay with my sister for a time."

He looked Esther in the face, almost defiantly, this time. She could never betray him now!

And she did not. But her drooping mouth, her frowning brow, expressed none of the pleasure that her friends might have expected her to feel.

Lady Charlotte glanced at her. "That will be very nice," she said, helping herself to cake, and leaving Andrews to supply the wants of her visitors: "very nice for you at any rate, and I daresay your sister will be pleased."

But Esther still kept silent, although every one was looking at her and wondering why she did not speak.

CHAPTER III.

MR. THOROLD OF HURST.

The Ellisons left Westhills about six o'clock, and walked back to the farmhouse where Esther was lodging and where Arthur had already spent one night. Silence lasted until they were well out of view of the windows, and then it was broken by Arthur, who put his hand quietly within his cousin's arm.

"Come, Esther, don't look so glum," he said. "I have only thrown a sop to the Cerberus of conventionality. What difference does it make whether I am your brother or your cousin?"

"I do not see why I should deceive people who have been kind to me."

"How have they been kind? What obligation have you to them? Lady Charlotte pays you for coaching her niece, that is all. I never heard that one was under such special obligations to one's employers."

"Lady Charlotte has been very kind to me in many ways, and I am very fond of Lisa," said Esther. "It is horrible to me to think that I am conniving at a lie—"

"But such a harmless lie," said Arthur, coaxingly. "And only meant to deceive Mrs. Grundy a little. Why, we are almost brother and sister: we were brought up together—we could always say that we meant *adopted* brother and sister, if ever we were brought to book."

And, seeing Esther shudder, he went on lightly: "Besides, who is there to bring us to book? We have no relations living to dispute the relationship: we have no intimate friends. I don't know how far you confided in your college friends concerning your family—"

"I had not much to confide. But I may easily have said that I had no brothers—it is a question girls always ask each other."

"Exactly; and I have provided for that difficulty. I told Lady Charlotte that I was your half-brother. You can always say that you meant you had no brother of your own—that you scarcely knew your half-brother, and so on. Come, Esther, be sensible. Let us be brother and sister for the rest of our lives: it signifies so many things. You could keep house for me in London as my sister, you know, whereas you are too young to do it as my cousin. I can't see why Providence did not arrange for us to be brother and sister in reality: it would have been much more convenient."

"It would be more convenient, but since it is not so—"

"We've pretended it before now, you will remember."

Yes, she remembered. It was when she was seventeen and he one and twenty: light-hearted, uncontrolled, scorning the fetters of convention, they had gone for a three days' walking tour in Wales, calling themselves brother and sister at the inns which they had visited. Esther wondered now how she could have done it, and was thankful that the expedition had remained a secret to most of her friends. There had been no harm in it, but it would not have occurred if she had had a mother to look after her. To her father everything she chose to do had seemed right.

"I was a child, then," she said.

"Well," said Arthur, skillfully changing his ground, "if you don't like the plan, dear, we won't keep it up. I only did it to make matters easier for you. It was so much better to say I was your brother than your cousin. But you'll not be staying here forever, and when you are back in London, we can resume our pristine relationship—since you are so anxious to keep me at a distance!"

"I am not that, indeed I am not, Arthur," said Esther earnestly. "I want to be as like a sister to you as I can possibly be, and I shall always do everything I can to help you; but it seems to me that we have entered on a silly bit of deception that can do you no good, and which may some day result in serious harm to both of us. And I hate deceptions—of any kind."

"It was a silly trick, perhaps," said her cousin. "I don't quite know what prompted me to say what I did, unless it was that your Lady Charlotte, with her big voice and her grand airs, frightened the wits out of me. I sheltered myself under your wing, instinctively. You won't round on me, will you, Esther? It's only for a week or two, you know."

"For you," said Esther, in rather a choked voice,

"but for me—I hoped that they would be my life-long friends."

"Why, so they will. I shall pass out of their life like a dream. What does it matter to them whether I am your brother or your cousin? They will see no more of me, probably, when I have left the respectable Mrs. Brown's. Make your mind easy, my dear: we are a little bit Bohemian, you and I, but we don't go about the world preying on rich people and getting money on false pretenses. Our little frauds are quite innocently meant."

It was true—so far, at least, as Esther was concerned. She was perfectly straightforward in her friendships, "hoping for nothing again" when she gave her love. She could not scheme: she could not fawn; and the consequence was that she made few friends, perhaps, but the friends she made were, like herself, staunch and true.

But Arthur was not exactly like herself. She knew that. She had never had occasion to call him dishonorable: he would never have spoken to her again if she had attempted to do so; but she was struck sometimes by what looked like a certain meanness of nature, an incapacity for seeing anything from a higher point of view than his own self-interest. It seemed to him so important that he should succeed; that he should be happy and prosperous. The world must be, in his eyes, thoroughly out of gear when it did not afford him all he required. He felt injured by its failure to do for him what he thought it promised: he had the feeling which a starving man might be supposed to have when he steals a loaf out of a baker's shop—that he is justified in taking what the world ought to be ready to give him of its own accord.   Arthur Ellison appeared to think that he might be forgiven in breaking the ordinary laws of God and man, when a question of his own welfare was involved.

Esther recognized this tendency in him when he put aside her remonstrances concerning their relationship. If he could benefit, if even he could get pleasure, out of the deception (he seemed to say) why should he not practice it?   Abstract right and wrong were nothing to him: he always acknowledged that he thought them relative.   The thing that was right in one situation might be wrong in another: the moral law was a matter of geography and climate. She could only hope that in his life his practice would transcend his own precepts.

She had a very sisterly kind of regard for him: perhaps a more truly sisterly feeling than a sister by blood might have had. In the old days, when they had spoken of marriage, they had often wrangled and jarred; their opinions and principles were different, and differences were important when two people were going to marry each other.   They agreed much better now that they were bound only by ties of cousinship.   But in this matter of Arthur's self-introduction to Lady Charlotte as Esther's brother, Esther felt herself distinctly aggrieved; and Arthur considered that she attached an undue importance to the incident.

But he acknowledged later, with a little superior smile, that she might have reasons.

She was sitting at the window of the farmhouse par-
lor one evening, her little table drawn up to the window-sill, so that she could inhale the perfume of the late
roses and catch glimpses of the golden autumnal sky,
when her solitude was disturbed by a visitor. A quick
manly tread sounded through the passage of the house,
then a side door into the garden was opened, and a
man in shooting trim, with a brace of pheasants dan-
gling from one hand, came out into the garden, with
Mrs. Brown behind him.

"I think you'll find Miss Ellison and her brother out
here, sir," she was saying. "They were sitting in the
arbor not long ago."

So they had been; but Esther had come indoors to
do some work, and Arthur had removed himself and
his pipe to his bedroom. Both, however, heard the
words, which brought Arthur to his window, where,
hidden by the muslin curtain, he looked with raised
eyebrows at this unexpected visitor. Esther did not
seem to move: he wondered that she did not make
some sign of her presence. If he could have seen her,
he might have noticed that her pen fell from her hand
and the rich carnation stole to her soft brown cheek.

"I wonder who this is," thought Mr. Ellison, eyeing
the newcomer. "Very well got up: very well groomed
—has Miss Esther set up an admirer? Or is it only
some message from Westhills?"

"I think they have left the arbor, Mrs. Brown," said
a quiet, pleasant voice. "It does not matter: I came
only to leave these birds with Lady Charlotte's com-
pliments. Part of the day's bag, you know."

"They are beautiful birds, sir," said Mrs. Brown, with empressement. "You're quite a large party staying at Hurst for the shooting, I hear, Mr. Thorold, sir. I hope you're going to give it a mistress of its own before long."

The listeners wondered a little at her freedom. But Mrs. Brown had once been head of the nursery at Hurst, and had known its master since he was a baby in arms.

Justin Thorold laughed at the remark, but a keen observer might have fancied a touch of embarrassment in his answer.

"I shall let you know when I am thinking of it, Mrs. Brown. And now, if Miss Ellison is out—"

"I am not out, Mr. Thorold," said Esther, putting her head out of the window, between the sprays of rose and jessamine which made a many-tinted frame for it. Arthur felt that he could hear her smile in her voice. "I am listening to all you say, so I hope you are not talking secrets."

It was rather cheeky of her to say that, thought Arthur discontentedly: but then a man is always critical of the behavior of his female relations. "She must know him very well yet she has scarcely ever mentioned his name to me."

But perhaps her silence had been more significant than words.

Mr. Thorold started a little, and drew closer to the window with a somewhat eager look. He was a man of middle height, well-made but with a touch of student's stoop at the shoulder, though there was nothing peculiarly student-like in the resolute, intelligent, serious face, with its observant hazel eyes and the suggestion of satire in the proud and slightly supercilious lip. Arthur remembered the face, as that of a member of Parliament whose influence was already felt although he was a comparatively young man: he had a curiously cool and trenchant way of stating his opinions which gave him unusual individuality. He had published a pamphlet or two and he was beginning to be known as an authority on education: it was probable that he would one day be a man of mark.

"Esther flies high," said Arthur to himself, with a little sneer. But his smile grew more genuine as he thought of the position she might occupy, if she ever became the wife of a man like Justin Thorold. "She would be very useful to me," said the budding author and journalist.

"You heard my message then, or part of it," said Mr. Thorold, approaching the window so closely that Arthur almost lost sight of him, although his voice still floated up to the listener's ears. Evidently he had shaken hands with Esther through the window, and was now leaning on the sill. "Lady Charlotte sends the birds I brought, of which Mrs. Brown has relieved me, by the way, and hopes you will find them useful. Also she wishes me to convey her love to you, and to ask you and your brother to lunch at Westhills on Sunday."

"It is very kind of Lady Charlotte," said Esther. There was some indecision in her tone.

"You have no other engagement, I hope?" said Mr. Thorold.

"None—thank you."

"Then I may tell my cousin that you will come. I meant to make this an occasion of calling on your brother," he went on, "but I was detained till late at Westhills—we have been shooting all day—, and now I'm afraid Mr. Ellison is out."

"I do not know where he is: I saw him in the garden, just now, but—"

"Ah, don't move, please. I shall see him another day. I shall make his acquaintance on Sunday, if not before."

"You will be at Westhills on Sunday?"

"I hope so."

"But I thought your house was full of visitors—that you had a large party of shooting men at Hurst?"

He laughed lightly. "Most of them are going to-morrow, I am delighted to say; and the two or three that remain will have to entertain themselves on Sunday. I shall plead important business."

"Oh!"

"Does that shock you? I know—you are so wonderfully sincere."

"Oh, indeed, I am not—not, at least, more than other people."

"I beg leave to dissent, Miss Ellison. It has always struck me that you had more sincerity than most people. I believe you would be quite incapable of indirectness or deceit."

"Please don't say so," pleaded Esther, with genuine

distress in her tone. "I shall feel as if I were mas-
querading—as if you did not know me in my true
colors—"

"Confound the girl!" said the unseen listener to himself. "She'll make him think there's something shady
about her past if she gets on like that!"

But Esther's words conveyed no special meaning to
Mr. Thorold's mind.

"You have the unusual peculiarity," he said, "of not
liking to be praised. I have noticed it before. Most
women are fond of flattery."

"I think I like flattery very much," said Esther, rallying, and recovering her vivacious tone. "Only it has
to be administered with great care—and in small doses,
I think—or else it palls upon one. And it is a great
mistake, you know, not to economize one's enjoy-
ments."

"I am not reputed to fall often into the mistake of
flattering any one too much," said Mr. Thorold laughing.

"No, I have heard you are very severe."

"I am never severe when I—respect," he said.
There was a very long pause before the last word: one
might have thought that he was going to use a
stronger one. A little silence followed: Arthur wondered what the silence meant.

It did not mean so much, perhaps, as he imagined.
Justin Thorold was leaning against the window-sill,
with his eyes fixed on Esther's dark, brilliant, bewitch-
ing little face: Esther, with her dark eyelashes cast
down, was twisting a spray of purple clematis in her

fingers. Mr. Thorold slowly put out his hand and touched the flower. "May I have it?" he said, so softly that Arthur did not hear.

The flower changed hands. Esther smiled a little, but she made no reply.

"Well, I must be off," said Justin, moving to a more erect position as he arranged the purple blossom carefully in his button-hole. "We dine at eight, and I shall only just be home in time. You will be at Lady Charlotte's on Sunday, then?"

"Yes, thank you."

He ought by rights to have gone, but he still lingered. It seemed as if he found it hard to drag himself away.

"I am so glad you have been able to interest Lisa in her work," he said. "It is so good for her to have an object in life. Her friends are all very much obliged to you."

"I was half afraid that Lady Charlotte would not thank me for imbuing her with such an ardent desire to go to Oxford."

"It is a much more sensible thing for her to do," said Thorold with vehemence, "than to lead an aimless, useless life at Westhills, with nothing in the world to look forward to but marriage!"

"I think Miss Daubeny is incapable of that sort of life," said Esther.

He laughed suddenly, as if he were pleased. "I like to hear you say so," he said. "I like to hear you stand up for her. It is mutual, you know: she is devoted to you—already."

The last word was again said after a pause, and in a lower tone.

"Now I must really go. Good-bye, Miss Ellison."

"Good-bye, Mr. Thorold."

There was still a pause before he actually moved away. Arthur risked discovery by craning his neck over the window ledge, but he could see nothing.

Indeed, there was nothing to see. Only two clasped hands, and the long look of a man and woman into each other's eyes—a look that tells so much to them, and means so little to those who do not understand. Then Justin Thorold strode away, throwing a last look, a last "Good-bye" over his shoulder to the girl who had charmed the heart out of him for the first time since he was a boy and had been jilted by a woman who wanted to marry a lord instead of an English gentleman.

Esther stood for a time exactly where he had left her, with a happy wondering smile upon her lips. Was it possible?—she asked herself, without putting the question any farther into words. Was it possible, she meant, that a man like Justin Thorold, a man of intellect, wealth, social position, was actually in love with her, a poor little nobody, a mere school-teacher, paid to come down from London for a summer to correct Miss Daubeny's Latin exercises, and to point out the faults in her English composition. Esther was not without the grain of conceit which lurks in the mind of every girl who has done better than her fellows in an Academic course, and has competed successfully with men for Academic honors. But all her conceit, such as it was, seemed to have died down beneath a new-born faith in some one wiser and loftier than herself, a respect amounting almost to reverence for a man who could calmly put aside delights and live laborious days for a cause that he had at heart, who spent his life in thankless toil for a nation that would never bless him, probably never even distinguish his name from hundreds of other voluntary law-makers at St. Stephen's, jeered at by the public and considered only in the light of rank and file.   Not that she thought Justin Thorold deserving of so lowly a place; but that she knew the ingratitude of the world, and that he was willing to work without reward.

She did not think of Arthur: she supposed him to be out, and she did not imagine that he had listened from his window to her conversation with Mr. Thorold.   And when she mentioned that gentleman's visit, and his message, Arthur did not betray himself, but heard what she had to say with a perfectly unmoved countenance.   He knew Esther too well to dare to congratulate her on the conquest that she had made.

But as he sat at table and talked to her, he was conscious of a distinctly new idea which Justin Thorold's attentions had suggested to him.   "If she marries this man, why should not I marry Lisa Daubeny? There is no more disparity on the one side than on the other.   They cannot decently refuse her to me if Thorold marries my sister.   What a brilliant idea of mine to say that I was her brother—I hardly gave myself credit for such foresight!" And he laughed so loudly, as he thought of the possibilities of the future, that Esther was surprised and asked him why he was amused. But he did not take her into his confidence.

CHAPTER IV.

THE OPINIONS OF LISA.

Lisa Daubeny had led, on the whole, a lonely life.
It was not Lady Charlotte's fault; Lady Charlotte had
racked her brains for plans to make her niece happy:
she procured games, toys, books, governesses and
masters for her in unlimited quantity. She had taken
her abroad, and in due time had presented her at
court, where her dress had been one of the most beautiful and expensive of the year, just as Lisa herself had
been one of the fairest of all the debutantes. It would
have been, perhaps, a mistake to say that Lisa was not
happy; but she had a sense of something wanting in
her life, and she did not know exactly what it was.

Perhaps it was love. And yet Lady Charlotte did
love her niece very heartily; but it was not her way to
be demonstrative or sympathetic. And the natures
of the two women jarred even more essentially when
Lisa was grown up than when she had been a child.
Lady Charlotte, with all her literary gifts—and that she
possessed these all the world was agreed—was essentially an "out-door" woman. She could ride, row,
swim, shoot, as well as many a sportsman; she was
fond of mountain climbing and other forms of hard
physical exercise; she had even begun, of late, to
mount a bicycle, and bade fair to become an accomplished wheelwoman. Lisa shared none of these

tastes, although Lady Charlotte had done her best to develop them. The girl had been forced into riding and swimming and rowing, because her aunt had thought them good for her; but she disliked all forms of exercise except dancing and quiet walking along a country road. She was really very timid, although she tried to conceal the fact. She liked books, music, needle-work, poetry—all the things that are usually called feminine; and although there was nothing sentimental or namby-pamby about her, she was exceedingly sensitive to the touch of exalted feeling, such as we call romance.

When Lady Charlotte was out in the fields or in the woods—for she was a capital farmer as well as a sportswoman—Lisa was reading Shelley or Swinburne in a sheltered nook at home. When Lady Charlotte was skimming the Times and delivering herself of impassioned diatribes against prominent politicians, Lisa was weaving delicate fancies into exquisite needle-work of costly materials and rainbow hues. Or while Lady Charlotte dipped into the memoirs of the last century and wrote scathing reviews of modern books of which she did not approve, Lisa was playing Schubert's sonatas or the weirder melodies of Chopin and of Grieg. The aunt and niece had insensibly drifted far apart, and the gulf between them was widening every day.

Curious to relate, it was Lady Charlotte who was the more conscious of this division and it was to Lady Charlotte that it brought the more pain. Lisa was young and did not know exactly what she wanted: the

older woman understood better, and did not know how
to supply the want. For all her strong-mindedness
and her numberless interests in life, Lady Charlotte
felt her heart ache sometimes when she looked at
Lisa. The girl was so far away! And she had hoped,
when Lisa came first as a tiny child, that she would
be to her as a daughter. But she had lacked some
power of showing her love; and the child had grown
into a girl who was amiable, gentle, docile enough, but
—to Lady Charlotte's mind—a little cold.

When she had been presented and had gone to a
good many parties and seen something of the world,
Lisa suddenly grew restless. She began to have vague
aspirations after a Career, and to talk of the Higher
Education of Women. Whereat Lady Charlotte had
smiled, well-pleased, thinking that here she saw the
influence of Justin Thorold, whom she had always designed to be Lisa's husband. Justin was wild upon
education; and he had always been very kind and attentive to Lisa, lending her books and showing a
kind interest in her pursuit. It was a vexation to
Lady Charlotte that Westhills would one day pass to
Justin Thorold, as her husband had no nearer relative,
and did not wish to alienate his estate from his own
family; while she, on her side, had little of her own
and not enough to make Lisa a rich woman, although
the girl would, as Esther had surmised, have a fair
dowry on her wedding day. But Lady Charlotte's
affection for her niece made her doubly anxious that
she should marry Justin, and thus become ultimately
mistress of the house over which the imperious daugh-

ter of the celebrated Lady Muncaster now reigned in
supreme autocracy. So Lisa's interest in the subject
of education was hailed as a happy augury.

Then Esther Ellison came on the scene, and Lady
Charlotte still rejoiced. Lisa had expressed her desire for a woman-coach who would spend the summer
at Westhills or in lodgings close by; and the Warden
of the Women's College to whom Lady Charlotte had
applied gave Miss Ellison the warmest of recommen-
dations. She came, saw and conquered; but not exactly in the way that had been expected. She cap-
tured Lisa's heart; that was all right; but she seemed
rather likely to capture Mr. Thorold's heart as well;
and that was what nobody had designed or intended.

Lady Charlotte saw nothing, suspected nothing.
When Lisa, inspired by Esther's enthusiasm, began
to sigh after the pleasures of a College life, her aunt
smiled benignantly upon her and sent her to talk to
Justin. And although Lisa was fond of Justin in a
sisterly way, she knew very well that he did not care
very much to talk to her unless she made Esther
Ellison the subject of the conversation; and she felt
extreme enjoyment in doing so. There was a delightful sense of freedom, even of license, in encouraging
Justin Thorold to fly in the face of his relations by
choosing a dear little working-woman for his wife
instead of the well-born, well-bred, aristocratic maiden
who had been selected for him. Lisa had always been
conscious of instincts of revolt, and they had been
strengthened by her intercourse with Esther, and her
increasing knowledge of the intellectual world.

In the interval that had elapsed beween Arthur Ellison's first introduction to Westhills and the invitation to lunch which Justin Thorold had carried to the
farm, the young man had more than once visited the
Byngs.   Lady Charlotte took an interest in his literary
ambitions: Mr. Byng, an amiable, scholarly man in
rather delicate health, showed him his library; and
Lisa—what did Lisa do for the entertainment of the
new guest?

She kept rather aloof from him, regarding him
sometimes with a sort of serious curiosity, as a being
of different order from any she had yet encountered.
She had seen a good deal of the ordinary young man
of society, and did not admire 'the type; she had also
met a number of old and middle-aged men who were
celebrated in one way or another—as writers, trav-
elers, artists and politicians. Plenty of these men
came down to stay at Westhills, to be made much of
by Lady Charlotte and to compliment her in turn.
Lisa heard them talk, but she never said very much
to them   They generally thought her shy. She was
not so much shy perhaps, as self-absorbed.

After all, the young observer said to herself, these
men who had achieved a reputation were not so interesting as they must have been in their youth. They
were resting on their oars: they were no longer striv-
ing against the stream.   She often wondered what they
had been like when they were in the midst of their
strenuous efforts to succeed: they must have had more
life, more energy, more brilliance, she thought, than
they seemed to have now. Lady Charlotte was not a

person who greatly encouraged the presence of young aspirants about her, literary or artistic: men in their salad days would not attract her, she sometimes said. Lisa had, therefore, few opportunities of putting her theories to the test.

But now, she thought, she had an opportunity. Esther's brother, a young literary man, fresh from the vaguely beautiful land which she figured to herself as "Bohemia," full of hope and aspiration and endeavor, he must surely be one of these budding geniuses of whom she had so often heard. She was quietly glad that her aunt had let him visit Westhills; she was not always so hospitable to strangers. She wanted to study him: to discern the coming greatness of his name: to behold and admire.

And in all this she was not so simple as it might appear: for Arthur Ellison had in very truth a considerable poetical talent, as well as an acutely critical turn of mind; and Lady Charlotte, to whom he had submitted some of his productions, had deigned to speak very well of them and to offer him an introduction to her own particular publishers. This, from Lady Charlotte, was high praise and favor, as Lisa knew.

On the morning of the Sunday on which the Ellisons had been invited to lunch, Lady Charlotte treated her niece to quite a long commentary on some verses that Arthur had sent up to read. They were breakfasting in a sunny cheerful room overlooking a charming view of the Surrey hills. Mr. Byng was lazily cutting the leaves of his Spectator: Lady Charlotte, in a

loose tea-gown of flowered silk, alternately drank
chocolate and read aloud some lines of Arthur's poems:
Lisa, who had finished her breakfast already, sat with
her eyes fixed dreamily on a great bowl of yellow
roses and burning autumn leaves that adorned the
table, and listened to her aunt's reading and remarks.

"He really has something in him," she said at last,
slapping the last sheet down on the table-cloth and laying her hand upon it: "and judging from his attempt
at a sketch, I scarcely thought he had. It was the
most feeble thing I think I ever saw. I should advise
him henceforth to abandon the pencil and stick to the
pen."

"We cannot all have your versatile tastes, Charlotte,"
said Mr. Byng, with a complimentary little smile in
her direction.

"We may have them, but we need not give way to
them," rejoined Lady Charlotte dryly. "I sincerely
hope Mr. Ellison will curb them when they take the
direction of art."

"You think he does better in poetry?" said Mr.
Byng politely. He had not much interest in the subject, but he made a point of following his wife's lead.

"The man's a born poet," said Lady Charlotte
shortly. Then, as if not wishing to commit herself too
far, she added: "That is to say, he's got the poetic
gift. He isn't a Shelley or a Keats. But he will
make a very good singer of verses for the drawing-
room and the boudoir."

"But one hardly calls that being a poet!" exclaimed
Lisa, moved out of herself.

"Well, I will go a step further and say that he will be a poet for the study, for the library. His verses won't go to the hearts of men, but they will be accepted by the publishers. Your modern poet hardly cares for more than that."

Lisa looked down and bit her lips. But Lady Charlotte was unconscious of any desire to depreciate Arthur's verses She thought that she had given them a very fair meed of praise.

"I don't see why they shouldn't succeed," said Lady Charlotte musingly. "They are light and graceful, and he has tried some pretty metrical experiments. His prose is good too. He sent me a very pretty little thing on the pride of ignorance—quite a smart little thing. I think he ought to be pushed."

"An introduction from you to Mr. Dorian will go a long way," said her husband, alluding to the eminent publisher whom Lady Charlotte asked to dinner when she was in town and allowed to publish her books.

"Hm—I was thinking rather of a secretaryship, or something of that sort. However, he'll get on. He is the sort of young man that will. There is a certain kind of success—not the highest kind—written on his very face."

She caught Lisa's eyes fixed on her in a sort of curious doubt.

"Ah, you mustn't tell the gypsy all I say, Lisa. I think very highly of her brother's abilities, tell her that. I am glad she brought him down: we may be able to do something for him—though I am bound to say that she did not look absolutely delighted when he turned up at Westhills."

"That was Esther's delicacy of feeling, I think," said Lisa quickly. "She was afraid we should think she was trying to force her relations upon us."

"Esther's not a fool," said Lady Charlotte. "She knows well enough that nobody's relations could be forced upon me."

Then she rose, leaving the papers on the table, and walked towards the window, whistling as she went. It was a trick of Lady Charlotte's to whistle when she was absorbed in thought.

"There's the church bell," she said at last, very briskly. "Howard!"

"I don't feel well enough to go to church this morning, my love," said Byng, who answered to this name.

"Then, Lisa, you must go alone. I am much too busy. Dorian has sent me a manuscript that he particularly wants my opinion upon by to-morrow morning. I'll glance through it while you are at church. I expect it's some frightful trash or other. And, Lisa, you need not let out to the Ellisons that I read for Dorian now and then. Young Ellison would be expecting me to get all his things accepted; and that's too much of a good thing."

She left the room as she spoke, and Lisa silently gathered up the loose sheets of verse which were scattered about the table. Mr. Byng aided her with a sort of humorous politeness, which expressed itself more forcibly in the remark that he made in handing her the last leaf of the little bundle:—

"My lady's swans are usually parti-colored ones, I think."

Lisa smiled and took the sheets away.

She would have liked to dream over them all the morning instead of going to church; but her conscience smote her for this unholy preference, and she made haste to don her pretty Sunday hat and coat, and her perfectly-fitting gray kid gloves. Thus equipped, with an ivory and silver prayer-book in her hand, she looked as grave and devotional as any fair saint on a painted window; and all the while her mind was running on certain lines which Lady Charlotte had declared to have quite an Elizabethan ring, and which, as she did not seem to have noticed, were the only ones that bore date. They were by no means as good as some of the others: yet Lisa remembered them for some secret, undefined reason, better than the rest. How did they begin?—

> "Lady, serene and still,
>   That shinest as the stars above me,
> Had I the skill
>   I vow I would refuse to love thee."

and so on, through two or three verses which represented the lady of his love as an overmastering influence that took away from him all power to resist his fatal love for her. The date scrawled at the end was that of the day on which he had first visited Westhills.

Lisa told herself that she was absurd, that it was almost unmaidenly to attach any importance to this effusion—although it had evidently been written on the evening after his visit, and bore a half-effaced "To

L——" upon the wrong side of the paper. She could
not help remembering that he had looked at her a
good deal, in a furtive kind of way; and that once she
had met his eyes. * * *

Oh, what was she thinking about? In church, too,
upon her knees, with her eyes closed and her chin resting on her clasped hands! She was resolved to give
all her attention to sacred things; but it was very disconcerting to find that Mr. Ellison was sitting just
opposite to her, in such a position that he was almost
obliged to rest his eyes upon her face. Lisa bowed
her head lower and tried hard to forget that he was
there.

Coming out of church, they met the Ellisons in the
porch, and Justin Thorold in the churchyard. They
all walked up to Westhills together, pairing off when
the path was narrow in proper and conventional fashion: Mr. Thorold with Miss Ellison, Mr. Ellison with
Miss Daubeny. And it was then that Lisa found a
moment to tell her companion that Lady Charlotte
had spoken highly of his poems.

"And you? Did you read them?" he asked, with
a culpable negligence of what Lady Charlotte thought.

"Yes, I read them. I liked them very much."

Arthur's sensitive face flushed with gratification.
It was part of his charm—for he certainly had a
charm for women, young or old—that he was so
eagerly responsive to the opinions and judgments of
others. He was depressed if a chance acquaintance
disapproved of him: he was elated if a beggar called
a blessing on him from the skies. And when he

genuinely valued the good word of a person, he was ready to take almost any means of securing it. Praise was the breath of his nostrils: "recognition," as he called it, the pole-star of his existence.

Lisa could not be but pleased to see the pleasure with which her approval was received. Then she had to tell him which poem she liked best, and why; and she exerted all her powers to answer his questions in the way that she thought would satisfy him best. But neither of them mentioned those four scrawled verses dated "September 10," addressed "To L——". Possibly they had been placed with the others by mistake.

Innocent Lisa, in spite of her experience of the world, Arthur Ellison was not the man to make that kind of mistake.

"Ah, good people, here you are!" said Lady Charlotte cheerfully, as the party entered the hall. She had changed her morning robe for an unmistakably Parisian gown of bronze silk, heavy and rich, with old repousse-work gold buttons: she had donned with it the air of a woman of fashion, and was more conventional than usual—it was the customary effect of Mr. Thorold's presence, and her intimate friends described it by saying that he was the only person in the world who knew how to keep her in order. At any rate, she was always supremely agreeable to him, telling her best stories in his presence, and abstaining from expressions that might shock his ears: also, she neither smoked nor whistled (in public), if he were in the house. People attributed this self-restraint to her de-

sire that Thorold should marry Lisa; but it had in
reality a deeper root. She thoroughly liked and
esteemed Justin, and as she was very much the creature
of her moods, it cost her no trouble to be to him all
that she knew he liked a woman to be. She was frank,
genial, good-natured, witty: showing her generous
and noble side, not the scornful and defiant one with
which the world was so well acquainted. Justin liked
her in return, and was wont to say that he could never
understand why Lady Charlotte had so many enemies.

She seemed inclined that day to lay herself out to
make friends. She was infinitely charming to Arthur,
spoke of his poems in very complimentary terms, and
assured him that she would do all in her power to
get him work such as he desired. A secretaryship?
A readership in a publisher's house? A well-paid
clerkship even? These were the things that would
suit him. And thence—her mellow voice ran like
music through well-rounded periods—thence he
would rise to eminence in the world, to riches and
success, as other men had done, and his life would be
one of those fortunate ones which are held up as ex-
amples and incentives to those who should come after
him.

"What does Lady Charlotte mean by this rhodomon-
tade?" thought Justin Thorold, as he noted the gratified flush on Arthur's cheek, and the half-veiled interest in Lisa's eyes. He could not understand it; but
he consoled himself with the reflection that when Lady
Charlotte took up a notion, she never failed to overdo
it, and that she was never afraid of an extravagance.

But seeing that this young man was Esther's kinsman, and that he, Justin Thorold, had made up his mind to make this brown-faced little girl his wife, he got a little vexed and uneasy at the way in which, as he phrased it, Lady Charlotte was "making a tool of" his future brother-in-law.

CHAPTER V.

RELICS.

"Now," said Lady Charlotte after lunch, "I want Mr. Ellison to come into the library and look at the relics."

Arthur heard her with dismay. He had planned in his own mind to sit beside Lisa and turn over his own poems, one by one, with her. He had not counted upon Lady Charlotte's increasing friendliness. Why did she not retire to her own room and go to sleep, like other middle-aged ladies on a Sunday afternoon? Such energy in a woman of her age was almost indecent. But, of course, he could not refuse. Rather sulkily he followed his hostess's rustling brown silks along a wide corridor and into the charming, book-lined room which was called the library. What she meant by the "relics," he did not take the trouble to inquire. Some musty remains of antiquity, he supposed: utterly uninteresting to him.

Lisa followed, a few paces behind; but the others had disappeared. Mr. Byng knew the virtues of an afternoon nap, if his wife did not; and Justin had drawn Esther inside the conservatory to look at a remarkable begonia. How Arthur envied and hated them at that moment! He would have liked to go with Lisa—anywhere, to see a begonia or anything else in the whole, wide world, so that he might have her to himself. Love was like an epidemic among these young people in the soft September days; they fell victims one after another with curious facility, and it was almost pathetic to see Lady Charlotte's utter un-consciousness of the fact. She carried her queenly presence to and fro among them without in the least knowing that it was a disconcerting embarrassment. After all, as she herself would very sensibly have said, the duties of life and the convenances of society do not entirely come to an end because two pairs of young fools have fallen in love with each other.

She moved about the room a little, opening a shut-ter, unlocking a glass case, moving some papers to another place, all with that fine grace of movement which distinguished her. People who knew her slightly, who heard only of her untrammeled speech and daring modes of action, used to expect to find her a noisy woman; whereas, with all her eccentricities, Lady Charlotte had singularly polished manners, when she chose, and was capable of receiving a queen or an empress with as much well-bred ease as she received the wife of a curate. To Arthur's half-dazed mind, she seemed like a specimen of an unknown genius; the representative of a class with larger minds, finer cul-ture, and more complete possession of the world, than the men and women of our own day. But he was a little dazzled by what he saw.

"I thought I should like to show you some memorials of my family, Mr. Ellison. They came to me through my mother, of course," said Charlotte care-lessly. Mr. Byng's family, although highly-respectable, was not of remote origin, and Lady Charlotte was proud of her own. "That is Queen Mary's snuff-box, patch-box sounds better, perhaps; she gave it to an ancestor of mine at Fotheringay. And here is a lock of King Charles's hair: Charles the Martyr, of course, I mean. There is a letter of Strafford's in that case; and a book of Hours which is said to have belonged to him. Don't be shocked when I tell you that these two yellow papers are love-letters written by Prince Rupert to one of my far-away great-grand-mothers. But she was a very virtuous lady and would have nothing to say to him. You see that string of beads? It belonged to one of Queen Anne's poor little babies; and here's a letter written by the poor little Duke of Gloucester to his governor."

"They are most interesting relics of the past," murmured Arthur, rather vaguely. He was far more interested in the present, and let his eyes wander to Lisa's face even while Lady Charlotte discoursed of miniature, of which she had a goodly store, of charms, gauds and baubles, all of historic value, of royal love-letters, and original manuscripts of songs and dramas, more prized than all the rest. She had indeed a fine collection of valuable and interesting objects, which at some moments would have held Arthur's attention completely; but, try as he would on this occasion, to listen to Lady Charlotte's explanations, his mind would wander to the slender whiteness of Lisa's fingers, to the shining coils of hair on her graceful head, to the soft blue shadows underneath her eyes. He had a quick, sensitive imagination, and it was fascinated by Lisa's har-

monies of form and coloring: the peculiar essence
of her beauty had gone to his head like wine.

Lady Charlotte thought him less intelligent than he
looked; but finally hit on the idea that he had a social-
istic tendency and cared little for the relics of kings and
queens. Thereupon, with her usual decisiveness, she
shut up one of her glass cases before she had detailed
half its contents, and said:

"Well, we can keep these for another time. I think
you have seen the best. What I want you to see now
may be more interesting than these things to you,
Mr. Ellison; and I have something to ask you about
them too."

Mr. Ellison became aware that his inattention had
appeared discourteous, and was beginning to "confound" himself, as the French say, in excuses, when
Lady Charlotte cut him short.

"All right: I know everybody does not care about
curiosities; but the papers I am going to show you
are not curiosities exactly: they are family documents."

Arthur looked up eagerly. Why was she going to
show him family documents? If she had such confidence in him already, would she not be willing by
and by——

"They're in this cabinet," said Lady Charlotte
shortly. "I generally keep the key on this chain at my
waist, so that nobody has much chance of getting to
them, d'ye see? Lisa, child, go and see whether they
have brought up the tea, and make Miss Ellison have

some.   I'll bring Mr. Ellison back to the drawing-room
by and by."

Arthur's heart sank, but he felt that he had more
power of attending to his imperious hostess in Lisa's
absence than in her presence, and he resigned himself
with a sigh.   Lady Charlotte opened drawer after
drawer, and displayed piles of old-fashioned letters,
with funny little red seals, and square yellow sheaves
of paper covered with crabbed manuscript.   He looked
at them with repugnance: did she mean to make him
read any or all of these?

"I am not going to inflict them upon you," she said,
perhaps reading the secret dismay upon his countenance, "but I want you to look at one of them—any
one will do—and tell me whether you find the writing
easy to decipher."

"Not very easy," said Arthur, after a few moments'
survey of the sheet she held out to him, "but I fancy
a little practice is all that is wanted to make it perfectly.
legible.   One needs to know the trick of a hand like
that."

"Exactly what I say," returned Lady Charlotte,
nodding her head triumphantly, "now Lisa can't read
a word of it—says it is utterly undecipherable; and my
husband declares that the mere sight of it tires his eyes;
but I can read it easily enough, and so would you with
a little practice.   How are you at languages?   French,
Latin, of course: any Italian?"

Arthur discerned in these questions a purpose which
made his heart leap.

"I have read Dante," he said, "and of late I have been dipping into modern Italian novels."

"Ah, that would do perfectly well. It seems to me, Mr. Ellison, that you are the very person I have been trying to find for the last two or three years—if, at least, you are at all in want of a job."

"I am utterly idle at present," said Arthur lightly, "and want congenial work more than anything else in the world."

"I wonder whether it would suit you," said Lady Charlotte, eyeing him keenly. "It's a project of mine which I don't want all the world to hear. I was thinking of telling you something about it, and asking you whether you could do a little of it for me."

"I shall be very happy, if I am competent," said Arthur, with rising color.

"It would not be difficult or responsible work—what I want done. The chief thing is trustworthiness in the agent I employ, and fair knowledge on certain points. I need not question the trustworthiness of our dear little Miss Ellison's brother."

For the first time, Arthur felt really uncomfortable on the question of his relationship to Esther. He had not expected to owe anything more than an introduction to his supposed sister, and he knew in his heart that he ought to avow the truth but—if he did so, what would be the result? Lady Charlotte would certainly be angry; she was not a woman whom he could make a fool of with impunity: she would refuse him the commission she spoke of: she might even forbid him the house. And for what reason? A simple, harmless

little trick—a deception scarce worthy of the name—
would she say that it made him untrustworthy in her
eyes? She might; and he dare not run the risk.

These thoughts flashed through his mind in a very
short space of time. When he had made his decision
—a more important one than he knew—Lady Charlotte was again speaking, in a quiet narrative tone.

"These papers, I must tell you," she said, "consist of
the private memoirs of my grandfather, his correspondence with a number of celebrated people, and some
letters belonging to other members of my family. I
have long intended to weave them into a connected history of my grandfather's life, with some account of
my mother also, and of the part she took in European
politics. You can imagine how interesting and important such a book would be."

"Quite so," said Arthur.

"But you see, it can't be published," said Lady Charlotte, brusquely.

"Indeed? And why——"

"There are too many things implicating other people: too many scandals, too many political jobs. He
left word that no memoir of him should appear—that
none of his journals should be published—until the
beginning of a new century. There are some years
still to run, and I am very sorry for it. I don't believe
in secret histories, and I daresay there is nothing but
what the world knows already. The book will appear
in 1900, and not a day before."

"You mean to compile a life of him then?" said Arthur, becoming interested at last, for he had heard

too much of the celebrated Earl of Belfield, father of Lady Muncaster, to be unaware of the importance that would attach to the publication of these memoirs.

"I want to begin the work. I am forty-nine already. I shall be growing old by the time the book can be published. I am the last of the family—except Lisa, my sister's daughter, and she has no capacity for that kind of work. I hold it the most sacred duty of my life to set these papers in order while I have health and strength to do it."

Lady Charlotte's voice dropped to a mellow recitative during the last sentence. She was sitting before the open cabinet, with her hands folded in her lap, her dark eyes resting on the papers, her mind evidently far away. She looked so like some majestic Sibyl of ancient days that Arthur did not dare to break in upon her silence with any commonplace question of his own. Yet he was growing anxious to know what she wanted him to do.

"The first thing to be done," said Lady Charlotte, rousing herself from her reverie, and speaking in an ordinary, practical tone, "is that the letters and manuscripts should be carefully transcribed. Some of this work I shall have to do myself, of course; but some of it can be done by any competent person. Certain letters will have to be translated from French or Italian originals. Will you undertake, Mr. Ellison, to try a little of this work under my supervision, if you are staying here with your sister for a time?"

"I shall be honored by taking any share in the work," said Arthur respectfully.

"Of course, I shall have to test you a little," said Lady Charlotte with a smile. "You will have to come for a day or two upon trial, and let me see what hand you make of it. I begin work at nine; if you could come from nine to twelve or one every day——"

"Certainly, Lady Charlotte."

"I think it would be worth your while if you have nothing else to do," she said indifferently. And she mentioned terms in an incidental manner, which made Arthur Ellison's heart glow within him with delight.

"In the meantime, you'll keep my counsel," she said, rising from her seat, and closing the drawers of the cabinet. "I must swear you to secrecy, you know. Tell your sister I want you to do a little secretarial work—copying of letters and so on. That will prevent her from asking any questions. And you understand, you are not to tell anybody of these memoirs"— she darted a look of fire at him, as she spoke.

"Your ladyship may depend upon my absolute silence," said Arthur, bowing, and speaking with unwonted gravity and ceremoniousness. He felt that it would not be possible to refuse anything that Lady Charlotte demanded, or to break his word to her when once passed. A want of good faith would be the last thing she would forgive. And she would not easily stay her hand if an offender came within reach of punishment. Arthur felt sobered by this conviction.

"Then we'll go back to the drawing-room. They'll wonder what has become of us," said Lady Charlotte, her face which had been for a moment overcast, clearing as if by a sudden flash. "I am much obliged to you, Mr. Ellison," she added, so cordially that Arthur almost proposed for Lisa's hand upon the spot.

He followed her to the drawing-room in a state of suppressed exultation which he was careful not to betray. He did not want Lady Charlotte to suppose that her proposition was at all wonderful. But he was filled with the greatest gratification. She was about to take him into her confidence, to associate him with herself in what she termed the most sacred duty of her life: did not all this imply increasing intimacy, such as would warrant him in asking very soon for Lisa's hand? And she knew so little of him too. She must have formed a very high idea of his abilities; and Arthur's heart glowed at the thought. The only draw-back to his satisfaction was the remembrance that he was bound not to speak of his work, even to Esther; and as he always had an uneasy consciousness that Esther thought less well of him than he believed to be his desert, he would have liked to have convinced her of Lady Charlotte's appreciation. He even debated with himself whether he might not make an exception to the law of secrecy in Esther's case, forgetting that Lady Charlotte had decisively excluded her from confidence. Esther would promise not to betray him, if he told her: was he not justified in counting on her loyalty? And it would be an immense comfort to him to have her sympathy, and sometimes even the assistance of her judgment. But very reluctantly he gave up the idea; she might be questioned as to her knowledge, and although she would not expose him to harm, if she could help it, he knew her to be ab-

solutely incapable of a lie.   It gave him a greatly increased sense of importance that he should be admitted
to a confidence which Esther did not share.

Naturally, the Lady Charlotte Byng's views on the
matter differed from his own.   When the visitors had
left the house, she flung herself down on a lounge in
the hall, clasped her hands high above her head, and
said, in a tone of satisfaction:

"I've done one good stroke of business, Howard.
I've secured that idle young man to transcribe dear
grandpapa's papers for me."

She did not see that Lisa turned a little, with a quick
movement, and a rising flush, as if to protest against
something in her speech.   It was Mr. Byng who pro-
tested openly, although in rather a different way.

"My dear Charlotte," he said, putting up the single
eyeglass which gave a look of fictitious keenness to his
mild, pale face, "how has Mr. Ellison managed to im-
press you with his fitness for so important an under-
taking?"

"Oh, I don't want very much," said Lady Charlotte
carelessly.   "A little literary facility, a sufficient acquaintance with Latin, French, and Italian—German
also, if possible—of which I have yet to judge; a good
hand o' write, as the Scotch say, and the morale of a
gentleman—that's all I require, and I have been seeking it these seven years."

"Which proves that it was not so easy to find as it
appeared," said Mr. Byng sententiously.   "How do
you know that he has the morale of a gentleman, for

instance? You have not known him more than ten days or a fortnight!"

"Oh, Uncle Howard! Esther's brother!" Lisa breathed, rather than spoke, in gentle deprecation.

"Well, yes, Esther's brother," said Lady Charlotte boldly. "It is a recommendation in itself, for Esther Ellison is a lady to the fingertips. I don't fancy that a brother of hers could be wanting in the essential elements of honor. I have told him that the book is not to be talked about, and he has given me his word not to mention it."

"It would be a pity if your distinguished grandfather's wishes could not be carried out in their entirety on account of the imprudence or the want of faith of this young gentleman, who, we must remember, is a journalist by profession," said Mr. Byng, resuming his book quietly.

"Good Lord!" said Lady Charlotte, raising herself a little, and bending her beautiful dark brows at her husband. "You don't suppose I am such a fool as really to entrust any documents of importance to his hands? Until I know him better than I do now, I shall be extremely careful as to what he sees, I can tell you. It is just the unimportant papers that I want copied; there's a mass of minor matters and official correspondence that I cannot undertake to wade through. All I want from Ellison is mechanical, secretarial work—clerk's work, if you like."

"I should have thought that Mr. Ellison's abilities deserved better employment," said Lisa, not·so much with resentment—she dared not show resentment—as with a touch of polite remonstrance in her tone.

"He has not done much yet," said Lady Charlotte. "He's clever, yes, but he has much to learn. It will do him no harm to associate and be associated with us for a few weeks, and I shall make it amply worth his while. I thank the gods for sending me so suitable an assistant, here in the very wilds of Surrey. Without my looking for him, he has dropped from the skies. It simplifies my work very much for the next six months, and I'll give him an excellent testimonial and dozens of introductions if he does his part respectably. Oh, I'm quite prepared to treat him handsomely. He and his sister have been a great find to us this autumn."

"I am glad you are prepared to treat him with caution," said Mr. Byng. "But I find a difficulty in seeing how you can prove whether he is trustworthy or not, until it is too late to withdraw from the arrangement."

Lady Charlotte showed her strong white teeth in a laugh that lighted up her face like sunshine.

"Oh, you men have no ideas," she said good-humoredly. "I have laid my plans with very great care, although you seem to think me so imprudent. I have one excellent safeguard—Lisa, you are not to repeat what I say to the Ellisons; do you hear?"

"Yes, Aunt Charlotte," said Lisa obediently.

"I have warned the young man against telling even his sister about the book. Miss Ellison is the soul of truthfulness, and if he tells her anything, I shall read it in her eyes. And in that case I shall drop him like a hot coal, for if he is unfaithful in that matter, I shall feel no trust in him when it comes to a greater one."

"It is rather like setting a trap for him," said Mr. Byng.

"Is it quite fair, Aunt Charlotte?"

"Quite fair. You are rather sentimental in your ideas, you two," said Lady Charlotte, with perfect good temper. "Don't you see that if the young man is a gentleman, with right principles and a sense of honor and all the rest of it, my 'trap,' as you call it, will not affect him in the least. And if he is devoid of these right sentiments, the sooner he is trapped the better!"

She took up a book as if to end the discussion, and Lisa, with flushed cheeks, stole away to muse over the poems that her hero had left behind, and to marvel at the suspicious tendencies of elder folk.

It crossed her mind, of course, that she might warn Esther of the "trap" set for Mr. Ellison, or even speak to Arthur himself upon the subject; but she decided that such an action would be lowering to herself and insulting to her friends. Esther was the soul of truthfulness, as Lady Charlotte had said, and her brother must be like herself.

So it was, perhaps, just as well that Arthur had made up his mind to keep the secret of his work under Lady Charlotte's tutelage.

CHAPTER VI.

IN THE CONSERVATORY.

While Arthur was inspecting the relics and con-
ferring with Lady Charlotte in the library, Esther had
been drawn away by Mr. Thorold to admire the flowers in the conservatory. Mr. Byng was as passionately fond of his "glass" as Lady Charlotte was of
her garden and her farm; and his begonias and his
orchids were the pride of his heart. He went with
his visitors through the houses, expatiating on the
beauty and rarity of his specimens; he even cut a
few choice blossoms for Esther, who knew enough of
his preferences to appreciate the honor he did her;
and finally he returned to the palm-house for a quiet
cigarette, while Justin escorted his companion to the
long conservatory that ran the length of the dining-
room, where he found her a comfortable seat among
the fragrant flowering plants.

"But where is Arthur, I wonder?" Esther said, a
little uneasily. She had already noticed dangerous
signs of a desire on Arthur's part to gaze rather too
persistently in Lisa's direction, and she was anxious
about him when he was in Lisa's society. But Justin's answer reassured her.

"He is in the library still with Lady Charlotte. I
think she has some designs on him. I know she has
been wanting a secretary for some time." He didn't

say a "copyist," lest he should hurt Esther's feelings; but he believed that Lady Charlotte's requirements would really be best described by that word. "Do you think he would care for work of that sort?"

"It is what he has been looking for. It would be delightful for him! But Lady Charlotte cannot want a secretary for any length of time?"

"No; it would be a mere temporary thing, but it might be worth his while to take it. I should consider association with Lady Charlotte a privilege in itself; she is a woman of very wide information; as was said of another lady, 'to know her is a liberal education,' and especially valuable to a literary man. Your brother has literary tastes, I believe?"

"Yes," said Esther. "He writes for newspapers— and poems sometimes," she added with a smile.

"It is a delightful facility," said Mr. Thorold, sitting down beside her. "I often wish I had time and talent for it; but Blue-books and Parliamentary reports do not form the best kind of preparation for poetry."

Esther was struck by the unusual amount of formality in his tone. His manner was generally considered cold and formal; the young legislator seemed to find it rather difficult to unbend in general society; but with Esther his tone had generally relaxed. She found it hard to imagine that it was he who had asked for the purple clematis in her hand a few nights before; the voice, the accent, seemed to her studiously different. She wondered what the change portended; and why he should stay beside her at all if he were so cold and indifferent. Perhaps he was staying only for

politeness' sake, and it was her part to relieve him
of an unpleasing social duty.

"Lady Charlotte is perhaps expecting me in the
library," she said, making a movement as if to rise.
"I want to see the miniatures again so very much——"

"Won't the miniatures wait for another day?" he
asked, quite quietly. "I have not so very often the
chance of speaking to you, and I thought we might
have had a little talk."

She settled herself again into her seat without a
word. It was foolish of her, she thought, to be unable
to reply to so simple and commonplace a remark; but
there was something disconcerting in his tone—or in
his eyes, she did not know which; and under its influence she could not find a word to say.

"I am afraid sometimes," he went on, "that Blue-
books and Reports do not make a very interesting
companion. May I speak of myself a moment? You
may have heard that my cousin, Howard Byng, is
almost my only living relation; I suppose very few
people are so much alone in the world as I."

"You are like me in that respect," said Esther, finding her voice again when his accents became cold and
dry. "I, too——"

She stopped suddenly.

"But you have your brother—a much closer relation than a cousin," said Mr. Thorold.

Esther colored hotly; the yoke of Arthur's "harmless little deception" weighed very heavily upon her.
She would not endure it a moment longer; at any
cost, she must speak!

"But Arthur is not—not my brother," she began, hurriedly and indistinctly. "He is only——"

"Of course—of course, I remember. He is your half-brother; Lady Charlotte was telling me. That accounts for the difference in your complexions—his so fair and yours so dark—I suppose. Still, a half-brother is much nearer than a cousin, especially when you are such good friends; and as you can see for yourself, Howard Byng and I have not much in common; he cannot be said to count for much in my life."

"No," said Esther, trying to nerve herself to interrupt him again. But he had a calm, deliberate way of speaking which seemed to impose delay upon her; she resigned herself perforce to making the disclosure another time.

"I have always felt a little lonely at Hurst, ever since I left the University and took up my abode at the old place," continued Justin. "You see, I can remember such a different kind of life there: a family life, with father, mother, a nursery full of children, every kind of thing that goes to make up enjoyment and delight. The place even now seems strange to me sometimes; I fancy I hear my brothers and sisters shouting and playing in the garden—it is an odd delusion——"

"You are too much alone," said Esther, sympathetically, as he paused.

"Yes, I am too much alone. I fill the house with acquaintances from time to time, shooting men, political friends, men whom I like and whose society I enjoy; but it does not make the place a home to me, as it used to be in the days gone by."

Esther was afraid of pauses. She spoke again, when his tongue halted. "You had several brothers and sisters?"

"There were six of us; I am the only one left. Three died in one week of diphtheria, and my dear mother never held up her head again. Then the two boys were drowned—a boating accident on the Thames —and for a time my father and I were left alone together. He died before I went to College, and since then—oh, well, I have had as many friends as most men, but I have had no home life. And I am rather a domestic man by nature, I believe; I should like to have a home."

"You are fond of Hurst?"

"Yes, I love Hurst. I have been asked to let it— even to sell it; but I have never entertained the idea for a moment. The home of one's childhood always stands first. You have never seen Hurst, have you, Miss Ellison?"

"Never."

"It is not a big grand place like this," said Justin, waving his hand towards the house, with a little smile. "It is quite humble and unpretending—a little red brick house among the trees, with a good deal of ivy growing almost over the windows. They say it is not very healthy—but I should have it looked to if it were going to be used again." He added the last words quickly. "I should set about cleaning, painting, redecorating, and all the rest of it!"

"Oh, wouldn't that be a pity!" said Esther impulsively.

He looked decidedly gratified.

"I should leave it as much unaltered as possible," he said; "but it would not do to risk the health of one who is dear to me——"

"Your own health may be in danger, then? Oh, Mr. Thorold, if that is the case, do let me beg of you to make all necessary improvements as soon as possible."

"Wouldn't it be a pity, as you said just now?" he queried, smiling.

"A life so valuable as yours ought not to be lightly risked."

"I wish," he said, bending towards her and speaking in a lower and very earnest tone, "that I could hear you alter that expression, and say—'a life that is dear to me,' as I did just now."

Esther remained silent, startled by the form of his remark. She hardly knew at first how much—or how little—it signified.

"I have been saying that I was lonely," Justin Thorold went on, in a voice that was no longer either calm or cold, "and I was going to say that, although I have often tried to find one whose presence would make a home of the old house, I have never met one whom I would willingly have set in my mother's place until—until I met you."

Again there was silence. The color flickered backwards and forwards on Esther's face; he tried to read its expression, but he could not interpret the meaning

6

of those transient blushes, of those downcast eyelashes
and the mutely bitten lip.

"I want a companion, Esther; I want someone to
love. And I love you; I will try to make you very
happy, if you will consent to be my wife."

He was simple and explicit; it did not occur to him
to wrap up his desires in fine language, or endeavor
to soften her decision by the use of a honeyed phrase.
And the few straightforward words went at once to
Esther's heart. They brought up her eyes to his face,
and the words to her quivering lips.

"Yes, I love you," she said, as simply and honestly
as he himself had spoken; "but—oh, wait, hear me,
please!"—as he put his hand on her and tried to draw
her closer to him—"I do not know what to answer;
I am not sure that I know what to say."

"Say?" he repeated, smilingly, as his fingers closed
upon hers; "there is only one thing to say after that
confession; you must say that you will be my wife."

"Oh, I don't know—I don't know," said Esther,
drawing herself away and looking before her with a
puzzled, almost distressed expression, which seemed
to him difficult to understand. "It is just because
I—I—love you that I am not sure whether I ought.
You know you were meant—you were expected to
marry Miss Daubeny."

"Nobody seriously expected it," he said. "And Lisa
would never consent—I am sure of that."

"But—Lady Charlotte—and Mr. Byng?"

"They are not my masters," he said, smiling. "Why
should I care what they say?"

"But Mr. Byng is your nearest relative, and I have heard—if it is not wrong to speak of it—that, as he has no children——"

"I am his heir? That I shall come in for Westhills, and all the rest of it? Well, that is true," said Justin, good-humoredly. "But is not that a reason for accepting me?"

"Not in my eyes."

"No, you unworldly little woman, I am sure of that; so you need not flame out at me like that. What is it you mean about Howard Byng, dear?"

"I think you ought, perhaps, to regard his wishes," said Esther, bravely, but without lifting her eyes.

"So do I, but not to the extent of regulating my choice of a wife by them. I have no reason also to suppose that he will object to my choice. You are a great favorite here."

"They are very kind to me," said Esther tremulously, "and I cannot bear that they should be displeased, and that all my pleasant relations with them should cease—for I am perfectly certain that Lady Charlotte will be very angry——"

"Well?" said Justin, less patiently than usual. "You are not going to give me up because Lady Charlotte is angry, are you?"

"Oh, no, no! But—may I speak to Arthur before I say anything more?" said Esther, in a voice that was almost inaudible. She had turned very pale.

"You may do anything you like, my sweet, now that I know you love me. Certainly I see one thing— it may be a little awkward for you if I precipitate matters while you are here. How much longer have you to stay, Esther?"

"Three weeks, or a little more. I begin my High School teaching about the middle of October."

"Had you not better write to the High School people and tell them to find someone to take your place?"

"Oh, no! I must fulfill my engagements." .

"It is not that I have any objection to your teaching, but you see, I want you at Hurst as soon as possible. But concerning Lady Charlotte: I will defer any announcement of my intentions until you are safe in London. Will that do? It may save you some embarrassment."

"And I will defer my answer until then, so that you will have no announcement to make," she said, the color returning to her cheek and the light to her eye. "I will write to you from London, and until then there is nothing between us—nothing."

"Nothing but our love for each other. Is that nothing?"

"It is a great deal—oh, it is all the world to me—but you are not bound. We are both free—quite free."

"Esther, is there any obstacle? Have you any other tie? Anything that could ever come between us?"

"Nothing of the kind—nothing. Only—you know me so little—would it not be better to wait a little longer—till you knew me better?"

There was a breathless agitation about her speech, which made Thorold look at her keenly. She was not like herself. Surely—surely she had nothing to conceal? No, there was truth in every feature of her face, every glance of her honest, expressive eyes.

"I do not quite understand you, Esther," he said gently, after a little pause. "You are not usually so distrustful as you seem to be of me; and I do not see why you should think so much of Lady Charlotte's approval. But I will do exactly as you wish, and you shall tell me when I may tell the world of our—engagement."

"I have not answered you yet."

"Oh, yes, you have," he said, and this time his arm went around her and drew her close to his side. "You have said you loved me; and that is enough, my darling, and I can trust you for all the rest." And then their lips met in a kiss which seemed to Esther the realization of all she had ever dreamed of human happiness.

But they had been left undisturbed a long time, and it was no wonder that Andrews looked rather grim when he announced that tea was served in the drawing-room. Andrews was a servant of the highest respectability, and he did not like to see Mr. Thorold sitting in the greenhouse, as he phrased it, with the governess. Esther was not a governess, but that was all one with Andrews, who knew that she taught for her daily bread. It seemed to him a light-minded and frivolous proceeding on the part of the future master of Westhills.

If Esther had not been very much preoccupied, she would have noticed the curious alertness, which came from suppressed excitement, of Arthur's manner. She alone could have properly appreciated its meaning, for to comparative strangers he did not seem differ-

ent from his ordinary self. But she saw nothing, heard
nothing—so absorbed was she in the wonderful revelation that had been made to her, the marvelous
change in all her future life which Justin Thorold's
love would bring.

She was so silent and dreamy as she walked home
with Arthur after tea that he grew almost angry with
her at last. "I don't believe you have heard a word
I have been saying," he said in a peevish tone, as
they entered their little sitting-room.

"Oh, yes," she said, sitting down on the first chair
within reach and looking at him absently. "You have
been seeing Lady Charlotte's relics, and telling me
about them. I have seen most of them already."

"Did you hear me say that I was going up to the
house at nine o'clock to-morrow morning to do some
—some writing for Lady Charlotte?"

"No, I did not hear that. But Mr. Thorold mentioned that she wanted a secretary. Oh, Arthur, has
she really offered the post to you?"

"Not actually. But I am going to help her a little,"
said Arthur, with a nonchalant air, which at any other
moment would have made Esther smile.

"If you do the work well, whatever it is," she said
eagerly, "Lady Charlotte is the very person to recommend you to others and get you a good position.
The only thing that troubles me, Arthur, is—her believing you to be my brother still."

"As if that mattered!"

"It matters a good deal to me," said Esther, coloring. "I cannot let the concealment go on much
longer."

"Cannot let it?" said Arthur, in much displeasure. "I think that you forget that you promised not to speak, that you said you would not betray me!"

"Circumstances have altered the case. Arthur, I have something to tell you. You must keep my secret," she said, trembling, yet half smiling, "for we do not want the world to know it just yet. Mr. Thorold——"

"He's asked you to marry him?" said Arthur, interrupting her. "Gad, Esther, you are in luck!"

"He has asked me," she answered, with downcast eyes, "but I have not answered him yet. I am to wait till I get to London——"

"But you will accept him then, I suppose? You are not going to be such an idiot as to refuse?"

"I love him," she said simply, and turned her face away. For a moment Arthur was silent; her avowal gave him a curious pang. He did not care for her except as a cousin; and he was falling hot in love with Lisa Daubeny; but there are few men that can be absolutely pleased to hear that the woman whose heart was once theirs, has given it to another.

"That means that you will marry him then," he said, with sudden roughness. "You've done very well for yourself, Esther. You were quite right to throw me over and wait for a wealthier man."

"Don't speak in that way, Arthur—especially now, when I am so happy."

"Well, well!" he said, with a short and bitter laugh, "I'll be amiable and do the heavy father on the great occasion! There could be no more suitable person to give you away, could there? The brother takes the father's place at these times."

"The cousin in this case," said Esther steadily.

"Now, Esther, what's the use of making a fuss? Why not let me be your brother to the end of our respective lives? No one will take the trouble to investigate the records, if we hold our tongues."

"I could not keep anything from the man I am to marry, Arthur. It may not be a very great thing, but——"

"In one sense, it is a very great thing—to you," said Arthur dryly. "If you tell Thorold that I am your cousin, he will ask a good many other questions—as to whether there was ever any love-making between us, for one thing. Thorold's a fastidious kind of man; I doubt whether the marriage will ever come off if he gets to know the truth of our relationship to each other before the wedding day."

Esther's face turned white. "You are wicked to say such things!" she broke out indignantly. "Mr. Thorold will believe what I tell him."

"And what I tell him, too," said her cousin, with a look that was almost malignant. Then recovering himself, he went on more pacifically: "I assure you, Esther, that you will be doing a very foolish thing if you enlighten him at present. Wait at any rate until we have left the place. We shall not be here long. You promised to keep the secret, and, as long as I am working for Lady Charlotte Byng, I will not have it told. You must make up your mind for silence until my work at Westhills is done."

CHAPTER VII.

A GOOD MEMORY.

Lady Charlotte had no cause to regret even the partial confidence that she had reposed in Arthur Ellison. He came punctually, did his work carefully, was quite competent for all that she wanted, and said not a word about the papers that he copied, either to Esther or to anybody else. Of course he was quick to see that his work touched the outside fringe only of the great minister's life; still less was he allowed any glimpse of the scandals that were reported to cling around Lady Muncaster's memory; but he came across gossip enough, and incident enough, to interest him considerably, and he could not but acknowledge that Lord Belfield's memoirs would probably create a tremendous sensation when it appeared with the new century. It was a pity that none of it could be published before then.

He suggested to Lady Charlotte in a tentative kind of way, that there would be no breaking of Lord Belfield's commands if she compiled a volume of gossip and anecdotes from her grandfather's memoirs, without publishing the political record which would form the weightier matter of the book. But Lady Charlotte despised the suggestion. "What! Pick out the plums and leave the solid pudding till 1900? Who would read the book then, I should like to know? No; it shall all come out together, or not at all."

Arthur did not dare to shrug his shoulders, but he thought her a very unpractical woman. He wished he had the handling of these memoirs; he could make his name and his future without fail. He had not been three days at work before he had realized the wealth of piquant information which lay stored in Lady Charlotte's locked cabinet.

The pity of it was, he said to himself, that she intended to "edit" the memoirs of her grandfather. He knew what was meant by a woman's editing. Lady Charlotte was clever and large-minded, but not entirely above the foibles of her sex. She would cut out the most amusing of the risque stories; she would omit the witty but profane expressions; she would soften down the gallant adventures of her immediate relatives. The work should have been put into the hands of a man!

And what a bore it was to think that it could not appear until the year 1900! By that time he, himself, would probably have forgotten the stories that had been left out. "And it's the stories that are left out which count," said Arthur. "If only I remembered all I read, I am pretty sure I could supplement Lady Charlotte's book admirably, when it appears! And, by Jove, why shouldn't I?"

His lip curved itself into a curious smile; he stopped —for he was walking home from Westhills when the idea occurred to him—and gazed at the distant horizon with an abstracted and dreamy air. There was a vague vision before him of infinite possibilities, of a world in which fortune might perhaps be ready to his hand, if only he had the wit and the courage to seize it.

"I believe," he reflected, "that I could write down all that I have read and copied to-day. A memory like mine stands one in good stead sometimes, although it is not a tenacious one." And this was true; he was able to report with very fair accuracy long passages from books or whole columns of newspapers after reading them once or twice; and although he could not retain for long what he had thus casually committed to memory, he had often found the faculty an extremely useful one. "If," he went on, still standing with his eyes fixed on the blue distance, "if I were to chronicle every night for my own pleasure— of course, simply for my own pleasure—what I have read during the day, it would do no one any harm, and it would give me the satisfaction in after years of checking Lady Charlotte's anecdotes. It would not injure the book; and it would not be telling anybody, for nobody would see the record; and it would save me trouble sometimes, for I could look up my own notes instead of referring to originals. I'll just try it to-night—just to see whether I can recollect enough to make it worth my while."

He hastened home, intent on the new idea, which, as he rather persistently repeated to himself, was a perfectly harmless one. And it was only for an experiment that he would write down his recollections of the day's work.

Esther was out. He shut himself into his own room,

sought out a thick note-book, ink and pens, and set
to work. After a moment's pause, he wrote on the
first page, in a neat text-hand, "To be burned unread
in case of my death," and felt almost heroic when he
had written it. "Now," he said, "it cannot fall into
unauthorized hands."

He wrote for a couple of hours, steadily. When he
had finished, he drew a long breath, and laid down
his pen with a jubilant air. "I had no idea I could
remember so much," he murmured. "My memory's
better than ever; by Jove, it is!"

He had written down almost every word of the letters and journal of which he had that morning made
a transcript; and of the two or three preceding days'
work, he had made a very full resume. It was a feat
of memory of which he felt proud. There was no
doubt about it—he had faculties which transcended
those of other men; and he would be foolish indeed
not to make use of them. He might not be able to
publish the result of his labor or to make money by it;
but it was a satisfaction to think that he could do
things of this sort if he chose. How tremendously
aghast Lady Charlotte would be if she knew what he
had written! He must be a little careful about letting
her find out that he possessed this somewhat abnormal
power of "memorizing" what he read, and more especially what he wrote.

He had turned over the leaves of his note-book
with great pleasure. There was nothing of profound
significance, of course, in the manuscript that Lady
Charlotte had permitted him to read; but there was

some pleasant gossip about the Court, some perfectly new anecdotes of people in power, some hints of a scandal, the nature of which did not transpire. Arthur began to feel a gnawing desire to get to the bottom of the story. He wondered whether he could piece it out from the fragments which it was evident Lady Charlotte meant to place only in his hands. He resolved to make great efforts to recommend himself to her, and to do his work for her so excellently and yet with so little apparent curiosity, that she would not hesitate to let him see even the most important and most private of her grandfather's papers.

In pursuit of this end, he labored well. Lady Charlotte praised him in public, and reposed more and more confidence in him. He was very exact, very quick, yet very reticent; she thought him rather wanting in knowledge of the world, however, and in the power of putting two and two together. She found him rather peculiarly simple, she said, in many ways. And she came to rely on his simplicity more than she had at first intended. At the end of ten days or so, Arthur might look through the papers as much as he pleased. Lady Charlotte would even leave her keys upon the table. "There was no need to take such precautions," she said once, when Mr. Byng uttered a few words of warning, "Mr. Ellison was a gentleman." And for some time, indeed, Arthur rejected the thought of using the keys for his own ends, with indignation. But perhaps Lady Charlotte would not have considered it the act of a gentleman to write down every evening all that he had learned through an attentive study of the Belfield MSS.

There came a point at last when it seemed to Arthur that his opportunities were coming to a close, and that he had not yet solved one or two problems which had suggested themselves to him rather early in his work. It had not been proposed that his engagement as Lady Charlotte's secretary should continue longer than Esther's engagement as coach; but he had hoped to make himself so invaluable that he would be asked to go on with his work—perhaps even to stay in the house! Ah, then what delightful chances he would have of ransacking the old cabinet and discovering all the family secrets! Not that he wanted to make any use of them; but he had a natural thirst, he said to himself, for information. And he had early got upon the track of what seemed to him an important (and possibly scandalous) family secret; ignorance of it left several passages in Lord Belfield's letters inexplicable, and Arthur felt that he must at all hazards secure the clew.

He seized his opportunity one morning when Lady Charlotte had been called away to London for the day. She had left him plenty of work to do, and told him that he would be undisturbed. Lisa accompanied her to London, and Mr. Byng was confined to his own room by an attack of sciatica. He was quite alone. It would be untrue to say that he had no scruples of conscience. He felt very uncomfortable when he thought of what he was about to do. Once or twice he almost resolved not to pry further into

Lady Charlotte's affairs. Then came the remembrance
of his incomplete note-book, and the incompleteness
appealed to him as it can only do to the professed
literary man. He really could not bear to feel that
it was incomplete. The key was in his hand, and
although his cheeks burned and his fingers trembled,
he turned it in the lock and opened Lady Charlotte's
private drawer.

Perhaps she had not been so careless as she seemed.
Some of the papers which Arthur most wanted to see
were hidden away in a secret drawer which he could
not open. He tried diligently to discover the spring
or sliding panel, which he felt sure must be in existence, but his efforts were utterly unsuccessful. But
he did come upon one paper, which Lady Charlotte
certainly never meant him to see: a letter to Lord
Belfield from his daughter Lady Muncaster, which
contained the key to the mystery that had baffled
Arthur Ellison so long.

He read and re-read the letter with gathering stupefaction. It threw a new light on the family history altogether, and yet it was a secret that had never
seen the light of day. Arthur knew well enough that
there were plenty of stories connected with old fam-
ilies which were sensational or tragical enough; yet
here was one which nobody had suspected, and which
would not perhaps have much effect upon the public
mind so long after its occurrence; yet which, if known,
might have changed the fortunes of Lord Belfield's
family completely.

Lord Belfield had been twice married, first to a

Miss Anketel, who had run away from him and been drowned at sea; secondly to the Honorable Maria De Vaux, who had become the mother of the celebrated Amelia, Marchioness of Muncaster, whose daughters had been respectively the wives of Howard Byng and William Daubeny. It seemed from the letter which Arthur held in his hand, that after the second Lady Belfield's death and the Lady Amelia's marriage to the Marquis, a story had got wind that the first Lady Belfield was not drowned at all, but was still living in America, the reputed wife of a Californian gold-digger. As she had not been divorced, owing to the rumors of her death, the marriage with Lord Belfield would of course still hold good, and the second marriage be invalid. Lady Muncaster wrote in great haste and indignation to her father, asking if the story were true, and stating that her husband with whom she lived unhappily, had already taunted her with the stain upon her birth.

Arthur devoured the lines eagerly. But where was Lord Belfield's answer? It would be interesting to see what he said in reply. A hurried search among the remaining papers convinced him that the letter was not there. It was probably among the papers which Lady Charlotte kept locked in her private drawer. Arthur swore a little under his breath, for he was growing desperately angry, when he realized that there was probably no way of possessing himself of these papers, and that he would be obliged to leave Westhills without establishing the fact, as he rather thirsted to do, of Lady Muncaster's illegitimacy.

He had no ill-will to Lady Muncaster, but he had
a curious taste for garbage, for unsavory scandals of
all sorts. It comforted him for his own obscurity to
know that persons of noble birth were sometimes, if
not generally, unworthy of respect. And for a few
moments he positively chuckled with delight at the
picture of Lady Charlotte's mortification and horror
if this blot upon the family escutcheon were made
known to the world. Even although it affected her
mother and not herself, Arthur knew that publicity
would pain her greatly; for she had never scrupled
to show her pride in being the daughter of Lady Muncaster. He felt that his old quarrel with the world
might be avenged if he could bring the blush of shame
to Lady Charlotte's haughty brows. There was no real
shame in the matter, for Lord Belfield had married
again in ignorance of the first wife's continued existence; but there was a sort of technical shame which
Arthur was certain that Lady Charlotte would especially dislike.

But there was no use in thinking of it. He acknowledged as much, regretfully, while he replaced
the paper and locked up the cabinet. He must not
quarrel with Lady Charlotte, and he must not betray
the family secrets to the world, if he meant to win
Lisa Daubeny's hand. He wondered whether he could
not use his knowledge as a method of bending the
Byngs to his will when the time came to avow his
passion for Lisa. A strong man, he imagined, would
threaten Lady Charlotte, and force her to submit to
his will. But he did not think he was strong enough

7

for that. Lady Charlotte always cowed him a little
in spite of himself. No, artifice and cunning must
be his weapons; or rather, as he called them, ingenu-
ity and intellect. With these he would win the day.

A step at the door, a rattle of the handle, made him
start. He had not yet quite finished his work of shutting the drawers and locking the cabinet, and he had
to turn back to the table with an uncomfortable suspicion that one or two papers had not been restored
to their proper places. One indeed had actually fallen
to the ground. He had time only to pick it up and
thrust it into his pocket, when the door was opened
and—and of all people in the world—Lisa came in.
She was flushed but smiling, and Arthur involuntarily
flushed also. If she had come upon the scene a moment earlier, what could he have said or done? Only
she was so innocent-minded that it would have been
easy to throw dust in her eyes.

"Why, I thought you were in London by this time!"
exclaimed Arthur, in amaze.

"We ought to be. There was a railway accident on
the line, and Aunt Charlotte would not go on. So
we came back to surprise you at your work."

"I am afraid I have been rather idle," said Arthur.
"I had a headache this morning, and have been taking
my time, thinking I should be able to work late as
Lady Charlotte was out."

"Then I am afraid you are not glad to see us back
again?"

"Don't you know that I am always glad to see you?"

He had adopted this tone with her several times

of late, at first timidly, latterly with more boldness
and ardor. After his recent discovery of a family secret, he felt more than usually bold. And Lisa had
never seemed displeased by his advances.

She looked very lovely as she stood beside the
library table, dressed in a jacket and skirt of soft
gray cloth, with silver buttons, and a little soft gray
fur-chinchilla, he thought, around the neck and throat,
and a gray hat with gray and white feathers and silver
buckles to match the dress. The gray suited her fair
complexion and bright hair admirably, and there was
a joyous light in her soft eyes.

"Always?" she asked. There was a happy playful-
ness in her tone.

"Always," he re-echoed fervently. "And there will
never be a moment of my life when I feel differ-
ently."

"One cannot answer for all one's future life," said
Lisa, shaking her head and beginning to draw off her
gray gloves.

"I can."

"Ah, Mr. Ellison, Aunt Charlotte always says that
you are remarkable."

"Is it so very remarkable to know when one has
seen the most perfect woman in the world?"

She drew back a little, and the smile flitted from
her face. Arthur saw the change, and was alarmed.
Had he gone too far?

"For heaven's sake, don't be angry with me!" he
said, in a voice rendered tremulous by the agitation
of his nerve rather than by his love for her—genuine

although he considered this to be—"I would not offend you for the world. Indeed I would not."

"I am not offended," said Lisa, drooping a little as he again drew near.

"Mayn't I tell you then that I think you—perfect?"

"No one is perfect, Mr. Ellison."

"A woman is perfect in the eyes of the man who loves her," said Arthur, in a low voice. Then as she did not answer, he pressed the point. "Don't you think so? Has no one told you so before?"

"I don't know. I think it would be rather foolish to say so," faltered Lisa, beginning not to know what she said.

"I shall have to go away very soon, and I want you to know what I think of you," Arthur whispered. He was already shaken up by the sharp fear of detection that had rushed over him when he had heard Lisa at the door; and the rapidly rising tide of passion swept away all the weak barriers of will that caution and duty had erected between himself and Lisa. He couldn't control himself any longer; he was obliged to speak. "I love you, Lisa; I love you, I love you," he stammered, not able to think of any other words. "Lisa—darling!"

It was plain that she could not speak. Her eyes were swimming in tears, but still she was not displeased. She was not going to send him away. There was a smile upon her lips.

"Lisa, darling, you love me. Let me—let me kiss you—just once, and then I shall feel sure," he said, scarcely believing in his own good fortune, but sure that she would not let him press his lips to hers unless she loved him in return.

It was true then? He had kissed her passionately many times; he lost all sense of prudence, as he stood with his arms around her, his face bent close to hers. He had forgotten that at any moment an interruption might occur.

"Good Lord!" said a voice from the doorway that caused the lovers to start apart hurriedly. "May I ask what this means, young people?"

And Lady Charlotte marched into the room.

CHAPTER VIII.

LADY CHARLOTTE INTERVENES.

Lady Charlotte's handsome brows were particularly
stormy, and if the dark lightnings of her eye could
have struck Arthur with instant death, she would probably not have been unwilling that they should do so.
She was still dressed in her London panoply—the
fashionable bonnet, the perfectly hung dress, the handsome velvet mantle, which to Arthur's eyes always
conferred new dignity upon her. He was not the man
to see dignity in undress. Yet he vaguely felt that
he would have been able to meet Lady Charlotte on
more equal terms if she had worn the rough tweed and
gaiters of her ordinary morning wear, or the loose
artistic tea-gown of her afternoon.

He had instinctively quitted his hold upon Lisa
when he heard Lady Charlotte's voice, but he had
manliness enough to put his hand upon hers and draw
her forward, as he said, with apparent calm:

"I love your niece, Lady Charlotte, and she is good
enough to reciprocate my affection."

"Reciprocate your fiddlesticks!" said Lady Charlotte rudely. But she sat down suddenly, as if she
had received a blow, and her lips turned a little pale.
After a moment's pause, however, she turned to Lisa
with an air of indulgent ridicule. "You silly child,
what nonsense! Run away just now and leave me to

talk over the matter with Mr. Ellison. I can speak
to you later."

Lisa lingered, her hand in Arthur's still. Her eyes
were bright, her cheeks flushed, she, usually so timid,
did not, to Arthur's astonishment, look afraid. "Aunt
Charlotte, you will listen to him? You will remember
that I—I care for him?" she said.

"Oh, yes, I will listen to him; I will remember
what you say," answered Lady Charlotte, with a sort
of ominous calm, rather belied by the fiery gleam of
her eyes. "You had better go now; young ladies are
not usually present at these interviews."

"But this is an exceptional one," Lisa pleaded.
"May I not——"

She could not continue her entreaties, for Lady
Charlotte rose, splendid and terrible, with the lightning and thunder of her eyes and brows, as she
pointed with her finger to the library door, and said
succinctly: "Go!"

And Lisa went. She would have been bold indeed
if she could have defied the power of that majestic
monosyllable. She pressed Arthur's hand before re-
linquishing, gave him a lovely smile, and departed,
while Arthur hurried forward to open the door for
her with all possible grace and courtesy of manner—
eager indeed for a moment's breathing-space in which
to recover his self-possession before turning to en-
counter his formidable opponent. For he felt that
she was only waiting for Lisa's departure to let the
storm break upon his head.

He turned back, leisurely enough, with his hands

thrust into the pockets of his loose velvet coat; his
face pale, a touch of insolence in his bearing and in
his cool blue eyes. In thinking of him afterwards,
Lady Charlotte acknowledged that she had never seen
him look so well. The independence of his bearing
was just the kind of thing that she could appreciate,
although at the moment it incensed her beyond measure. As he had expected, she dropped all pretense
of civility when Lisa had left the room.

"Now, sir, will you tell me what you mean by this
dishonorable conduct?" she said, in tones which admitted of no doubt as to her opinions.

"I deny that it is dishonorable in any way for me
to pay my addresses to Miss Daubeny," said Arthur
hardily.

"Pay your addresses! Is it paying your addresses
to make love secretly to the daughter of the house
in which you have been admitted on the footing of
a friend? Or, to put it another way, is it considered
honorable in an employe to win the affections of his
employer's niece or daughter?"

"It has been done before," said Arthur, with an exasperating smile.

"It has been done before, but not by gentlemen,"
said Lady Charlotte. "And I had the impression, to
begin with, that you were a gentleman, Mr. Ellison.
I am exceedingly sorry to have to alter my opinion."

Her voice was not passionate any longer, but cold
and cutting. Her nostrils worked slightly, and her fine
lips and brows expressed a lofty disdain. Arthur

bowed and answered with such exaggerated politeness that it seemed ironical.

"I must beg your ladyship's pardon if through my ignorance of the laws of society I have erred, in securing the affection of the niece before I applied for the permission of her guardians," he said. "But seeing that the error has been committed, may I now ask your sanction to an engagement between Miss Daubeny and myself?"

"Of course you know that is absolutely out of the question," said Lady Charlotte, with great composure.

"Even if Lisa loves me——"

"Lisa love you! Pray, how long has this nonsense been going on?"

"I have loved her ever since I saw her! It is sober earnest, Lady Charlotte; there is no 'nonsense' about the matter. I shall love her to my dying day."

"Love her by all means! There is nothing to prevent you," said Lady Charlotte with curling lip; "but what I mean is, when did you speak to her first?"

Arthur hesitated. He wished he could say that he had spoken before that morning. From the point of view of honor and honesty, it was of course better that he should not have spoken earlier; but this point was not always the first that presented itself to Arthur Ellison. It would have given him keen pleasure at that moment to pain and vex Lady Charlotte by saying that he had declared himself to Lisa several days before. But he reflected that Lisa could contradict this statement, if it were made; so he contented himself with saying:

"I have not tried to hide my feelings toward her, but I have not perhaps made them quite clear to her until to-day."

"Oh, then there's not so much harm done," said Lady Charlotte, with sudden briskness. "If she has a fancy for you, it will soon die out, and when once you have left Westhills, we shall hear no more of the matter. You have mistaken my niece's character entirely, Mr. Ellison, if you think that she would have lent herself to any underhand behavior or to clandestine correspondence."

"You have scarcely given us time to show what we were going to do, Lady Charlotte," said Arthur, in an exceedingly injured voice, "I assure you that I should have come to you at once. I spoke to her only on the impulse of the moment—only because I could not keep silence any longer——"

"Then it is very fortunate that I came in just then," said Lady Charlotte dryly. "I can certainly not employ a secretary who cannot control his feelings. You know very well, Mr. Ellison, that you ought not to have spoken a word to Lisa without consulting me first. You did not consult me simply because you knew perfectly well what my answer would be. In the case of an equal, it would be different. I could understand that a man perfectly suitable in fortune and position might take our consent a little for granted, and try to win Lisa's heart without asking for her formally; but with you—you must see that the case is different."

"You said just now that I was a gentleman," said

Arthur. "Penniless gentlemen before now have aspired to the hand of women much more highly placed than themselves."

Lady Charlotte uttered a short, harsh laugh. "I'm afraid I used the word gentleman in a very conventional sense," she said. "Everyone's a gentleman now. What claims to gentility in the real sense have you? Who was your father?"

Arthur turned red and white by turns. "My father —he was——"

"A schoolmaster in a little country town. I've heard that from your sister. She at least makes no pretension to be what she is not. He was a good man, I am sure, and an intellectual man, but I am unable to see that he gives you any claim to marry Lady Muncaster and the great-granddaughter of the Earl of Belfield. I am not a snob," Lady Charlotte went on hastily, "and I don't say that you might not make her as good a husband as many a man of higher rank; but it is as plain as a pike-staff that you are not a suitable match for her. You force me to say things that I don't like to say, Mr. Ellison. You have been to neither a public school nor a university. You have no profession; you live from hand to mouth by doing hack-work for newspapers; is it possible that you consider yourself a fitting husband for Lisa Daubeny, who not only comes of a noble family but has been used to every indulgence and every luxury that wealth and position and strong family affection can give?"

"If I were rich, I suppose that you would forget my other drawbacks," said Arthur, a little bitterly.

"Well, it is better to be frank; I suppose I should.
If you were a millionaire, I suppose we should not
scrutinize your family tree too closely. It sounds brutal to say so, but in these modern days, it is absolutely
true. And so—as I don't see much prospect of your
becoming a millionaire—I think it would be advisable
for you to take this afternoon's train for London, and
make up your mind not to see Lisa any more."

"You delight in putting things cruelly, I think, Lady
Charlotte," said Arthur, with quivering lips. He was
so thoroughly pained and overwhelmed that Lady
Charlotte smoothed her brows and looked at him
pityingly.

"I don't delight in anything of the kind," she said,
"and I am very sorry that you have allowed your heart
to get the better of your head, Mr. Ellison, more especially as you have been very useful to me in several
ways; but you should have remembered in entering
this house that you were received here with perfect
trust and confidence, and should have been very careful not to abuse it."

"I had forgotten the claims of rank," said Arthur,
speaking more savagely than he knew. His evil temper was getting the upper hand of him again. "I ought
to have remembered, as you say, the position of Lady
Muncaster—and her legal status—before I made love
to her granddaughter."

He regretted the words before they were well out
of his mouth, but it flashed across his mind that if the
story recorded in Lady Muncaster's letter to her father

were untrue, his shaft would fall unheeded to the ground.

Lady Charlotte flashed a sudden, keen, questioning glance at him, and changed color a little. Then she sat perfectly still, as if considering something. Arthur's heart beat fast; he knew now what he had done. He had taunted Lady Charlotte with the slur upon her mother's name. Would she ever forgive him? Or would she try to conciliate him, and make terms, so that he should not give the story to the world?

He had not long to wait.

"It appears to me, Mr. Ellison," she said at length in the quietest of tones, "that you have been prying into things with which you have no business. By the bye, do I not see my key hanging from the lock of the cabinet? And by what authority have you dared to use that key, which was left in this room on the presumption that you were, as you told me just now, a gentleman?"

The gathering scorn in her voice crushed the listener. He stammered out some sort of excuse or denial, but Lady Charlotte took no notice. She walked, with a firm and stately step, to the escritoire, opened it, and tried one or two of the small inner drawers. One was open a little way, and the paper had evidently been disturbed. Lady Charlotte pointed to it, and turned her proud face, with a sarcastic smile, towards her whilom secretary.

"I do not think that I ever gave you permission to look at those papers," she said. "And if you have seen them, I really do not know what good they can do you or what harm they can do to us. But I think it settles the question as to the propriety of your proposing for Lisa. Her future husband must at least be an honorable man."

"I have looked at nothing—I know nothing of your affairs," said Arthur angrily. "It is common report——"

She looked at him full in the face. "Oh, no, indeed it is not," she said. "You have been quite—misinformed."

She smiled contemptuously. "It is not worth discussion. All that remains for me to do is to write you a check for your services, Mr. Ellison, and express my regret that our connection is come to such a disastrous end. I should advise you to return to London as soon as possible. I think your talents would be more appreciated there than in this quiet country place."

He writhed under the lash of her tongue, but he could not reply. Her scorn took away the very power of speech. He looked on helplessly while she sat down at the open desk, deliberately drew out a checkbook, and wrote a check, payable to his order. He could see by the turn of her pen that it was a very handsome check: fifty pounds, apparently, although he had hitherto been paid by the week—ten guineas a week, which was an altogether ridiculously high sum and had been given by the Byngs only as a way of showing kindness. The fifty was evidently meant in lieu of notice.

Arthur debated within himself as to whether he

should take it. The high-spirited thing to do was to
tear it in twain, and walk out of the house penniless;
but—penury had grown more than ever distasteful to
him. He had thrown up his regular work in London;
he had nothing laid by, and he was in debt; he would
have to borrow of Esther and look for something to
do, living, meanwhile, in those mean little London
rooms which he hated with such intolerable hatred.
He could not do without Lady Charlotte's fifty pounds,
even if it were flung to him as a bone is flung to a
dog.

She inclosed it in an envelope, and laid it before him
on the library table with a queenly air of dismissal.
"I think you will find that all right, Mr. Ellison,"
she said with a carelessness that was almost cheerful,
"and I wish you a very good-morning."

"You will hear of me again," said Arthur, as he
sullenly pocketed the envelope.

"In the newspapers, perhaps," returned Lady Charlotte, with significance.

"I mean, Lady Charlotte, that I shall not give up
my hopes of winning your niece's hand."

Lady Charlotte's bow and smile were absolutely
exasperating, in that they were unconcerned.

"Lisa used to be fastidious," she said, standing by
the table, and drawing towards her the manuscripts
upon which Arthur had been engaged. "I do not
suppose that she has entirely lost her power of dis-
tinguishing between right and wrong."

"You send me out of the house without allowing
me to see her again?"

"Certainly. Why should she see you?"

Arthur flushed hotly. "You are a hard woman, Lady Charlotte, but you may one day regret your hardness," he said.

"Is that meant for a threat?" said Lady Charlotte, with a curiously inscrutable face.

"You can take it as one if you like. If I can win Lisa, by fair means or foul, I shall do it."

"I am obliged to you for the warning, Mr. Ellison. I do not know whether it will be of any interest to you to learn that if Lisa marries without my consent, she does not receive one penny of the dowry that we intended to settle upon her. She has nothing of her own, and is entirely dependent upon us."

"That," said Arthur grandly, "is a matter of no moment to me."

He walked towards the door, Lady Charlotte watching him with her inscrutable face. "Good-morning, Lady Charlotte," he said, with punctilious politeness.

"Good-morning, Mr. Ellison. I hope you will some day find out the advantages of honorable and straightforward dealing. You should take a lesson from your sister."

Arthur turned around sharply. The last remark was one that he could not bear. No motive of prudence withheld him, for he knew that he had offended Lady Charlotte beyond redemption, and what he said or did was of little consequence now. He would fire his last shot and reduce Esther from her high position of trust to the same level as himself.

"My sister!" he said, with an unpleasant laugh; "as

you disapprove of me so highly, you may be pleased to hear that Esther is not my sister at all."

"Eh?" said Lady Charlotte, with a frown. "What is that? Not your sister! She told me so."

"I don't think she ever committed herself to the statement. She let it pass—that was all. Esther is my cousin, and we have always been very fond of one another; I thought at the time that she did me a good turn when she let me pass as her brother. We were once going to be married, but we thought better of that arrangement."

Lady Charlotte was not easily shocked; but she was shocked—inexpressibly shocked on this occasion. "I cannot believe it," she said. "I cannot believe it. Surely—are you lying, or are you mad, Mr. Ellison? I would have trusted Esther as I would myself."

"I will let her make her own apologies," said Arthur with a smile that was singularly distasteful to Lady Charlotte. "I do not suppose that she will deny it when she finds that I have been beforehand with her."

If Lady Charlotte had not been startled out of her usual calm, she would have seen Mr. Arthur Ellison off the premises, without letting him have the chance of meeting Lisa again. But his intelligence so far amazed her that she sat down to consider what Esther had said and done when Arthur first came to West-hills, and to remember that they had all agreed that her brother's coming seemed to be no matter of pleasure with her. And by the time she had recovered a little from the shock the lovers had had time for a hasty meeting, and a good deal of mischief had been done.

Lisa met Arthur at the door of a little morning-room, and drew him at once inside. "What did she say? How did she take it? Was she very angry?"

"Ah, my poor Lisa," said the young man with a sigh, as he held her two hands and looked into her eyes; "it is all over. We are never to meet again."

Her pretty face whitened; her eyes grew large with tears. "Arthur, then—do you mean to give me up?" she said wistfully.

"My darling, I shall never cease to love you, but I dare not ask you to bind yourself—it would be too hard for you."

"Nothing would be too hard."

"Will you be true to me, Lisa?"

"Always—always. Arthur, I shall see you again?"

"If we are true to one another, dearest, I am sure we shall. You may be able to win the day for both of us, if they see that you are determined to be true. Will you promise me, Lisa—promise yourself to me?"

"I promise," she murmured, in a frightened voice and with her eyes full of tears. But there was resolution in her face.

They kissed and parted; and for a time, Arthur, who was really in love with her, forgot his wrath against Lady Charlotte and the humiliations to which he had been subjected, in his fond thoughts of Lisa's tenderness. It was only when he reached the farm-house and began to unfold, partially and by degrees, to Esther what had occurred, that his anger and his sense of humiliation returned.

When his words had sent Esther flying up to Westhills to know the worst, he went up to his bedroom
and began in a dogged manner to pack his port-
manteau. During the process he had to change his
coat, and therefore turned out the contents of his
pockets upon the bed. There was a yellow crumpled
sheet of paper among them which he did not recognize.
On looking at it again, he remembered with some dismay that it was the paper which had dropped from
the cabinet drawer when he was trying to close it
hastily. He picked it up, straightened it, and, still
standing beside the bed, began to read the contents.
Presently he flung it down, and seated himself with
his head between his hands, his breath coming heavily
as if he had held it for a time, as one holds one's
breath in moments of intense surprise.

He had brought away with him the letter for which
he had searched so eagerly that morning and never
found: the missing letter from Lord Belfield in reply
to Lady Muncaster.

CHAPTER IX.

DISMISSAL.

By the time Esther reached Westhills, Lady Charlotte had had time to lash herself into a condition of storm and fury, which was far more intense in view of Esther's delinquencies, than with regard to those of Arthur. "I trusted you entirely," she said to Esther as the latter stood before her like a culprit, "and you have utterly abused my confidence."

"I have nothing to say," Esther responded, wringing her hands nervously together at the reproach. "I ought never to have let the mistake—the deception —continue for a single moment. But I never thought —I never for one single moment thought that Arthur would take advantage of it in this way." Here she broke down and cried bitterly, with the effect of irritating Lady Charlotte more than ever; for Lady Charlotte hated tears.

"It is no use crying," she said in her sharpest tones. "Of course you will see for yourself, Miss Ellison, that it would be inadvisable for you to remain here any longer. I don't say that you acted from bad motives, but really the whole thing is intolerable. Your cousin wanted to worm himself into the house, to get what he could out of us—perhaps even to marry Lisa—I never heard of such impudence in my life; and you— you aided and abetted him! I really was never so much astounded as when he told me that you were not his sister after all."

Esther took her hands from her face. "No," she said, with a novel spirit and dignity, which took her accuser by surprise; "you must not say that of me, Lady Charlotte. I never aided and abetted Arthur in any of his schemes; I did not know of them. He took me by surprise when he claimed to be my brother before you, and I didn't like to contradict him, to put him to shame, as it were, before you all."

"Very weak of you," commented Lady Charlotte. "I suppose it is a weakness that proceeded from the fact of your attachment to him?"

"My—attachment?"

"You were engaged to him once, I think?"

"Yes—once," said Esther, utterly confounded by the question, for Arthur had not given her a very full report of what he had said and done. "But—"

She meant to explain that it had been only when she was seventeen years old—a boy and girl attachment that had very soon come to an end on both sides. But Lady Charlotte cut her short.

"It would be a good thing, Miss Ellison, if you were to renew and consummate the engagement as soon as possible," she said very stiffly. "It is the only way of repairing the mischief that has been done, and to remove any aspersion on your character. I must say that I shall sincerely hope to hear of you and your cousin once more—and once more only," she added with emphasis, "and that is on the day of your marriage."

Esther stood silent. What about Justin? And what would he say when he heard Lady Charlotte's version of the whole affair? She thought for one moment of trying to see him first; then she hung her head and wondered how she could justify herself in his eyes. No, it was impossible! Having done wrong, she must accept her punishment: and even if Justin decided that she was no fit wife for him, she felt that she could not in conscience protest against her fate.

She looked so pale and miserable, that Lady Charlotte was almost surprised to hear the resolution of her clear tones as she spoke.

"That is out of the question. I would never marry Arthur if he asked me a thousand times. And also, that is not likely: he cares for—Lisa."

"Keep my niece's name out of all connection with his, I beg of you," said Lady Charlotte, severely. "I hope and trust that when Lisa is completely severed from you and from your—h'm, cousin, she will turn her mind to other things. I shall take her abroad, if necessary, or let her see a little modern society. She need no longer think of college life or anything of that kind; this—this escapade puts an end to those plans. I shall not trust her away from home without me."

"I may be to blame, and Arthur, too," said Esther, flaming, as she sometimes did, into sudden wrath, "but it is quite unjust to blame Lisa; Lisa was not to blame."

"Miss Daubeny's conduct is not under discussion, I think. I have my own opinion of hers—and of yours. In fact, I think you have all three acted disgracefully, and I am ashamed of my niece!" cried Lady Charlotte, whose temper was hotter than even Esther's own. "I can only hope for her sake that we shall see no more of you and your family."

"You shall certainly see no more of me, unless you can acknowledge that you are doing me an injustice," said Esther, quivering with mortification, and too much moved to know exactly that she was committing herself to a course of action which might cause her some difficulty in the future.

"That is hardly likely," said Lady Charlotte, with a short laugh. "Well, it's no use prolonging this extremely painful interview. I hope you will not think it necessary to correspond with Lisa, for I warn you that I shall open and return your letters, and I do not think that she is as yet prepared to enter upon a clandestine correspondence."

"Neither am I," said Esther. "And I do not think that my one error altogether justifies you in insulting me, Lady Charlotte."

Lady Charlotte glanced at her, but made no further answer. Esther was bitterly conscious that the scorn conveyed in that glance was too deep for words. But in reality, Lady Charlotte was reflecting that the girl's tone was spirited and genuine, and that she was very far superior to that wretched cousin of hers, who was no doubt chiefly to blame. She was very angry with Esther still, but she did not despise her.

Esther, however, read nothing but contempt in the gesture with which her late employer pushed an unsealed envelope to her across the table. As in

Arthur's case, Lady Charlotte was prepared to act handsomely. She had written a check for twice the amount due, although she did not consider herself really bound, under the circumstances, to make compensation for instant dismissal. But, in spite of her anger, she wasn't altogether surprised when Esther, with an upward lift of her proud little head, took the check out of the envelope, tore it in two, and deposited the pieces on the table.

"That's folly," said Lady Charlotte, who knew nevertheless, that she herself would have done the same: "You may want the money. I shall send it by post."

"I hope you will not give yourself that trouble. I shall not accept it," said Esther, looking very white and fierce. "I would not accept a penny from a person who said that she could not trust me."

"As you like, Miss Ellison. But you must at least take what is owing to you."

"I will take what I have worked for, and nothing more." Esther named the sum: it was not a large one. "I have no right to decline what I have earned, for I shall have to pay my landlady. But nothing more."

Lady Charlotte wrote another check in silence, and gave it into Esther's hand. Then, looking at her with a touch of mingled kindness and compunction, she added. "I am always ready to be referred to as regards your competency to teach. And I wish well to you, Miss Ellison, but I strongly advise you to marry your cousin as soon as possible, and to persuade him to set about earning an honest living."

With which words she swept out of the room, not

choosing to wait for the hot answer that hovered on Esther's lips.

It was with a sore heart that the girl went back to the farmhouse, and began to pack up her things. She found, as she had expected to find, that Arthur was gone. Probably he did not care to face her after her interview with Lady Charlotte. There was a note for her on the table. "I am going back to my old quarters: shall see you when you come to town. Let me know where you are. I suppose you too have been thrown overboard by the Westhills people. Would advise you to make the running with J. T. as soon as possible—before the Witch of Endor gets hoid of him." Arthur had often spoken in private of Lady Charlotte as the Witch of Endor. "He is at Hurst to-night; see him before you leave. This is disinterested advice, because I know that you will throw me over as soon as you are allied to the Byng family. Yours A. E."

Esther tore the letter into little pieces and then sat down, buried her face in her hands, and thought.

She hated Arthur's suggestion, and yet she wished that she could act upon it. If she could see Justin before Lady Charlotte spoke to him—for it was certain that the whole history would be poured into Mr. Thorold's ear—she would have a much better chance of justifying herself in his eyes. She was prepared to say that she had done wrong, yet she could not bear to think of his hearing the unqualified condemnation which Lady Charlotte would pour upon her name. If she could but tell him herself! Should she send him a note?—But no, it would make people talk: it might even come to Lady Charlotte's ears and make her angrier than ever. Should she go up to his house and ask to see him? Ah, no, that was quite out of the question. Perhaps, by some lovely, lucky chance, he might come to the farm that evening, as he had come before, and then she would have the opportunity of pouring out her heart to him. But it was only a chance; and what if he did not come? Could she go back to London without a word?

After long reflection, she decided that she would wait at the farm until the following morning, and if by that time she had heard nothing from him, or of him, she would write to him by post. He had at any rate a right to know where she had gone. And then she thought of Lady Charlotte's wrath and chagrin at finding out that not only had Lisa fallen in love with Arthur Ellison, but that her paragon, Justin Thorold, had made a proposal of marriage to Esther Ellison herself. She went on languidly with her packing until nearly four o'clock. She had had no lunch, but she wanted none. At four o'clock Mrs. Brown brought her a cup of tea and looked at her pale face and swollen eyes with great sympathy. Mrs. Brown had no doubt at all as to what was wrong. She had never liked Mr. Ellison, and she was sure that he had got himself into some trouble at Westhills, and that both he and his sister were to be "sent away" in consequence. Mrs. Brown knew no better than to talk as if Mr. and Miss Ellison were a sort of superior valet and ladies'-maid.

Esther drank the tea and felt slightly depressed. She had almost dropped into a doze when a noise in the room awakened her, and starting up, she saw Lisa Daubeny looking down at her with the sweet face of a pitying angel. Esther, gazing at her, thought curiously that she was scarcely discomposed. Her eyelids might be a little reddened, her cheek a little pale; but there was no other change. Yet all this overturning of her friend's life was in part her doing. Why had she chosen to give her heart to one so unworthy of it as Arthur Ellison? "You look at me coldly, Esther," Lisa said. "Dear, dear Esther, it is not my fault. I could not help loving him!" Esther felt as though she had unintentionally spoken aloud. Lisa had answered her very thought.

"Why are you here?" she said almost coldly. "You know that Lady Charlotte would be very angry—"

"I told her that I was coming to see you and to say Good-bye," said Lisa. It seemed to Esther that she had never before observed the determination denoted by Lisa's square chin and steady mouth. "She could not prevent me, of course, although she told me that she wished me not to come. But I said that, under the circumstances, I must take my own way."

"I am sorry," said Esther. "Not sorry to see you, dear; but sorry that Lady Charlotte should be displeased. I wonder, Lisa, if it would have made any difference to you if you had known that Arthur was not my brother?"

"None at all," said Lisa. "But it was just that which brought me to speak to you. Esther, Aunt Charlotte says that you are engaged to Arthur—"

"No, no! That is not true."

"And that it would be the greatest kindness on my part to give him up to you. You know I love you, Esther, and if this were true—"

"But it is not true," said Esther, with sudden energy. "Listen, Lisa: the truth is this. Arthur and I were brought up together in the same house, almost like brother and sister. When I was seventeen and he one and twenty, he—we—became engaged for a little while. We cared very little for each other, I think—at any rate, in three months we found out that we did not care at all, in that way. We broke off the foolish engagement and went back to our old relation of adopted brother and sister. It was this long knowledge of each other, this long intimacy of childhood, which made it seem less terrible to me than it ought to have done, when Arthur declared himself to be my brother. It seemed so very like the truth!"

"I understand," said Lisa: but there was a wistful look in her clear eyes. She added presently, in almost pathetic tones, "How was it that he said so? Why—"

Esther answered, without thinking of the effect that her words might have; "I suppose he was so anxious to get an introduction to you—all;"—the word "all" was an afterthought—"that he did not mind what means he employed."

She was sorry that she had said it. The pink deepened in Lisa's cheek, and spread to her ears and brow and chin. It was evident that she thought Arthur's deception to have proceeded from his love to her; whereas Esther knew it to have been simply a matter of self-interest.

"I am afraid," she said, trying to find words that should not sound too brutal, "I am afraid he thought that Lady Charlotte might recommend him or help in some way."

"That is not like you, Esther," said Lisa reproachfully. "To attribute a low motive, when you can't be sure of it, it is not the action of a friend."

"I am not at all sure that I am Arthur's friend at present. Lady Charlotte is right: he has behaved disgracefully. Lisa, dear, put him out of your mind—out of your heart. He is not worthy of your love."

"You are indeed unlike yourself," said Lisa. "If you cannot trust him, I can."

"Trust him!" echoed Esther despairingly.

"I shall be faithful to him all my life. I shall never love anyone else. You can tell him so from me when you see him."

"I shall take no messages."

"I shall find another way then of letting him know. Good-bye, Esther. I thought you would be glad to know how much I loved him."

She held Esther's hand in her own, and looked with steady inquiry into Esther's sorrowful eyes. Reading there the answer that she wanted she laid down her friend's hands with a smile and a sigh. "It is not that, then!" she said.

Esther understood. "It is not that, certainly. I love another man."

Esther kissed her. "You don't wish for my happiness," she said reproachfully, "but I will pray for yours."

"Ah, Lisa, Lisa," cried Esther. "I will pray for yours too—but it will not come with Arthur or Arthur's love."

In a little while she was again alone, and then she changed her dress and washed her face, and hoped that Justin would come to her. But the day wore to a close, and the night deepened, and Esther waited in vain. For Justin Thorold was dining that evening at Westhills. Lady Charlotte had sent him a hasty note of invitation soon after luncheon, and he had responded to it in some wonderment. From his first entrance he knew that something was amiss. Even the servants looked mysterious. Lady Charlotte's brow was ominously black, and Mr. Byng wore an air of extreme annoyance. Lisa was not visible: she had retired to her room, feeling unable to sit out the long dinner, in the presence of a visitor before whom she felt sure that her misdemeanors would be laid. Nobody ever attributed to Mr. Thorold more than the slightest possible passing interest in the Ellisons. His grave and usually impassive demeanor had very successfully hidden any traces of his passion for Esther.

It was not until dessert was on the table and the servants had gone that any free conversation could take place; but at the earliest opportunity, Justin put the question:

"Is anything wrong?"

"Everything," said Lady Charlotte vehemently.

"It's a bad business," said Mr. Byng, shaking his mild head. And then the story came out, head first, so to speak, so confused and entangled by Lady Charlotte's wrathful metaphors, that Thorold could not tell for some time whether it was Lisa that had been sent out of the house, or Esther who had been "rummaging" Lady Charlotte's drawer or Arthur who had torn up a check and thrown it in Lady Charlotte's face. When at length light began to shine upon his mind, he looked very grave indeed.

"It is a very extraordinary story," he remarked soberly.

"I was never so much deceived in my life!" cried Lady Charlotte. "The young man does not want for brains, but he is a cad—a thorough-going cad, an impostor."

"To make love to Lisa was certainly carrying matters very far, you must acknowledge, Justin," said Mr. Byng, with an inkling that his cousin was somewhat lukewarm in his denunciation of the culprit.

"It was presumption, certainly. But one can make allowances—one does not always consult parents and guardians before winning a lady's heart, I believe," said Justin, with a glance at Lady Charlotte. It was well known that she had married Mr. Byng quite against her father's will.

"Things are very different where there is no disparity of position," said that lady. "He should have married his cousin—it seems they were once engaged—"

"His cousin?" said Mr. Thorold.

"Oh, didn't I tell you? Miss Ellison is not his sister at all—his cousin only—and they were engaged to be married—"

"Miss Ellison his cousin!"

"One would not have thought it of her," said Lady Charlotte, with an acrid kind of laugh; "she seemed so frank and open, but I'm afraid she is as much a schemer as her cousin. Almost as much, at any rate," she added with an impulse of candor. "She owned to me with tears that she had allowed this young man to deceive us—I don't know why—I suppose for the sake of getting a footing in this house. She seemed distressed, but I do not wonder at that: it must be rather a blow for her to lose her post here and to know that she has really no chance of getting another."

"Why not? What have you done?" said Mr. Thorold with something that startled Lady Charlotte in his tone.

"I dismissed her at once, of course, my dear Justin. It would never have done to keep her here, in constant intercourse with Lisa. And although I shall always be willing to speak highly of her attainments, yet—as to truthfulness and straightforward conduct—"

"Forgive me for interrupting you," said Justin, rather hoarsely. "I cannot let you go on, Lady Charlotte, without making a somewhat important announcement."

He pushed back his chair and rose, looking pale, but stiffer than ever. "I was only waiting until Miss Ellison had concluded her duties in this house to tell you that I had asked her to be my wife, and that she had consented. Under these circumstances, you will see that I cannot allow her to be accused of untruthfulness."

"You must be mad, Justin!" cried Lady Charlotte. "The girl's beneath you in every way."

"No, not in mind nor in character," he said firmly. "And those are things I value most."

"She is engaged to her cousin, I tell you!"

"That I cannot believe unless I hear it from her own lips."

"You can't be in earnest, Justin?" said Mr. Byng, in a tone of feeble remonstrance.

"I am quite in earnest. I believe nothing against her, and shall marry her as soon as I can get her to fix the day."

"I shall not receive her."

"Of course you can do as you please in that respect, Lady Charlotte." His voice was civil, but perfectly firm.

Lady Charlotte fell back in her chair. "I thought I had reached the end of our troubles with the Ellison family," she said, "but I see they are only beginning. For God's sake, speak, Howard, and speak out! Tell him that you do not intend to put Westhills at the mercy of that girl—that you would sooner leave the place to a beggar in the streets! Let your cousin know that he forfeits all friendship, all countenance from us, if he marries that wretched little creature. Let him choose between us—and surely he will see his mistake."

"If I have to choose between Esther and Westhills, I choose Esther," said Justin manfully. But Lady Charlotte's words came upon him like a blow. For although Mr. Byng had done nothing so far but groan

9

distressfully, Justin was well aware that Lady Charlotte would have her way. He could not look to be
master of Westhills, if he married Esther Ellison.

He took leave immediately and went away, but he
did not call at the farm on his homeward way. It was
too late, he thought, to disturb Esther that night. And
when he called next morning, she had taken the early
train to London and he did not know her address.

CHAPTER X.

A WANT OF TRUST.

A day or two later, Mr. Thorold received a short note from Esther. It was an odd little note, without proper beginning or ending and signed only by her initials. But it gave her address in London, which was what he was chiefly concerned about. And on the afternoon of the day on which he received it, he went up to London and knocked at her door about five o'clock, the time when she said she should be at home.

Mr. Thorold was certainly not pleased at the turn which things had been taking, and it was perhaps for this reason that his bearing had an involuntary stiffness, his face an unconscious gravity and coldness, as he waited at Esther's door. Lady Charlotte had given him great annoyance during the last few days. She had caused Mr. Byng to write to him a solemn letter warning him that Westhills was not entailed and he should consider the claims of other relations before leaving it to a man who had "contracted a mesalliance." The expression made Thorold laugh in spite of himself, but he felt hurt as well. There was no mesalliance, to his eyes, in a marriage with Esther Ellison. She had spoken to him quite frankly—or so he believed, with the one exception of her relationship to Arthur—on the subject of her family and connections. Her father had been a chemist in a country town: her mother, be-

fore her marriage, a nursery governess. The family
of neither had any pretensions to anything more than
respectability, but Esther's father and grandfather had
been book-lovers, and it was probably from them that
she derived her studious tastes. Mr. Ellison had not
been a successful man, and the three hundred pounds
that he had left his daughter was the only sum he had
been able to put aside. But Esther's perseverance and
energy had conquered all obstacles between her and the
fulfillment of her desires for knowledge; and she had
risen rapidly in academic circles to "the top of the tree"
as represented by a first-class in history, and a very
high reputation at Oxford for brilliant cleverness. It
was a kind of success which appealed particularly to
Thorold, who valued it far more highly than wealth
or social position. And it seemed to him, therefore,
a peculiar misapplication of terms to call his marriage
with Esther a mesalliance. But he knew that there
would be no use in remonstrating either with Mr. Byng
or with Lady Charlotte, who could do nothing but
breathe flame and fury against the Ellisons. All her
magnanimity seemed to have deserted her. In his
own mind, Thorold silently pronounced her ungenerous. He was quite determined to remain uninfluenced
by anything she might say against Esther: at the same
time he was more influenced than he knew.

Esther had taken lodgings in the Bloomsbury district, not far from the Museum. Justin frowned at
sight of the house, which struck him as shabby and
dingy, but, as he walked up the narrow street, he said
to himself that she should not remain there very long.

Why should he care for Lady Charlotte's opposition? He felt bitter against his cousin as he knocked at Esther's door.

She herself opened it, and he entered the little shabby sitting-room without exchanging more than a perfunctory greeting until the door was shut. Then he turned to her with a quick, eager movement, and took the little figure straight into his arms. He expected her to cry a little, or to say some tender word of gladness that he had come; but she neither moved nor spoke, only let herself rest against him in a passive way that struck him as unnatural. Presently he turned her face up with his hand and kissed it. He saw a very pale, tired little face, with dark rings round the eyes, and a look as if all the beauty and color and life in it had been wept away. Justin kissed it again, before he spoke.

"My poor little girl! I do not like to see you look like this. It's a miserable business."

"Yes," said Esther faintly. She disengaged herself partly from his arms and looked up at him. "You know everything, I suppose?"

"I think so. Lady Charlotte did not spare me details. But I don't understand."

"No, I suppose not. That was why I wanted to see you." She paused and made an effort to command herself. "I must not forget my duties. There is tea here—you will have some?"

"Speak first," he said, rather abruptly. "I would rather that we go over all that there is to say, then we can be comfortable together. Just now things seem in such an unsettled state: I hardly know what to believe."

"I don't know that speaking will make things much better," said Esther rather wearily. "But let us talk by all means. Sit down; there is one easy chair at least; and you shall tell me what you want to know."

He seated himself as she desired, and looked round with an air of dissatisfaction. The room was dark, dingy, low-ceiled and—to his thinking—almost squalid. "I must get you out of this," he said, in a tone of disgust which made Esther smile for the first time that afternoon.

"This is a palace compared with some of the rooms I have had," she said. "We working women are not used to luxuries, and I shall be quite happy here for the next three months, while I give my lectures at B— Street School."

She seated herself on a low chair beside him and timidly laid her hand upon his knee. He knew quite well what the gesture meant. She was beseeching him to judge her mildly, to listen with kindness and sympathy to all that she had to say. He was not at all disposed to do anything else. He laid his hand over hers, and looked down almost tenderly at her bowed dark head.

"Your—your—cousin is not here, I suppose?" he said at last, as if struck by a new idea.

"Oh, no. He is lodging in Kensington, I believe. I have not seen him."

"Little woman, I can't think how you came to submit to his desires."

"But I did, you see, Justin. We can't get over the fact," said Esther, sadly. "I was weak: I did not like

to say that he was not telling the truth before everyone, and I let it pass.   It was very wrong."

"I can't see that you were so very much to blame,"
said Justin, who would have blamed her more if she
had been less hard on her self.   "Of course you did not
know what he was going to do.   He did not take you
into his confidence with respect to Lisa, I suppose?"

"Oh no, I never thought of such a thing."   Then
with the color rising, she added, "You have heard perhaps, that I was engaged to him—once."

Justin was silent for a moment.   "I must say," he
replied at last, rather icily, "that I should have preferred to think that Lady Charlotte made a mistake
upon that point."

"It was when I was very young," said Esther.   "It
lasted a very little while and I never really cared for
him.   Oh, Justin, you don't think that?—you don't
think that I cared?"

"No," he said—almost unwillingly, as it seemed to
her.   "I don't think you cared.   But it has been an unfortunate business altogether.   I should like to say,
Esther, although I do not wish to hurt your feelings in
any way, that my doors can never be open to Mr. Arthur Ellison."

Esther started a little.   "It is not that I wish to be
friendly with him," she said, "for I think he has not behaved well—but I should like to know exactly on what
grounds you mean to refuse him admission to your
house.   Is it—like Lady Charlotte—simply because he
wanted to marry Lisa?   Because, you know, he and I
are in the same position."

"Not precisely," said Thorold. "A man's wife takes his position: that is just the difference. Your cousin has no position at all to offer Lisa. But apart from that, I would rather not receive him, because I hold that he has acted in an ungentlemanly manner, by passing himself off as your brother and placing you in a very unpleasant position. He has, in fact, shown himself not a trustworthy character, and I should very much object not only to admitting him to my house, but to allowing any intercourse between him and my wife."

Esther paused a little while before she replied. "I daresay you are quite right. I wish to have as little to do with Arthur as possible. But I am not sure whether I should be able to promise never to see him or speak to him—or help him, again."

"I am afraid I can give you no choice," said Justin very gravely. "I must insist that all acquaintance between your cousin and yourself cease at once. If he wants help, I will undertake to supply it; but it must not come from you."

"You make me feel as though you did not trust me," said Esther, with some indication of anger in her tone.

"It is not that at all. I trust you perfectly. But he has implicated you already in what might have turned out to be a worse business even than it is. Have you not heard that Lady Charlotte accuses him of ransacking her private papers?"

"No!—oh, that is impossible!"

"I am afraid not, from her story. Your cousin hardly denied it. I cannot possibly admit to my house a man who cannot rebut an accusation of this kind, and neither can I think him a suitable person for my wife to know."

Esther bit her lips. "I am afraid," she said, in a choking voice, "that your wife is not a very suitable person either. Your friends are sure to say so."

"They are not my friends if they make such observations."

"Lady Charlotte makes them, I am sure. You have told her?"

"Yes."

"And what did she say?"

Justin hesitated. "It is hardly necessary for me to repeat her words. She was not in the best of moods—she did not choose her phrases."

"Ah!—have you seen her since?"

"No."

"But you have heard from her? Dear Justin, don't hide the truth from me: it is very important to me that I should know what your friends say, before you marry me."

"I do not see that it is important. Lady Charlotte can be uncivil; that is all." But he did not look her in the eyes as he spoke, and she felt that there was something more.

She sat for a moment lost in thought. Then some words that she had heard came back to her.

"What about Westhills?" she queried almost sharply. "Have I not heard that Westhills will come to you from Mr. Byng?"

"Well—it is a possibility," he owned reluctantly.

"It depends upon Mr. Byng's choice of an heir?"

He nodded silently.

"Then tell me, Justin, I hope—they have not threatened—they have not been so offended with you as to say—"

She stopped and looked into his face. There was guilt on every line of it. She felt perfectly sure that marriage with her would entail on him the loss of Westhills, and that he had not meant to tell her so.

"They mean to leave it away from you if you marry me," she said quickly, but with the manner of one no longer in doubt.

"My dearest—"

"I should be your 'dearest' indeed, if I lost you Westhills," said Esther, in whimsical despair. "A dear bargain. Tell me. It is so, is it not?"

"A man may change his mind half a dozen times before he dies, Esther. Even if Howard Byng and his wife choose to say disagreeable things, it does not follow that they will carry out their threats. Besides, I am not dependent upon them. I have Hurst, and am content with it: it is there that I want you to make my home for me."

She only said "I see," with a curt little nod and remained silent for a time, with her hands propping her chin and her elbows on her knees. Justin watched her with a secret anxiety, but he did not offer to speak. He felt aloof from her: he had simply no conception of what might be passing in her mind.

By and by, she raised her head and flung out her hands before her, with the gesture of one that rejects a proposition. "It won't do," she said. "I've been thinking of what our life would be and it is intolerable."

"What?" said Mr. Thorold, with emphasis.

"I mean it. When I saw Lady Charlotte last, she said that she hoped she should see no more of me and my family. I said—she never should, unless she could acknowledge that she had done me an injustice."

"That was a useless thing to say, Esther. Lady Charlotte never eats her words."

"But I can't be your wife, Justin."

"My dear child—"

"It is impossible," said Esther, vehemently. "I could not go with you to Hurst and live there, knowing that I had cast you off from your only relatives, that through me you were impoverished and disgraced. I should be miserable, and so would you. I will never let a man quarrel with his family on my account."

"You mean that you will sacrifice my happiness,— and me—to your own pride, Esther?"

"It does not mean that. And—oh, it would be different, if you gave me absolute trust, Justin. But you don't—you don't!"

"I have told you I trust you entirely," said Mr. Thorold, turning a little pale about the lips, and looking sterner than was his wont.

"Yes, you have told me so; but—I know I have forfeited your trust. I was weak once, and you think I may be weak again. It is a just punishment, perhaps, but it is hard—it is hard!"

"I think nothing of the kind, Esther. Indeed, you are mistaken: you have all my trust and all my love."

"I will test it," said Esther, looking at him through the tears that had risen unbidden to her eyes. "Do you leave me free to act as I think fit with regard to my cousin Arthur? If I choose to write to him, to speak to him, will you admit that I have every right to act as I choose?"

Justin hesitated. "I can't go quite so far," he said at last. "I must be able surely to say whether I like a man or not."

"That is not the question. May I do as I like or not?"

"I am afraid I could not give my consent to your friendship with your cousin, Esther. After all that has passed—"

"Ah, you see!" she said, turning away her head. "I knew. You have no confidence in me."

"My dear Esther, what nonsense this is! I love you, at any rate, with all my heart, and you love me. Marry me, dear, and these little differences of opinion will right themselves. You and I are not the people to quarrel."

She shook her head, then rose from her seat and walked silently to the fire-place, where she stood with her hand resting on the mantel-piece and her eyes fixed on the glowing embers of the little fire which a wild north wind had made necessary, even in September. There was a look of subdued melancholy in her attitude, which Justin found unspeakably touching; but his tongue seemed tied: he could find no words in which to express himself.

"I know what it would be," she said presently, "if I

married you on this basis. You would be cut off from your old friends: Lady Charlotte would spread these stories about me and Arthur, and people would say I was not a proper person to be presented to their daughters; and then you would be ashamed of me, and think that after all there was some reason for their gossip, and we should both be miserable—No, no! For your own happiness, Justin, I must give you up."

He approached her and put his hand on her wrist, trying to draw her towards him, but she resisted.

"Esther, you cannot be in earnest."

"I am in deadly earnest."

"Have you no love for me?"

She gave him a look of such mingled agony and reproach that he was ashamed of having asked the question. But the look lent words to his tongue. He broke out into rapid speech: he argued, he implored. But although Esther listened, she was not moved. She grew paler and paler, but she set her face like a stone.

"You are more cruel than you know," he returned, in a tone which vibrated between intense anger and the bitterest reproach. "But you have never loved me—never; or you could not treat my love as lightly as you do."

She made no answer, but turned so that he could not see her face. And after waiting a moment, he left her, without another word.

Then she locked herself into her bedroom, and cried her heart out for the love she had cast away.

CHAPTER XI.

BETWEEN TWO WAYS.

Lady Charlotte carried out her intentions, as she had a habit of doing. At the beginning of November, she shut up her house, and carried Mr. Byng and Lisa away with her to Italy. Here they passed some months, chiefly in the larger cities, such as Florence, Rome and Venice, where they not only studied Art and saw the great sights, but were immediately plunged into a vortex of society and received by the English Colony with open arms. Not that Lady Charlotte confined herself to English people. She had plenty of acquaintances among the higher classes of Italian society; and her apartments were crowded every Wednesday afternoon by princes, statesmen, and soldiers of all nations, as well as by soft-voiced monsignori. The latest novelty in Italian poets or novelists, and a sprinkling of artists and sculptors. Among these various guests Lisa moved like an angel of light —or so her admirers averred—always sweet, gentle, attentive to every one's wishes, yet with the faint unearthliness of expression which a great artist had divined, becoming more and more perceptible and decided. She was painted, sketched, modeled, by many hands and in half a dozen media; but that curious aloofness in her eyes appeared in every representation, and gave Lady Charlotte a great deal of annoyance.

"She looks as if she were dreaming of heaven!" said one of the admirers, in a devout tone; and Lady Charlotte had hard work to restrain herself from saying, "She looks to me as if she were dreaming of her lover!"

For Lisa steadily refused to disguise the fact that she had not given up the man she loved. She even wrote to him sometimes, and she did so openly, always telling Lady Charlotte of the letter and showing her the envelope. "I am not a child," she once said steadily, "I am over age, and I can do as I like." Whereupon Lady Charlotte ceased to mention the subject; but she felt with intolerable bitterness, that if Lisa had loved her more, she would have been more tolerant of her wishes. Discussion died down, but the feeling of resentment on the one side and resistance on the other, remained alive.

When the gay winter was over, and spring was melting into summer, Lady Charlotte and her husband held a consultation. Mr. Byng was pining for his orchids, Lady Charlotte for her farm and her literary work; both wanted the comforts of Westhills, and repined at the prospect of another winter abroad. "Surely she has got over her infatuation by this time!" said Mr. Byng.

"Not a bit of it: she is more besotted than ever. And the man had the impudence to send her his poems the other day, dedicated 'To Lisa!' Dorian published them: I am amazed that Dorian should accept such trash."

"You gave him an introduction to Dorian, did you not, my dear?" said Mr. Byng, not without malice. "I daresay he thought you would be pleased by their appearance."

"It does not much matter whether I am pleased or not, as far as Dorian is concerned," said Lady Charlotte brusquely. "I am not going to entrust the publication of any other book of mine to him. I am sure he swindled me tremendously over the last. But what are we to do about Lisa?"

"You might ask her to promise not to meet him again."

"She refuses to promise anything. I expect that she will see him as soon as she can after reaching London. One can't be always chaperoning her."

"I suppose she knows that we should do nothing for her if she married him?" asked Mr. Byng doubtfully.

"Oh, dear, yes," was the impatient response. "What a nuisance these love affairs are! I'm tired of threatening and scolding. Look what a fuss we had to make before Justin would give up the Ellison girl."

"I don't think he gave her up to please us," said Mr. Byng, who had his flashes of insight. "I think she refused to marry him when she heard of our opposition— that was the impression he gave me."

"Oh, fiddlesticks!" said Lady Charlotte.

"At any rate, Justin was very much cut up about it." And Mr. Byng returned zealously to the perusal of the Secolo.

"The Ellisons seem to have cast a charm over every one they came in contact with;" said his wife, somewhat pettishly. "I can't understand it—though, of course, Esther was an attractive little thing in her way." She paused for a moment with a softer look in her fine dark eyes. "I hope she is getting on all right: I have not heard of her since she left us. She refuses to write to Lisa—a different way of acting from her brother's—cousin's, I mean. She had some good in her; and she knew when to yield. Lisa does not."

"Lisa comes of a family distinguished for strong will," said Mr. Byng politely.

"You may as well say obstinacy and have done with it," remarked Lady Charlotte. "Well, let us go back to London. We shall be in time for the fag end of the season, at any rate. And I don't suppose Lisa will do anything very mad: Ellison couldn't support her, and you may depend upon it he will not marry a poor woman—he's not the sort."

She made the same remark to Lisa, hoping that she would lay it to heart. But Lisa said nothing, and the sudden flush and compression of lips that followed did not give Lady Charlotte much information concerning the workings of her heart.

In fact, Lisa was going through a severe struggle with herself. She did not want to disobey her aunt and uncle, to whom she felt that she owed affection as well as duty; but her whole soul had gone out to Arthur, and she was all the more attached to him because of their enforced separation. If she had seen him more frequently, it is possible that she would have discovered the extent to which he was actuated by self-interest, even in making love to her; but she had not seen him since he had left Westhills, and in the meantime he had written her several impassioned, poetical

10

letters which seemed to her to be worthy of a Shelley
or a Keats.   Arthur Ellison had in truth a very considerable amount of talent; and his letters to Lisa were
charming.   She did not often answer them, for she
would not write in secret, and she did not like to vex
her aunt by writing too frequently; but now and then
she sent him a reticent, simple little note, which, by its
very reticence, perhaps added fuel to Arthur's flame.
And she could not make up her mind as to her duty
in the future.   Did it lie in obedience, or in love?
Arthur said "In love," and wrote passionate appeals
to her to be true to herself, to her higher instincts, to
the claims of an ideal passion, such as theirs should be.
What all these appeals amounted to, she could not have
said exactly.   He proposed nothing definite; he did
not ask her to marry him out of hand, which Lisa would
at once have consented to do; but he made much
lamentation over his own poverty, and the cruelty of
the guardians who kept them apart.   And Lisa
brooded silently over these letters, and wondered,
night and day, what she ought to do.

She consulted no one, because, in her heart of
hearts, she knew that every person of sense would tell
her to obey Lady Charlotte, and not hamper a man
who had his way to make in the world.   She was
dimly conscious of this; but her mind was confused
by the false lights that Arthur's letters threw upon her
path.   It sometimes seemed to her when she had read
them, that all her notions of duty were inverted; that
what she naturally deemed true and beautiful, Arthur
called low and base; that nothing was imperative but

love, and the claims of others upon one's consideration, regard, or obedience were as dust and ashes when compared with the claims of love. He cast a glamour over her eyes, and she saw only as he bade her—until too late.

There were two reasons why she was glad to leave Italy. For one thing Lady Charlotte had committed the error in tactics of bringing prominently forward a suitor for her niece's hand, and a suitor whom Lisa especially disliked. He was a middle-aged, uninteresting man of enormous wealth, and he was quite bent upon marrying Lisa who thought, not unnaturally, that if she could get away from Rome, she would leave him behind. But, as she soon discovered, Mr. Greville was determined to follow up the chase in London, and there was no escape that way. Her other reason lay in the fact that during the last month or two of her stay in the Eternal City, it seemed to her that a change had come over Arthur's letters. They were no longer so poetical as they had been, nor so ardent, nor so long. He excused himself by saying that he was extremely busy: he had obtained some important commissions, and was gaining quite a large connection in the literary world. He added something that Lisa did not altogether understand about his publisher, and his publisher's daughter, a lady of very literary tastes. But what, Lisa wondered, had Arthur to do with the daughter of his publisher?

The Byngs had a house in Mayfair, which they had intended to occupy until the end of the season. And it was not long before Lisa and Arthur Ellison found a way of meeting, even under Lady Charlotte's angry eyes. It was impossible for her to make a scene when Arthur came up to them at a private view, lifted his hat to her, and shook hands with Lisa. Audacity was the best protection. Lisa greeted her lover with a shy smile and allowed him to sit beside her on a red velvet settee, whispering soft nothings into her ears, while Lady Charlotte frowned in impotent wrath and could not possibly interfere. There was one other meeting, also, when Lady Charlotte was not present, and Lisa was accompanied only by her maid: a meeting in the park, which had in the long run a very important result.

Lisa was troubled and shed tears. Her aunt had been extremely displeased with her: Mr. Greville was importunate, and even Mr. Byng had gone over to Mr. Greville's side. She could not bear it much longer, she said; yet what was she to do?

"There is only one thing, my darling," Arthur said. "When life gets unbearable, you must come to me."

"But we have no money: we could not live."

"I am making a fair income, now," said Arthur, which was not quite true, unless one could call a hundred and twenty pounds for sub-editing a paper, and a few small sums for short stories and poems, a fair annual income. "And I suppose," he added, tentatively, "that if we were actually married, your people would come round and do something for us."

"No, I don't think so," said Lisa. "Aunt Charlotte has told me over and over again, that I should have nothing if I married you."

"That's awkward," Arthur muttered to himself.

"Do you mind so much?" Lisa murmured, with her ungloved fingers twitching a little in his hand. They were sitting on a bench under the trees in a retired corner; and the maid was discreetly absorbed in a Family Herald romance, though not perhaps quite unobservant of the romance which was going on under her eyes. Arthur gave the slender fingers a careless pressure, and answered promptly.

"Only for your sake, dearest! I could not bear to see you submitting to the discomforts and privations of poverty."

"If it is only for my sake, then, it does not matter," said Lisa, radiant once more; and Arthur laughed and caressed her, with distinct pleasure in outwitting Lady Charlotte, but an equally distinct impression that his love for Lisa was on the wane.

It had been a pretty distraction while it lasted. But for Lady Charlotte's opposition it would never have lasted so long. He had been stimulated to persevere by Lady Charlotte's anger, her insults and her threats. Lisa was not piquante enough to keep him faithful; she was too sweet, too gentle for him. Her tone of mind was tiresomely elevated; he had to be very careful what he said to her, and no one could go on talking Shelley forever. Even her beauty, he thought, had deteriorated. The slight thinness, the liquid look of her sweet eyes, the transparent shadows about her mouth and temples, which had given the etherealized expression of which the painters had raved at Florence and Rome were not particularly admirable in Arthur's estimation. He wanted something more fleshy and material. But as long as he could annoy Lady Charlotte by his courtship of Lisa, so long would he continue it —unless indeed, it became inconvenient in other ways.

"Tell Lady Charlotte," he said to Lisa before they parted, "that she has me to reckon with, that I am always ready to be your protector, my darling."

He kissed her on the lips, and wondered a little why he had gone such lengths in his admiration for her among the Surrey hills: he supposed that the fresh air and the pleasant surroundings had made him think her prettier than she really was. Certainly she was very pale, and looked worn and fatigued: it was rather a pity that she did not marry Greville after all. He himself was growing tired of the comedy; and he yawned over the thought of it as he went back to Kensington.

For a beginner, he was doing fairly well. He had pleasant enough rooms, and knew how to economize with discretion. He did not approve of running into debt, nor of seeming poor. He liked to keep up a certain appearance, yet not to spend his whole income. With such admirably prudent sentiments, he was likely to get on. Yet in his walk to Kensington that day, he admitted that he had been rather rash in his expressions of tenderness, and sincerely hoped that Lisa understood men well enough not to take him at his word. "Let us hope she will not insist on marrying me," he said to himself lightly. "I shall really have to find a way of explaining to her that I cannot marry her; it would be suicide for me to marry unless my wife brings me an income."

On reaching home he found a note from his publisher, which pleased him very much.   Mr. Dorian invited him to join his family party in Kent from Saturday to Monday: he mentioned that his daughter was
a great admirer of Mr. Ellison's poems, and would be
pleased to renew the acquaintance which he had made
with him some weeks previously.   This was the Miss
Dorian of whom Arthur had spoken in a letter to Lisa.
She was thirty-eight years old, tall, thin, managing, but
with a sentimental turn: Arthur had a strong impression that he might marry her if he liked, and that she
would bring her husband a substantial dowry.   "I
might do worse than think of it," he reflected, as he
wrote an acceptance of Mr. Dorian's invitation.

Then he sat down to a book which he had begun to
write, and in which he was greatly interested.   In the
evening he looked in at the Empire, and amused himself; but when he went home, he set to work again.
Sleep did not actually come to him until late; and on
this particular night it did not seem inclined to visit
his eyelids at all.   After a time he rose from his bed,
lighted a lamp, and took from a drawer a bottle of
clear-colored liquid, of which he took a considerable
dose.   He had begun to look upon a bottle of chloral
as one of his greatest consolations in life, and laughed
at the idea that there was danger in the practice of taking narcotics.

On the Saturday he went down to Mr. Dorian's
house, and found, as he expected, that Miss Dorian of a
decidedly "coming on" disposition.   He laughed at
her in private, but he was quite ready to respond to

her advances. He lounged with her in the garden, read poetry sitting at her feet, turned over music for her, all with such assiduity that Miss Dorian credited him with keenest appreciation of her charms and talents. By Sunday evening, if he were not exactly engaged to her, he was so far committed that he felt his position serious. "I must think over this," he said to himself," before I go any farther: if it were to come to old Dorian's ears that I was making love to Lady Charlotte Byng's niece, while I flirted with his daughter, there would be the devil to pay."

So he drew back a little, sighed a good deal, and mourned over the poverty that would not permit him to marry.

It did not escape his notice, for Arthur's blue eyes were keen—that Mr. Dorian and the three younger daughters were all quite anxious to encourage his attentions to "dear Fanny." It is not a good sign when a whole family so distinctly wants one of its members to be out of its way. Arthur debated the matter with himself and took warning. Still he was of opinion that a stalled ox was infinitely preferable to a dinner with herbs, and love might be left out of the question.

"My daughters think very highly of your verses, Mr. Ellison," the publisher said to him on Sunday night, as he passed the whisky and hot water to his guest. "I hope the public will do the same."

"I am afraid the public will not be so lenient as your daughters," said Arthur politely.

"They are not usually lenient, I assure you: Fanny is by way of being quite a critic," said Mr. Dorian, wagging his gray head. "She says that she is sure of your ability, that you ought to make a great reputation. I have a good deal of confidence in Fanny's judgment."

"I have thought lately of launching into prose," said Arthur, with a touch of nervousness in his manner.

"Fiction?"

"No, not fiction. The fact is," said the young man, with engaging frankness, "I came into contact a good deal at one time of my life with members of the old Blundell family, and studied their records and papers with great interest. They gave me every facility, and I was much delighted with what I found."

"Ah, indeed. Let me see—the Blundell family: it is nearly extinct, is it not?"

"Lady Charlotte Byng and her niece, Miss Daubeny, are the only representatives, I believe."

"There is always a good deal of curiosity about old Lord Belfield's memoirs," said Mr. Dorian. "But Lady Charlotte refuses to publish them at present."

"I believe I could supply a good deal of what would be most interesting to the public," said Arthur, lowering his voice.

"I should be glad to see anything of the kind that you may attempt," said Mr. Dorian, cautiously; but Arthur felt that his words almost implied acceptance of the manuscript, and he was satisfied.

He did not get back to London until late on Monday afternoon, and as he went upstairs to his rooms he was indulging in a secret debate with himself as to whether he had become accidentally engaged to Miss Dorian or not, when his landlady intercepted him on the landing with a mysterious air.

"I beg your pardon, sir," she said, "but I suppose you know that there's a young lady waiting for you in your room."

"What?" said Arthur.

"I thought it might be your sister, sir, seeing as your 'air and eyes is a good deal alike," said Mrs. Pearson deferentially, "but she says not. Says she's your young lady, sir, and has been here ever since eight o'clock this morning."

Arthur felt a sudden chill. It couldn't be Esther, whom he seldom saw: surely it was not Lisa, escaped from the trammels of home life by sudden freak of willfulness! He turned pale at the thought, but had the prudence to say a reassuring word to his land-lady.

"It's all right, Mrs. Pearson: I expected her to-day, but not quite so early. I hope you will make us a cup of tea," he said in his most ingratiating manner: and then he strode forward and hastily opened the sit-ting-room door.

It was Lisa who sat by the open window, and rose to greet him with appealing hands and eyes.

CHAPTER XII.

HER OWN CHOICE.

"Lisa! What brings you here?" said Arthur, in real dismay.

He foresaw endless complications. But there was perhaps some explanation possible: he must wait for it without frightening her. She was already pale: she had grown paler at his tone.

"Aren't you glad to see me, Arthur?" she said, pathetically. Her eyes were red, he noticed, and the handkerchief that had fallen to her feet was wet with her tears.

"I am always glad to see you," he said hypocritically, "but you look as if you were in trouble of some kind, and it distresses me to see you like that. What is the matter?"

He kissed her as he spoke, but in rather a perfunctory manner, and led her back to her seat instead of holding her to him in the close embrace which Lisa had perhaps expected. The coldness of his manner made her evidently nervous. She began in a timid voice:

"It was so unfortunate that you were out this morning: I left home quite early, hoping to find you——"

"You left home—left Brook Street?"

"Yes, and for ever," said Lisa, her eye suddenly dilating, her cheek suffused with color. "I have come to you: you told me to come if life became intolerable. I could bear it no longer."

"My dear child, do you mean to say that you are not going back?" said Arthur, laughing uneasily. "What nonsense! I will give you some tea and then get a cab for you: you will reach Brook Street in time to dress for dinner."

"You don't understand," said Lisa. "I can never go back. I left a letter for Aunt Charlotte, telling her I had gone to you and that we were going to be married. I can stay with Esther for a few days, if you like: I thought we should have plenty of time to arrange things if I came early. I never imagined that you would be out of town."

"Are you out of your senses, Lisa?"

"No," she answered with a look of surprise. "You told me to come, did you not? If things grew too bad to be borne? Aunt Charlotte and I had a great quarrel last night. A Mr. Greville asked me to marry him, and I refused; and then my uncle and aunt were both very angry, and Aunt Charlotte told me that I must either marry Mr. Greville or go away into Yorkshire, to live with an old governess of mine. They would not keep me in their house any longer, unless I did what they wished. Aunt Charlotte said I was going too far—that they must put a stop to my meeting you; so I said that they should have no further trouble: I was of age and could do as I pleased, and I would leave their house."

"And what did they say to that?" said Arthur. He was standing beside her, with one hand on her shoulder, in a caressing fashion, but his brows were contracted and his eyes were singularly cold.

"They said that I was at liberty to go my own way, but that I must not expect any help or assistance from them. I said I expected nothing, and I would wish them good-bye and go as soon as I could get my things ready. And then, Arthur, a most extraordinary thing happened——"

"What?"

"My aunt Charlotte—you know how hard she seems, how indifferent?—I never thought that she cared for me particularly. But she must have cared a little, for she suddenly burst out crying and walked out of the room. I ran after her, feeling as if I must yield, must do anything she wanted, rather than make her cry— for, after all, she has been very good to me—but she waved me back—would not speak to me, and went upstairs with her handkerchief pressed to her eyes. So, after that——"

"Yes! After that?"

"There was nothing for me to do but come away. It was either banishment or marriage to Mr. Greville. There was no alternative; so, Arthur, I came to you."

Like Lady Charlotte, in whose tears, however, Arthur scarcely believed, Lisa began to cry, and Arthur was obliged to devote himself for some minutes to the task of soothing her and of making her drink the tea which Mrs. Pearson sent up, before conversation could be renewed.

His mind was in a ferment. A few months—even a few weeks—earlier, he would have shrugged his shoulders and bowed to the inevitable. That is to say, he would have married Lisa as soon as the preliminaries could be settled, and trusted to Lady Charlotte's real generosity of nature to provide means for a menage. But now—he had other views. The chance of marrying a fairly wealthy woman was before him, and his fancy for Lisa sank into insignificance beside the prospect of bettering his position in the world. "One can't be sentimental," he reflected. "My whole future depends on making her understand the situation. Fortunately matters have not yet gone too far. But it is rather awkward to have to explain them. Girls ought to understand!" And a dull rancor against Lisa began to rise in his mind: she presented herself to him merely as an obstacle to his future plans.

"Now, Lisa," he said, when she had drunk the tea, "let us have a little talk together. Have you any plans?"

She looked at him helplessly. "You told me to come," she said, in a low voice, "So I thought——"

"Yes, yes, to apply to me in any trouble or perplexity: that would have been all right. But of course I expected a letter or a telegram first. You see, we have arranged nothing: you can't stay here, and I suppose you have no friends that could take you in."

"I have some money with me," she said, her color rising, "I had twenty pounds saved out of my allowance; and this morning I found an envelope pushed under my door with a cheque for a hundred pounds—from uncle Howard; so you see, he was kind after all. I don't suppose Aunt Charlotte knew what he had done.   I thought that I could go to a hotel or a boarding-house until——"

"Until you have made your peace with your relations and they have taken you back again," said Arthur.   "That is the only thing possible, Lisa.   It would not be right for me to advise anything else."

"It is a little late for you to advise it," said Lisa, smiling anxiously.   "I have broken with them completely.   For your sake, Arthur."

"I am afraid I am not worth such a sacrifice.   Surely, there was some way out of your difficulties—some *modus vivendi* —without doing a thing which will cause such a terrible scandal!   To come straight to me!   It's a thing unheard of!   Why not have gone to the old lady in Yorkshire for a few weeks?   The Greville business would have blown over, and you could have made it up with the Byngs."

She looked at him with her mouth quivering, and her eyes full of tears.   "Arthur, I thought you would be so glad to see me!   You so often said——"

She could not go on, and Arthur made an impatient movement as he replied: "I may be glad to see you without wanting you to ruin yourself and me for the rest of our respective lives!"

"Arthur!   What do you mean?   How could I ruin you?"—She asked no questions about herself.

"It would ruin me," he said, averting his eyes from her, "to marry."

There was a short silence.   He waited, not knowing what else to say, and greatly dreading the effect of his words upon her mind.   He dared not look at her, and was relieved when, with a great effort, she began to speak.

"Why did you talk to me of marriage then?" she said. It did not sound like a reproach, for her voice was very gentle. But it made Arthur wince.

"I meant—at some future time—when I was better off. You see, Lisa, what is enough for one is not enough for two. I could not undertake the responsibilities of marriage in my present circumstances. It is quite out of the question."

"Oh," she said, her face clearing, "but you are getting on—you are doing well: you have often told me so. Before very long you will be able to carry out all your plans. I can wait for you, Arthur: I will gladly wait."

"You were waiting at home," he said, a certain hardness coming into his voice. "How have you mended matters by coming away?"

"I have shown them at home—that my mind is made up," she said, with a little catch in her breath. "And it is better for me to be away from them: I want to learn—to work—to live my own life. Esther will show me how. Let me go to her—since we cannot be married now—and she will teach me all the things I ought to know."

"You might go to her for a time," said Arthur reluctantly. "But what would be the good of it? You would have to return—ultimately—to your friends."

He did not know whether she understood. He hated to appear unkind—to say harsh and unkind things to her. He would have liked to stand well

with everybody: to be universally popular and be-
loved. But it was imperative that she should understand that he did not mean to marry her. Of course
she must go back to Lady Charlotte Byng.

"Return—to my friends?" said Lisa, very slowly.

"Yes, it would be better."

"But—if I did not promise to give you up——"

"My dear Lisa, let us look things in the face. It is,
as I said, impossible for me to marry. It would be
tying a mill-stone round my neck: unless, of course,
I married a rich woman. I am too poor for the luxury
of a wife and—a home." He tried to conclude with a
smile, but he was very uncomfortable. It was so difficult to tell a woman who loved you that you did
not want to be bothered with her! And especially
when she was slow to comprehend. He began to feel
angry with her for her stupidity.

"But it will not always be so, Arthur?" she said,
soberly and quietly, as if trying to measure the force
of his words.

"As far as I can see—I'm sure I don't know when
the present condition of things will end. And uncer-
tainty of this kind practically means that it is useless
to look forward to anything different."

"But—you asked me to marry you, Arthur!"

"Then I was a fool!" said Arthur angrily. "I have
no means of supporting a wife, and I ought never to
have thought of marriage. Your aunt was perfectly
right; and I should strongly advise you to go back to
her and marry Mr. Greville."

He had said it now, and he ventured to turn and look

11

at her.   She was sitting erect, with her hands crossed
on her lap, her face as white as snow.

"I see," she said, in a curiously stifled voice.   "I
have made a mistake."

"We have both made a mistake," said Arthur, impatiently.   "And the sooner we repair it the better.
Come, Lisa, be sensible.   People can't live on nothing,
and it would be very selfish of me to condemn you to
a life of privation and poverty.   I release you—I set
you free.   Your best plan will be to go back at once
to Brook Street, tell Lady Charlotte that you left the
house in a willful fit, but that you have not the slightest
intention of marrying me, and let her send at once for
Mr. Greville."

"And you?" she said quietly, with a suspicion of
satire in her tone.   "You: what will you do?   Is
there some one for whom you will send?"

The question approached the truth so perilously
that he was startled.   He had not given her credit
for so much penetration of his motives.   But a glance
convinced him that she had hit the mark by hazard
rather than of deliberate intention; for she proceeded
hurriedly:

"Forgive me!   That was an ungenerous thing to
say.   But I understand now what you mean.   Everything is at an end between us, and I will not stay here
any longer."

She rose to her feet, pale but perfectly composed.
Arthur looked at her with distrust.   He would have
been better satisfied if she had wept.

"You must see that I am driven only by necessity

to this decision," he said lamely. "It is entirely against my will."

She said nothing, but rose from her seat, and took up her hat, which lay on a side-table. Her fingers trembled as she pinned it into its place on her shining hair, but no sound escaped her lips. Arthur brought her her cloak: she signed him to put it down upon the sofa. He felt a pang of shame at seeing that she would not accept even this small courtesy from his hands.

"You don't forgive me, Lisa," he said reproachfully.

Then she found words. "You mistake. It is that I cannot forgive myself. I do not want to trouble you: I will go as quickly as I can."

"Shall I send for a cab?" said Arthur, falling back a pace or two. He was irritated by her tone.

"Yes. At least—does Esther live near you? I am going to her. You must give me her address."

"Indeed, I shall not! You are going back to Lady Charlotte's in Brook Street."

"That is quite impossible. She would not take me in."

"She must take you in. I will go with you and explain. Or, I will go first, if you like, and then come back for you."

Lisa's pale smile abashed him for once in his life. "You do not suppose that you would be admitted, do you?"

"Oh, then, confound it! I will write!"

"You will not write, you will let me do as I choose,"

said Lisa, in a vibrating tone which had the very ring
of Lady Charlotte's voice. "Do you suppose for one
moment that I am going back to them, to say that the
man I loved, and who, I thought, loved me, has cast
me off already?" She paused, and then said with
biting emphasis, "I would die first."

Arthur cowered, as if she had struck him. It flashed
across his mind that this gentle Lisa was not so gentle
as she seemed. Sometimes she had presented herself
to his mind as actually insipid. But she had the Blundell blood in her after all: the blood that ran in the
veins of the audacious old statesman, Lord Belfield; of
his beautiful and celebrated daughter, the Countess of
Muncaster; of Mrs. Daubeny, her mother, the sister
of Lady Charlotte Byng. Injure her, insult her, and
the proud spirit showed itself. After all, the girl who
had chosen her lover and held to him in Lady Charlotte's despite, who had left her kinswoman's home
sooner than give him up, and now refused indignantly
to confess to the world that she was a woman scorned
—this was not a girl whom any man need call spiritless or insipid.

Arthur Ellison felt this quality in her, and suddenly
shivered as if, according to the old saying, some one
had walked over his grave. It occurred to him for the
first time that bad faith sometimes brought bad luck.
He almost wished that he had not told her so flatly,
so insultingly, that he would not marry her. But he
had never thought that she would make it a reason for
not returning to her aunt's house. He stammered out

an apology, a remonstrance, but all in vain: she turned from him in quiet scorn and would not hear.

"Esther's address," she said, in such a freezing voice of command that he felt himself forced to give it to her, although he would have preferred very greatly to withhold it. But Lady Charlotte herself could not have assumed a more imperious tone.

He was glad to slip away from her and call a cab, and he sent the maid upstairs to tell her that it was ready. When she came down, closely veiled, he was waiting on the step, and offered to hand her to the cab, but she refused the aid with a gesture of scorn. It was a four-wheeler and the cabman leaned from his box with a gruff "Where to, Miss?"

"For heaven's sake, let me come with you," said Arthur, "and take you back to Brook Street!"

"I shall never go back to Brook Street."

"Lisa——"

"To you, I am 'Lisa' no longer, Mr. Ellison. We are strangers."

"Why should I not still be your friend?" said Arthur, to whom the dusk of the evening gave courage. He stood with his hand on the door of the cab, and tried to interpret the meaning of her pale, veiled face. "It is not that I have ceased—ceased—to care for you, believe me——"

"I do not believe you," said Lisa, very distantly and very coldly. "My eyes are open now. If you had ever loved me, you would not drive me away from you as you have done to-day."

"I was a fool! Forgive me: it all came from my love and care for you."

And for a moment, he believed what he said.

"It is too late," she said, and he thought that in the semi-darkness he could distinguish a smothered sob. "You spoke the truth and it is too late to contradict it now."

"Then, for God's sake, go home, Lisa!" he cried, almost losing his self-command. "Don't let me feel that I have spoilt your life in this way. I'd no idea that you would refuse to go back. Tell Lady Charlotte you have never been with me—tell her you threatened to come to me out of bravado—tell her anything you like, but go back—go back!"

"I will not go back," she repeated. "Take your hand off the door, Mr. Ellison, and give your cousin's address to the cabman, if you please. Good-evening."

He was defeated and he knew it. Slowly and sullenly he withdrew his hand, gave the address to the man, and lifted his hat as the cab rolled away. For some minutes he remained motionless upon the curbstone, lost in thought. At last he seemed to come to a sudden determination, plunged his hands in his pockets and exclaimed "I'll do it!" in a decided tone. In two minutes he was seated in a hansom cab, on its way to Lady Charlotte's house in Brook Street.

"Not at home, sir," said Andrews, in a funereal voice.

"I must see Lady Charlotte," Arthur insisted, "or Mr. Byng. I've special reasons——"

"Not at home, sir."

"But if you were to take in my name——"

"Very sorry, sir. I have special orders not to admit you, sir, if you called. Nor Miss Daubeny neither, sir," said Andrews.

"I'll write my errand on my card——"

"I've not to take in any messages, sir. My Lady and Mr. Byng leaves town to-morrow for the country." And then Andrews shut the door in his face.

"By Jove, they are in a rage with her," thought Arthur, with an uncomfortable laugh, as he walked back to Piccadilly. "Poor little girl! I'll write and let them know where she is: no doubt there'll be a general reconciliation in a day or two."

Meanwhile Lisa had made her way to Esther's lodgings in Bloomsbury, and having found her at home, alarmed her inexpressibly, by falling down in a dead faint as soon as she was inside her friend's dingy but hospitable door.

CHAPTER XIII.

CURED.

Some days elapsed before Esther could get at the reason for Lisa Daubeny's sudden appearance in her rooms. The girl was completely overcome, in a state of collapse which baffled all her friend's attempts to rouse her; and when Esther, kneeling beside her bed, begged to know what was wrong and whether she should send for Lady Charlotte, all that Lisa seemed able to do was to weep gently and say "No, no, do not send for any one—I will tell you by and by," with an accent of such heart-rending pathos and desolation that Esther was afraid to trouble her more.

But on her own responsibility, she did what she could. She wrote a note to Arthur, of whose correspondence with Lisa she was aware; and she sent two telegrams to Lady Charlotte Byng, one to the Brook Street mansion and one to Westhills. To neither of these did she receive any answer, and, in the meantime, she summoned a doctor, for it seemed to her that Lisa was very ill. The doctor looked grave, talked of nervous prostration, and possible injury to the brain, recommended great quiet and care, and promised to send in a sick-nurse, who would share with Miss Ellison the burden of long-protracted sick-nursing.

Esther was ready enough to accept any burden.

But her funds and her time were alike limited: she had been successful as a teacher and lecturer, but her profession did not make her rich. Her rooms too were small. Fortunately her landlady was a kind-hearted woman, and gave up one of her own apartments to Esther's use, while Esther surrendered her own to the nurse and her patient; but on the fifth day of Lisa's illness a change of circumstances was brought about, and Esther's responsibility was to some extent relieved.

It was the arrival of Lady Charlotte's man of business that produced the change. He was a little dried-up old man, with gray whiskers and piercing gray eyes behind rather large round glasses; and Esther knew him by name as a solicitor of repute. He bowed ceremoniously to her as he entered and was extremely polite, but she felt that he was surveying her keenly through his spectacles. Perhaps, from all he had heard of her, she was not exactly the kind of person whom he had expected to meet.

Esther's brilliance was dimmed. She had lost the crimson of her cheek, the ruby color from her lips: her face was thinner, her dark eyes more deeply hollowed. Even her curls were combed and pinned with neatness, and the plain black dress, which did not suit her brown complexion, was relieved only by the primmest possible line of white at the neck and wrists. Red and yellow were Esther's natural hues in dress; the life and color seemed to die out of her when she took to black and white. But the keen intellectual look was intensified: the cleverness of her face was more apparent than ever, and Mr. Furnival noted it with considerable interest. "Brains rather than beauty," he commented to himself, "and that was how she caught poor Justin's fancy, I suppose. Still, I should have thought Justin had an eye for a pretty girl," he added in some perplexity; not having seen Esther in her glorified days.

"I've come on an embassy from the Lady Charlotte Byng," said the little lawyer. "Or scarcely an embassy, perhaps: more for the sake of an informal conversation."

As Esther looked at him, she could hardly believe in the possibility of his doing or saying anything that was not formal.

"You wrote to Lady Charlotte a few days ago, concerning her niece, Miss Daubeny, I believe?"

"Yes," Esther answered. "Miss Daubeny is here, and seems to be very ill; I thought that her friends ought to know."

"Exactly," said Mr. Furnival. "Now will you tell me the day and the hour at which she came to you, Miss Ellison?"

Esther complied, wondering why he wanted information on this point.

"And you know, I suppose, where she spent the day?" insinuated Mr. Furnival.

"I have no means of knowing," said Esther. "She has told me nothing."

"And you have heard nothing from any one else? You do not know when she left her aunt's house?"

"No, I know nothing."

The lawyer asked a few questions, then, putting up his note-book with a snap, he said, in a more kindly tone:

"The fact is, Miss Ellison, Miss Daubeny has left Lady Charlotte's house, in consequence of a little dispute, relative, I believe, to your cousin, Mr. Arthur Ellison. You know probably that there was some understanding, some attachment, between them?"

Esther acknowledged that she knew so much.

"The Lady Charlotte," said Mr. Furnival in measured tones, "is a lady of strong will, strong feelings, strong prejudices, I may say. She wished her niece to become the wife of a Mr. Greville, a gentleman eminently fitted, in my opinion, to be the husband of Miss Daubeny, had not Miss Daubeny most unfortunately contracted a great dislike to Mr. Greville, a dislike which no amount of remonstrance or reason availed to remove."

Esther smiled: she could not help it. It did not seem to her that remonstrances usually availed to make you like a person whom you abhorred. But Mr. Furnival did not see the smile.

"The difference of opinion between the two ladies became so acute, that at last, an alternative was presented to Miss Daubeny," said the old man in his old-fashioned pedantic way. "Either she must promise to accept Mr. Greville, or leave London and stay for a time with a lady in Yorkshire, a Miss Danby——"

"How could Lady Charlotte be so arbitrary—and so absurd!" said Esther sharply.

Mr. Furnival lifted his hand. "My dear young

lady, she thought she was acting for the best.   She
did not expect that Miss Daubeny would take the matter into her own hands, by declaring that she should at
once marry Mr. Ellison, and by leaving the house next
morning—presumably to go to him."

"But—but—she did not go to him?" said Esther,
now considerably startled.

"That we could only conjecture—at least until to-
day, when I made some inquiries at Mr. Ellison's lodgings.   I did not see Mr. Ellison himself; I understood
that he was out of town.   A lady answering to the description of Miss Daubeny was at his rooms last Monday: she must have come to you from him."

"I do not know: she fainted as soon as she came
in, and I have not been able to ask her anything."

"And Mr. Ellison has not been here to inquire after
her?"

"No.   I think there must have been some mistake
throughout," said Esther.   "For I wrote to my cousin,
thinking he might know what had brought her to
me; and he has not even replied."

"Ah, well, we shall know in time," said Mr. Furnival; and then he added, rather quickly, "My errand to-day, however, concerned practical matters.
Of course the family do not wish you to suffer any
loss or inconvenience from Miss Daubeny's present
illness.   It has transpired that she had a check—conveyed to her hands through Mr. Byng's kindness of
heart, I believe—but probably she has not been able to
use it.   Do you know if she had it with her, or any
other sum of money?"

"I have not touched Miss Daubeny's purse or other possessions," said Esther, stiffening.

"It would be well, perhaps, if we examined them now," suggested Mr. Furnival.

Esther hesitated, but thought that on the whole it would be best to make no objection, although she very much disliked the idea of an examination of poor Lisa's effects. It seemed as though she were already dead! However, she went silently to the bedroom, and brought back Lisa's dainty pocket-book and purse, which she laid before Mr. Furnival, who proceeded quite quietly to open them and look at the contents.

The check was there untouched; and there were twenty pounds in notes and some gold and silver besides. Mr. Furnival coolly tore the check in two, saying:

"I have Mr. Byng's authority to leave behind me the equivalent of this draft in cash, which I am to give to you for Miss Daubeny's present expenses, if she is not able to receive it in person. I am almost empowered to offer her a sum of three hundred a year, paid quarterly, if she will consent to give up her project of marriage with Mr. Ellison. Or at least, I should say, until she marries Mr. Ellison. On the day she marries him, her allowance will cease."

"I think that a very hard and unjust way of arranging matters, Mr. Furnival."

"Naturally it seems so—to a lady, and to one so nearly connected with the gentleman in question. But that is the ultimatum which I bring from Lady Char-

lotte and Mr. Byng. And I assure you that Lady Charlotte has her niece's welfare very much at heart."

"Lisa cannot answer for herself at present," said
Esther, more quietly. "So we shall have to leave the
decision until she is better."

"Until she is better," said Mr. Furnival, suavely,
"the money will be paid in advance. I am sorry to
trouble you, Miss Ellison, but I was requested by
Lady Charlotte to see Miss Daubeny for myself——"

"But she is ill—unconscious!"

"Whether dying or dead, were Lady Charlotte's
words!"

"Does Lady Charlotte think we are lying?" said
Esther, in high disdain; but she caused Mr. Furnival
to be admitted with as little delay as possible to the
darkened chamber where Lisa lay faintly muttering
to herself, with the white-capped, white-bibbed nurse
in attendance.

Mr. Furnival was visibly moved at the sight. "Poor
girl! Poor girl!" he said softly as he withdrew. "I
have known her since she was a baby. Such a pretty
little thing! A sad business!"

Then he went downstairs again and silently counted
out the money which he had brought, only asking
Esther to give him a formal receipt. Something in
his silence, and his grave looks, caused her to say, at
the close of this transaction:

"Lady Charlotte may feel quite sure that I shall do
all in my power to persuade Lisa to go back to her,
when she is well enough to hear reason."

"Ah, I'm afraid it's too late," said the old man,

shaking his head. "Lady Charlotte is not very ready to accept apologies or submission when they have been long delayed. She feels Miss Daubeny's conduct very bitterly."

And Esther could say no more.

As soon as she was free, and could leave the patient with the nurse for some time, she set out resolutely for Kensington. She felt that she must see Arthur and know what had happened. But she was unsuccessful in her quest. Arthur was out of town; and when she called again, she found that he had changed his lodging and left no address. Possibly he thought it safer to be out of reach of Lisa's friends for a little while. Esther began to suspect that something unforeseen in the relations between Lisa and her lover had occurred. But there was nothing to be done but to wait.

She waited; and in time, Lisa began slowly and painfully, to recover. But for many weeks she was so unable to bear the slightest excitement, that Esther dare not question her concerning the past. The summer vacation came before she was really strong; but she was able in August to go with Esther to a quiet little sea-side place, where they could sit on the beach all day in the sunshine, and let the breezes fan a little color into Lisa's pale cheeks. And it was there that Lisa at last spoke of Arthur Ellison.

"Esther," she said, very quietly, "do you ever hear anything of your cousin?"

"I have not heard anything of him for a good many weeks," said Esther, laying down her book.

"Not since I was ill?"

"No. And even before that. I do not know now whether he is in town or not. He has changed his address."

Lisa was silent for a minute or two; then, with changing color and in tremulous tones, she said:

"I do not remember very well what happened. I came to you one evening, did I not?"

"On a Monday evening, about nine o'clock, in May. You fainted as soon as you came into the room, you know, dear, and were unconscious for a long time afterwards."

"What trouble I have given you," said Lisa, the soft eyes suddenly suffused with tears. Then, after putting out her hand to give Esther's an affectionate pressure, she said, "I think it is time that we should talk things over a little. There are some things I want to ask you, and, perhaps, I have been thinking, there are some that you would like to ask me."

"Are you really strong enough to bear it, Lisa?"

"Bear it? Oh, yes," said Lisa, with perfect quietness. She even smiled a little as she spoke. "I have been longing to speak; but I thought that you avoided the subject. Tell me first—has my Aunt Charlotte asked after me, or thought about me?"

Esther replied by telling of Mr. Furnival's visit, and the message that he had brought. She even went on to mention, with bated breath, the condition attached to the allowance that was to be made to her friend. Then she was almost afraid to glance at Lisa, but, to her surprise, the girl answered at once, in a voice that was perfectly clear and cool:

"There will be no difficulty about that. Every-thing is over between Mr. Ellison and myself."

"But, Lisa, when you left Brook Street——"

"I know what you are going to say," said Lisa calmly. "All was not over then? No, I left my aunt's house, resolving to go to Arthur's immediately, and thinking that there could be only—at most—a few days' delay before our marriage. I went to his lodg-ings, and waited for him all day. He came in at last, and I told him why I had come. It was between six and seven in the evening, was it not? I know it was growing dark when I came to you."

"Lisa, what did he say?"

"Don't vex yourself, Esther; it is not worth while. I assure you he is no more to me now than yonder fisherman drying his nets, or the passing tourist on the quay. I lost my love for him, I think, when I heard him tell me, that although I had given up my home, my position, perhaps my reputation, for him, he would not marry me."

"He wouldn't marry you, Lisa?"

"He said he was too poor; he could not afford a wife. He advised me to go home and marry Mr. Greville."

"But—he loved you!" cried Esther, amazed and disconcerted.

"He thought he did—once. His love was not strong enough to bear even the prospect of poverty," said Lisa, in a tone which was faintly indifferent, faint-ly contemptuous, but expressive of no deep feeling at all. "He said that my aunt was right."

12

"Lisa! My poor Lisa!"

"Why do you cry, Esther? Don't you see that it was much better that I should find out in time how slight a regard he had for me? When you peril all that is dear to you for the sake of a man who is ready to cast you off as an old glove—then you find out how much love is worth. I am cured now; I do not care."

"But it is worse than all, if he has taught you to think little of all love," said Esther.

"I do not think little of all love; I am glad of yours," said Lisa gently. "But I do not want to talk of a man's love any more; I think I should be glad if I could never hear of it again. Do not speak to me on the subject, if you care for me, Esther; it only gives me pain."

But she spoke dreamily, listlessly, as if nothing on earth could make her feel either grief or joy again. And Esther recognized, with a great pang, the fact that in some natures great sorrow, a great shock may sometimes numb or even kill the inmost fibres of emotion; so that a person may emerge from it perfectly cured, as we say, perfectly sane, but with no great capacity of feeling anything any more. Was this Lisa's case? If so, it seemed to Esther as if Arthur had murdered her very soul.

"Oh, if I could only punish him! If only I could make him suffer!" she cried, vengefully striking her white teeth together and clenching a small brown fist. Lisa looked at her tranquilly and smiled.

"Why distress yourself?" she said. "If he has done

what is wrong, he will suffer, you may be sure. We all pay our debts. I am paying mine now." And she looked out to the heaving purple sea, with a curious expression in her eyes, half-pathetic, and yet as it seemed to Esther, half-cynical over her own pain.

Esther was silent, thinking of the words that had been said. Were they not very true? Was not she also paying her debt? Suffering the punishment of that evasion of the truth from which so many unlooked for events came about? Justin Thorold had left England: she did not know whither he had gone. She thought it probable that she should never see him again, and she resigned herself, as Lisa was doing, to "the paying of her debt."

"Lisa," she said at length, almost timidly, "you will go back to your aunt's house now, will you not? I am sure she will be glad to see you again."

Lisa brought her eyes back from the sea, and let them rest a while upon Esther's face before she spoke. "No," she answered at last, "I think not, Esther."

"But why—why not?"

"There was never much sympathy between my aunt and myself," said Lisa thoughtfully. "We were not congenial to each other."

"But would it not be right, dear, for you to go back?"

"Would it? I have thought of that. But I don't think I could. When I think of the way in which I left her house,—of the things we said to each other—I feel as if it would be impossible."

"It would be hard, I know," Esther murmured, only half convinced.

"And then," said Lisa, raising herself to speak with more animation and eagerness than usual, "think of your own lessons to me in the past, Esther! Think of what you used to tell me about girls who worked, who made a career for themselves, who did something in the world! Would it not be well for me to remember that teaching now?"

"Do you think of Oxford or Cambridge still," faltered Esther, her heart sinking within her.

"No, I have given up that idea. But I think, Esther, that if you will let me, I should like to live side by side with you for a time, seeing how you live, how other women live and what they do in the world. I am tired of seeing only rich people around me; of hearing talk about art and poetry and music; it seems to me that I want to get down to the bare bones of life, and see what the common people do. Will you help me to get what I want?"

"I will help you in anything," Esther said fervently; but secretly she shed a few tears over the disappearance of her beautiful dream-maiden, and the rising from her ashes of a sobered, saddened woman who wanted to know more of the realities of life. It seemed sad to her; but perhaps it was not quite so sad as it seemed.

So when Lisa was stronger, she went back to London with Esther, and the two settled down in the same house, "side by side," as Lisa had said; but not in the same room. There seemed a desire on Lisa's part to

assert and maintain that hardly won independence of
hers: she could bear no restriction upon her liberty:
she would scarcely tell Esther beforehand what were
her plans for the day.   And Esther left her perfectly
free, knowing that she would come to no harm: and
was complimented quarterly by Mr. Furnival on the
discretion and completeness with which she chaper-
oned Miss Daubeny.

Of Arthur they saw nothing.   He had sent Esther
his address, and she had once addressed a bitter little
note to him, but to this he did not reply.   Once Esther
heard that he was engaged to be married to Miss
Dorian; but she could not believe it to be true.   And
as the report was soon afterwards contradicted, she
never even mentioned it to Lisa.   Not that she fancied
that Lisa would have been disturbed.   The girl seemed
placid and happy in her new life; and but for a certain
restlessness, a sort of haggard look in her blue eyes
sometimes, Esther would have thought that she was
perfectly content.   But that expression sometimes
seemed to show that her heart was not quite at rest.

CHAPTER XIV.

PHILANTHROPY.

Among the many works on which Lisa cast passing
glances in her research for the realities of life, there
was one that particularly pleased her. It was a club
(conducted on purely secular principles) for rough
working girls, some of them of the lowest type, un-
taught, unkempt, almost savage in their appearance,
but curiously responsive to kindness, and extremely
affectionate. The club had been well managed for
some years, but owing to a recent change of head,
there had lately been tumult and rebellion among the
members; and, as it happened, on the night when Lisa
first visited the rooms, the disaffection was at its
height.

Lisa never forgot the effect produced on her by the
first sight of these girls at tea in the big room where
they could purchase that refreshment for a penny.
The room was close and overheated; the fumes of the
tea, the odor of bread and butter, mingled with the
odor of humanity, until the atmosphere was almost unbearable. The girls in their feathered hats, with little
shawls over their shoulders, or ulsters down to their
feet, some with white aprons, others with blue neck-
laces and gilt earrings, were drinking hot tea out of
their saucers, and talking at the top of their voices,
though lowering them if any of "the ladies" came near.

Some adverse decision in matters affecting their enjoyment had just been announced; and although the
judgment was a wise and right one, it excited a great
deal of adverse feeling. Lisa looked at the flushed
faces and broad shoulders—for many of the factory
girls were a sturdy, strapping type—and wondered
whether she would ever get the length of even speaking to these young working women, who were so different from any other persons she had ever encountered in the course of her carefully sheltered life.

They were girls like herself, but they had never
known the softening influences which had been
brought to bear upon her all through her two and
twenty years. They were utterly ignorant, without
any attempt at an ideal of conduct, loud, rough, ex-
perienced in drunkenness, in bad language, in the ways
of the streets. Were there any points of contact between them? Any matters in which they could hope
to sympathize? She felt vaguely oppressed by the distance, the difference between them.

Nevertheless, the girls themselves were immensely
attracted towards her. Fond of the shops, arrayed in
ragged finery, often only too ready to sell their very
souls for a brooch or a bracelet, they had a great appreciation of Lisa's pretty well-made frock. Miss
Daubeny was simply dressed, but she had not thought
of donning the costume of somber black which "workers" so often think necessary on similar occasions.
She wore a blue gown with a white vest, and a hat with
a sparkling clasp; one of the pretty costumes she
had worn a good deal when she was abroad the pre-

vious year. She had taken off her gloves and showed
the pretty multi-colored rings upon her white hands,
and the girls glanced at her enviously, and conversed
about her frock and her jewelry in undertones, while
one or two of the presiding ladies said something to
each other, with a look of annoyance, concerning the
folly of wearing ornaments in the presence of the poor.
Esther, who had brought Lisa with her to the club,
overheard the remark, but resolved not to tell Lisa of
it: her own opinion was that if you wore ornaments
as a general rule, you had better not take them off
simply because you were mixing with those who were
poorer than yourself.

Lisa was unconscious of the favor her attire had
gained her in the eyes of the girls, and felt sadly helpless and awkward. By way of doing something useful, she carried a cup of tea to a poor pretty-looking
girl, with a tired face and a small white baby on one
arm, who had just entered the room and seated herself beside the door. She looked so pinched and hun-
gry that Lisa was amazed when she said with a curt
sharpness that contrasted strongly with her soft con-
tours,

"No, thank yer, Miss."

"You look so tired; do have a cup of tea," said Lisa
gently. "I'll hold the baby for you while you drink
it."

She had a passion for babies and was already eyeing the little creature covetously, but the young
mother only said more sharply still, "No, thankee,
Miss."

"She ain't got a penny, Miss, that's what it is," said another pale girl in Lisa's ear. " 'Ere, Nelly, I'll treat yer. Cup o' tea an' bread an' butter for Nelly Hagan, Miss, please," she added, putting a hot and sticky penny into Lisa's hand; and Lisa went off well pleased to obtain the steaming beverage, which Nelly did not now refuse.

Then Lisa sat down beside her and held the baby, and heard how this child of seventeen had run away from home to be married to "a bloke" who was nineteen, and how he sometimes earned twelve shillings a week and sometimes nothing at all. And she heard how Nelly had lost her work, which was that of a laundry-girl, when the baby came, and that when the baby was two months old (it was now only six weeks) Nelly hoped to be able to put it out to nurse and to get work again.

To Lisa, it was more interesting than a romance. She had never before come into contact with the London poor, and she was struck with the girl's intelligence, with a sort of flower-like prettiness in her face, with the pathos of the story. She sat on, talking to Nelly, without perceiving at first that most of the girls had made a sudden and violent rush for the upper floor, and that yells and cat-calls were proceeding from the upstairs room with rather an alarming effect.

"They're a rough lot in to-night," said Nelly, with an air of superiority. "I think I must be gettin' 'ome; my chap don't like me to be out after ten. Thankee, Miss. I 'ope we shall see you another night shall us, Miss?"

"Thank you," said Lisa, quite gratefully. "I shall be glad to come."

"What are they doing?" pursued Nelly. "Are they smashing the crockery?"

For there was a great crash overhead, and at that moment all the gas went out. The girls had evidently organized a rebellion, and somebody had got at the gas-meter.

Lisa hastened upstairs to find Esther, and see what was amiss; and in the hubbub, Esther seized hold upon her and drew her into one of the inner rooms. It was perfectly dark, and the noise of laughter, shouts and uproarious singing was appalling.

"I've an idea," said Esther, rapidly in her friend's ear. "Sing, Lisa—sing!"

"How can I sing in all this noise?"

"Begin! They'll quiet down directly."

And Lisa began.

She had a sweet, well-trained voice of considerable power and compass, and some instinct made her choose a song which many people would have thought quite inappropriate to the occasion—a plaintive ballad, with a lilt in it, which she had often found very successful in drawing-rooms. It was just as successful here. After the first bar or two the noise began to slacken: some one called out, "Listen to the lydy!" and "'Old your jaw! She's singin'!" Before she had half-finished the first verse, there was absolute silence in the room.

In the darkness when she had finished, came a perfect storm of clapping. As Lisa afterwards found, a song without accompaniment would always be listened to with deference and in silence; whereas the sound of the piano, even with a voice, set every tongue to wag its loudest and fastest. "Another, Miss!" "Please, sing one more, lydy!" "That's worth listening to, ain't it! Go on, Miss! Go on, lydy!" such were some of the exclamations that ran on every side.

"If I sing again," said Lisa, by a sudden inspiration, "will you be quiet afterwards and do what we wish?"

"Yes, yes, oh yes! Sing, Miss, and we'll be as quiet as mice," cried the voices. And in the meantime the front door was softly opened and some of the ringleaders made their way into the street. The ladies went about the house relighting the gas. When the song was ended, and the room was fully illuminated again, the audience consisted of some twenty girls, as serious, sober, and well-conducted as girls could be. They came up to the ladies in authority afterwards to apologize for or to deny their share in the recent outbreak; and then slipped off in a shame-faced manner, to join their rougher companions in the street. Several shook Lisa's hand, saying, "You'll be sure to come again, won't you, Miss?"—and for that evening at least Lisa was openly mistress of the field.

The other ladies congratulated her on her success, although with some reserve in their tones. They thought Lisa rather too fashionable, rather too "worldly"-looking, to be of great use among the girls; but they invited her cordially to come again. And Lisa, unconscious that her dress could be the cause of any objection to her presence, promised very warmly that she would come back.

She came again and again, and Nelly Hagan became her special pet and protege; and she learned from her a great deal about the other girls, and about the habits and manners of the very poor. It was quite possible that Lisa did not do the girls very much good, but they did some good to her. They taught her the meaning and value of submission and obedience, of sincerity, of earnestness, of many things which she sometimes undervalued and misprized. They also taught her to think less of certain other things which she had all her life been trained to respect—luxury, for instance, and soft-living, and a good deal of what she had been taught to call refinement. "It makes me ashamed sometimes to think what I have spent on trifles," she said to Esther more than once, after recounting to her some tale of woe, with tears in her eyes. Esther, with her more practical matter-of-fact way of viewing things, had to check her indiscriminate charity sometimes. And she did not give unmixed pleasure to her fellow-workers, for she had not enough of experience to know always what to do for the best, and as the club was worked by a committee of ladies on a somewhat independent basis, there was no one to take Lisa seriously in hand and train her as to what she ought to do. But all went well for a little time, until one evening when it seemed to Lisa as if she were treated with exceptional coldness by the others, and when she heard one lady say to another—not in very subdued tones—

"Such a grief to the Byngs, you know. Quite unable to get on at home. In fact, they would not keep her. They make her an allowance and let her live where she likes. A very undisciplined character."

"Rather objectionable," said the other lady. "I think she is not a suitable person for our work at all. Why does she come?"

"Oh, for a little excitement, I suppose," said the first speaker, and then they moved away.

Esther was startled by finding Lisa at her elbow a few minutes later, with an unusually pale face, and a look of appeal in her clear and candid eyes.

"Esther," she said, "I want to go home. Shall I go by myself, or will you come too?"

"I will come too. You don't look at all well, Lisa. Anything wrong?"

"Nothing much. I will tell when we get home."

And it was not until they were safe in Lisa's pretty little sitting-room, that she told her friend the words that she had overheard.

"I suppose that is the way that people do talk about me," she said gently, but with a distressed look in her eyes; "only I have never happened to hear them before."

"There are ill-natured people everywhere," said Esther, not quite knowing how to reply.

"Esther,"—the words came very quietly—"do I strike people like that? Have I a very undisciplined character?"

"My dear Lisa! I hardly know what the woman meant. She is only an outsider, you must remember.

She does not come regularly to the club at all. I scarcely know her."

"But that has nothing to do with it. I mean—is it true that I was wrong, and that I ought to have yielded to my aunt's wishes? Tell me the truth, Esther, I really want to know."

"I can't answer in one word," said Esther, whose face had grown grave. "I do not think that you were wrong to refuse to marry a man whom you did not love; but on the other hand—"

"Yes?" said Lisa, as Esther paused.

"Well, I have often wondered how you could justify it to yourself to walk out of Lady Charlotte's house and renounce her so completely, when she had brought you up and been like a mother to you—"

"Not a mother," said Lisa, in a low tone. "A mother would not have shut her door against me as she did!"

"But you gave her very little chance of doing anything else, Lisa. Have you ever written, ever tried to make her understand that you were sorry for the pain you must have given her?"

"She would not read my letter if I write."

"Do you never mean to see her again?"

"What am I to say to her if I do see her?" said Lisa, with sudden passion. "Don't you know that if Arthur had been true to me, I should never have repented of leaving everything for him? If he had loved me, I should have been a proud woman, not one who has cause to be ashamed—who can be scorned and

maligned by two gossips who know nothing of my nature or my story!"

"But gossips may attack anyone—and almost always
unjustly," said Esther, sensibly. "What gossips may
say ought not to affect us! What affects us is whether
we are doing right or wrong."

"But if we do not know whether we are doing right
or wrong?" said Lisa.

"Is that possible?"

"You do not know my difficulties," said Lisa, in her
gentlest voice. It seemed to Esther a wonderful thing
that Lisa should look so gentle and speak so softly,
and yet be possessed of such a will of steel. Lady
Charlotte's high spirit was not more unbending, more
indisposed to yield. "You yourself always told me
that we ought not to yield tamely to oppression, but
try to lead our own lives. I am trying to be independent and lead my own life now."

"And much happiness it has brought you, my poor
Lisa!"

"Happiness! Is there such a thing?" said Lisa, putting her hand to her forehead, with a momentary look
of such mental and physical weariness that Esther was
alarmed for her. But it passed away and was succeeded
by a smile. "We all have to 'dree our weird,'" she
said, "and it is hard sometimes to make out the meaning of it. I am a little tired of philanthropy, Esther.
What is the good of our trying to benefit these working girls if we pull each other to pieces behind their
backs? Is that charity?"

"I think," said Esther, with some hesitation, "that

we have been beginning at the wrong end. Our club
. is on secular lines only. I'm inclined to think that we
can do no good to anyone without the religious influence. Perhaps we never tried to set the highest and
best things before the girls—and the workers have suffered too."

"Perhaps," said Lisa, languidly. "I never thought
much about these things. Aunt Charlotte said they
made people dull. But since I have come to this
point, what is there to do but be dull?"

She lifted her arms and crossed them behind her
fair head; her face slightly averted, looked inexpressibly sad. Something in her listless question struck a
passionate answer from Esther as fire is smitten from a
flint.

"Can it be dull to set ourselves to know God?" she
asked.

The vibration in her voice called Lisa back from a
melancholy fit of dreaming.

"You are full of life and vigor: you do not know
what it is to be dull. I am only a sort of crushed but-
terfly, I think. But lead the way, Esther; show me
what to do next, for I am terribly tired of the present
state of things, and—I hope you won't mind—I am not
going to that girls' club any more."

"But—Nelly Hagan? And the others?"

"They must come to see me."

"You have so much influence with girls, Lisa, that I
don't like to think of your giving up this kind of work.
Try the club in Marston Street: it is worked on the—
well, on the religious basis, I suppose," said Esther, a

little afraid of impressing her views too strongly upon her friend, "and I have always liked what I saw of the workers there."

Lisa made no objection, but for some days seemed so spiritless and out of heart that she went nowhere at all. Esther, in the meantime, paid a last visit to the club, took her leave of the presiding lady, who was not very sorry to hear that Miss Daubeny was not coming again; and paid two or three visits to various evening schools and girls' institutes before she could make up her mind whither to carry the offer of her services.

But this time it was Lisa who decided her choice. Lisa came in one day, with a face so expressive of a new desire that Esther looked eagerly for an explanation.

"Nelly Hagan is ill," she said, sitting down and plunging into her subject without any preface, "and I have been talking to her. She says she has left the club and means to go back to one that she belonged to before. It is in Marston Street."

"The very one I mentioned to you."

"Yes, I know. Nelly was telling me about it. She said she left it because some of the workers talked to them about religion. I almost laughed when I heard her say so; it was such a commentary on what you had been saying."

"But she wants to go back again!"

"Yes, and she implored me to go down to Marston Street and ask if she might become a member again. So I went, expecting to find some one like Mrs. Ledwith or Miss Clarkson, some one rather haughty and

13

austere, you know, and I found the gentlest, sweetest-faced lady in black, who was delighted to hear of Nelly Hagan and said she would do all in her power to help her—quite irrespective of political economy, you know, or any question of the housing of the poorer classes. And I saw a lady in uniform, whom everybody called Sister; and I have promised to go to-morrow and play for them when they practice hymns for their Sunday class."

It seemed to Esther a more hopeful opening than the other one had been. She had begun to feel that she wanted to see Lisa Daubeny laid hold of by some positive belief in something out of herself: as though she would never be happy so long as she sought her own will and her own way, and that perhaps the first lessons needed were those of submission to authority and faith in the unseen. She herself had been learning the same lessons, superadded to a resignation to the uncertain and perilous future, which Lisa could not feel to the same degree. For Lisa's future, in a material sense, at any rate, was provided for: she had a sufficient income for her life, without the necessity of working; whereas Esther knew very well that her own comfort, her own livelihood, depended upon the health of her body and the strength of her brain. She wondered sometimes what would become of her if she grew ill or unable to work, and she had difficulty at those moments in abstaining from some regrets for the prospect that had once opened out before her with such absolute fairness, and which she had with her own hand so resolutely put aside from her.

After her parting with Justin Thorold, she had heard no more of him for some weeks. Then she saw from the newspapers that he had resigned his seat in Parliament and gone abroad; and for many a long day her heart was sore within her with the consciousness that she had not only hurt him, but had hurt his work—the thing that he was pledged to do. With her fiery conception of duty, it seemed to Esther as if Thorold ought to have gone on with his work even while his heart was breaking—not thrown it all up and gone away to take his pleasure in foreign lands!

She had a sense of desolation which equaled that of Lisa, although she had not been formally renounced by her family, or slandered by unkind tongues. Arthur was no longer a friend of hers, and although she was bitterly angry with him, she could not help missing his companionship. He had always been ready in the old days, to drop in and smoke a cigarette in her room, while he told her of all that he meant to do and to be in the coming years; or to take her out for a stroll along the Serpentine. The old partisanship of Lisa's cause and affection for Lisa herself were not always successful in winning her mind from thoughts of days gone by. So the two girls lived side by side, and worked in their different ways and with gradually diverging aims; for as Esther was obliged to labor more and more arduously at her profession, Lisa devoted herself with constantly increasing fervor to her work among the poorest of the poor. For both, life seemed to pause a while; as if it waited for a crisis which approached and yet was long delayed.

CHAPTER XV.

THE MOODS OF LADY CHARLOTTE.

Lady Charlotte Byng was not a very easy person to understand. Every now and then she delighted her friends by some sudden manifestation of nobility of character: now and then she surprised them by an outbreak of passion or willfulness which must mentally lower their opinion of her and her own of herself. And again she would disarm them by a swift return upon herself, a frank penitence, a generous acceptance of blame, which went far in their opinion to atone for the ill that she had done.

But in the matter of her niece, Lady Charlotte's behavior had not seemed to conform to the ordinary rules of her character. She had had no generous or noble impulses where Lisa had been concerned. She had treated her with rigor, with harshness, and even when the girl was most to be pitied she had sternly refused to re-admit her to the house. In vain did Mr. Byng and Mr. Furnival, and even Justin Thorold, plead with her for mercy. They reminded her that she was treating Lisa as if she had really brought some great disgrace upon herself, some lasting shame upon her family. All the world would say that it was so, when Lady Charlotte's conduct to her niece was observed; and that Lisa had in reality only been willful and wayward, and had announced her intention of marrying a

young man whom her aunt disliked. Many a girl had
done this before, and had been ultimately forgiven by
her friends. And it would be particularly easy for
Lisa to be forgiven, seeing that she had not married
the young man after all.

"That's the worst part of it," Lady Charlotte had at
first cried out angrily. "Why hasn't he married her?"

"Her illness seems to have come on immediately,"
said Mr. Furnival. It was after his visit to Esther's
rooms. "Possibly the wedding was fixed for a day or
two later; and may be performed as soon as the young
lady is recovered."

"You can ascertain that, can you not?" said Lady
Charlotte, with an eagerness which was decidedly
sharp. "And you made Miss Ellison understand
that the allowance would cease at once if the marriage
were carried out?"

"My dear Charlotte," ejaculated Mr. Byng in a re-
monstrant undertone. Then, as she turned and
looked at him, he added, rather timidly, "We should
have to receive them, sooner or later, if they married,
you know."

"I should not," said Lady Charlotte, haughtily, and
turned her back upon him without saying more.

Some weeks then passed by without further discussion of the matter. Lady Charlotte rigidly abstained
from inquiries, but Mr. Byng questioned Mr. Furnival
closely whenever the old lawyer appeared at Westhills
with his budget of news. Mr. Furnival interviewed
Esther rather often about this time; but Esther never
guessed that every item of information she gave him

was conveyed to the house among the Surrey hills, and that Mr. Byng who was exceedingly attached to Lisa, would willingly have come to see her if Lady Charlotte would have allowed it. But Lady Charlotte would not allow it, and Mr. Byng had never been master in his own house.

After a time, the reports of Lisa's condition became more favorable, and Mr. Furnival came less often to the house. It was late in the autumn when he brought word on Esther's authority, that Lisa's engagement to Arthur Ellison was entirely at an end, and not likely to be renewed on either side. There was therefore no reason why the allowance of three hundred a year should not be made permanent.

He had, as usual, made these remarks to Mr. Byng, carefully choosing a moment when Lady Charlotte was sure to hear. As he had expected, the words produced an instant effect upon her. She turned round sharply and demanded, with flashing eyes and in a voice of thunder—

"Do you mean to say that the man won't marry her?"

"I have tried to ascertain all particulars," said Mr. Furnival, in his bland voice, "and I even managed to interview Mr. Ellison for a few minutes; but all that he would say was that the engagement was dissolved by mutual consent."

"I am quite sure that he deserves horse-whipping within an inch of his life," said Lady Charlotte, clenching her hand.

Her husband looked at her in amaze. He could not

see why—when she had been so anxious to obtain a
rupture of the engagement—she should yet be so
angry with young Ellison for breaking it off.   But Mr.
Furnival smiled.   He knew the world very well, and
he knew Lady Charlotte; and he fully believed that
the day of reconciliation between her and her niece
was not far off.

"Possibly," said the old lawyer slowly, "there was
an obstacle somewhere.   There often is.   Another
woman—"

"In that case, Lisa is safe," said Mr. Byng, with an
air of relief.   "I think, Charlotte, that a message from
(us—"

"To whom?" said Lady Charlotte, in a hard voice.

"To Lisa, of course, begging her to come home—"

"Oh," said his wife dryly.   She got up and swept
her long skirts to the door but paused with her hand
on the knob to say a parting word.   "The only message I can imagine sending is the one that my grandfather would have sent to Arthur Ellison in a similar
case.   In these degenerate days messages of that kind
are out of fashion; but there is no other I feel inclined
to send, either to Lisa Daubeny or to anyone else
whose name has been mentioned."

She closed the door behind her, not noisily or even
emphatically—she did not point her words by her
movements—but the two men she left behind felt
rather as if a thunderbolt had been launched at their
devoted heads.

"You see!" said Mr. Byng, nodding dismally at his
neighbor.   "She won't hear a word in her favor."

"Give her time! Give her time!" said the lawyer, shaking a little, but holding valiantly to his opinion. "She will come round."

She did not "come round," however, although the two men (and Thorold with them, until he left England) spared no pains to induce her to send some message of forgiveness or friendliness to Lisa. But she absolutely refused to do it. Mr. Furnival, who was perhaps less afraid of her than any other person on the face of the earth, took upon himself one day to tell her that she was not doing her duty to her dead sister's child.

Lady Charlotte turned upon him with a face, as he afterwards said, "of steel and iron," and reminded him that Lisa was of age and beyond her jurisdiction.

"Women need friends at any age," said Mr. Furnival sententiously.

"She has thrown off our friendship: and when she needs it, she can let us know."

"My dear lady! Is that likely? Miss Daubeny has got all the pride of her race. In some cases, it seems to me, Lady Charlotte, that a young lady—a young girl—should be helped in spite of herself. Miss Daubeny has laid herself open to the assaults of spiteful tongues, that cannot be denied; and your ladyship gives countenance to these evil reports by neither making public the cause of the quarrel, or receiving your niece back into your own house."

"I cannot help it, if people say nasty things. Lisa was quite old enough and had seen quite enough of the world to know that a flight from her guardians' house

would set everybody talking. I'm told there have
been paragraphs in the society papers about her—"

"And about yourself, Lady Charlotte," said Mr. Furnival, with great politeness of manner, but malicious
intent.

"It matters very little what they say of me," she returned; "I'm rather beyond the attacks of scandal-
mongers, thank heaven! It is Lisa herself who will be
affected by them, and she ought to know better than
to lay herself open to such assaults."

"She could guard herself from them only by coming
back to Westhills," said Mr. Furnival cautiously.

"To Westhills? Never!"

"You will not interfere to shield her?"

"Why should I?" said Lady Charlotte abruptly; and
Mr. Furnival held his peace. But while he was pre-
paring a retort which he hoped to prove effectual, she
faced round on him with her hands behind her back—
a favorite attitude of hers—and delivered herself un-
compromisingly.

"I don't wish to hear anything more about it—or
about her, Furnival. (In certain moods, Lady Charlotte always left out the "Mr.") I will not be trapped
into saying what I would do or what I would not do,
under circumstances which are not likely to occur. I
should never receive Lisa here again, unless she
chooses to humble herself, and ask pardon for her behavior. That, as you know, she is not a bit likely to
do. So why should we bother ourselves?"

"A word of encouragement," began the old man tentatively; but Lady Charlotte silenced him once and for all.

"I'll send no word of encouragement to anyone. And you'll please not say to her or to her friends that I shall be likely to listen even to the humblest of apologies. She has cast me off; and I cast her off in my turn. I don't want to hear her name again. I don't think any the worse of you for trying to plead her cause, you know, my good man; you do it better than Howard, who is a perfect idiot where she is concerned; but I am tired of the subject, and don't want to hear any more of it."

After that, Mr. Furnival had really no excuse for introducing Lisa's name into a conversation with Lady Charlotte; but he took good care to keep Mr. Byng well-informed as to the movements and circumstances of Miss Daubeny and Miss Ellison.

And thus the winter went by, and then the spring. Summer came again, but brought no hint of Lisa's return to her old home; and autumn glowed in the woods, but reconciliation was as far off as ever.

It was noticed that Lady Charlotte was beginning to look worn and pale: the outline of her cheek was sharper, the curve of her brows more persistently stormy, her activity was untiring. She managed all her affairs with twice her old spirit and assiduity; and when she was not engaged in outdoor pursuits, she devoted herself to literature. Several articles in magazines on biographical and historical matters at this time came from her pen: she was announced to have a book in the press, and there was a hint of her having accepted a post on a great critical journal. In addition to these employments, she visited and entertained a great deal. How she found time for everything, nobody could imagine. But it was reported that she could do with four hours' sleep only, and a great deal can be got into the superfluous hours gained by wakefulness.

Mr. Byng looked drooping and depressed. He was unaffectedly attached to Lisa, and the breach between her and her family gave him real pain. Lady Charlotte, who knew by instinct what he was thinking about, used to grow positively angry when he sat with her sometimes; for he did nothing but look beyond him and sigh. She was only too well aware that he was sighing for Lisa all the time.

On a wet day when even Lady Charlotte was confined to the house, she found this habit of sighing quite intolerable. She rose at last, and left him alone in the drawing-room, while she retired to the library and tried to pretend that she was busy. But for once the will to work had deserted her. She tried in vain to fix her attention upon the books and papers on her writing-table. The rain, driving against the broad plate-glass windows, made her melancholy. The rush of the wind, among the branches of the swinging poplars, with their wealth of golden leaves, gave her a shivering sensation. She drew a chair to the fireside, turning her back upon the rain-swept world without, took up a magazine and tried to read. But before long the book fell from her hands, and she was looking into the red embers of the fire, and dreaming of the past. She was not quite sure afterwards whether she had been asleep or awake. She was remembering the day when a little blue-eyed child had first come into her house, a child whom it had seemed to her so easy to love and care for. She fancied she saw the little Lisa, a fairy in white, with long golden hair, cut straight over her soft brows, running into the room—that room, the library—with arms outstretched, and she saw how the child tripped over a footstool and fell. All this had happened in reality many years before, and up to that point Lady Charlotte felt sure that she was wide awake. But then came something which certainly had not occurred in real life. The child seemed to have hurt herself: there was blood upon her face and on her frock: she stretched out her little hands for help—and Lady Charlotte could not give it. No, though she strained every nerve to rise and go to the child's assistance, she could not move. An anguish of powerlessness was upon her: she would have screamed for help if she could have found a voice. But she could neither speak nor move, and there lay the child, helpless, crying, perhaps even at the point of death.

Lady Charlotte started up, broad awake. It was eighteen years since Lisa had fallen over a foot-stool on the library-floor, and her aunt had picked her up and kissed her and consoled her. Why then should she dream of the scene? and give such a disagreeable turn to the story?

Perhaps, because—the idea occurred to her for a moment—Lisa was quite as much in want of help now as she had been when a tiny child in a white frock, not very strong for her age, nor steady upon her feet; and she, Charlotte Byng, the girl's nearest relation, had refused to help her in her extremity. The thought flashed through her brain, and was angrily dismissed; but the dream had shaken her. When she rose to her feet, she found that her hands were trembling and that there was a mist before her eyes.

"What a fool I am! I must be getting into my dotage!" she said to herself. She rang the bell in her usual imperious way; and it was answered at once by Andrews, looking as imperturbable and almost as young as he looked twenty years ago.

"Have the letters come, Andrews? Bring them to me, and a cup of tea."

The letters were brought: there was generally a goodly pile of them for Lady Charlotte. Andrews placed them carefully beside the little silver tray on which her tea was set. There was a rather big brown parcel: there were also several newspapers, some printers' proofs, and half a dozen letters.

She drank her tea before she opened any of them. Her hands were not quite steady yet, and she felt a little unnerved. She waited for a few minutes, and then set to work on the letters, leaving the papers for a later period.

The first three letters referred to invitations given or accepted. Then came a tradesman's circular, then a missive from Mr. Dorian, the publisher. Lady Charlotte had made up the little quarrel that had arisen between them. She had been all the more ready to make it up because she heard that he was not now very

friendly with Arthur Ellison, whose early poems he
had published, but who had acted rather shabbily (it
was said) with regard to the eldest Miss Dorian, to
whom he had once been almost, if not quite engaged.
Lady Charlotte had told Mr. Dorian pretty roundly
what she thought of Arthur Ellison, and she had not
yet gone so far in friendship as to offer him any of her
books in publication; but she had called on him once
or twice, and suggested that she still enjoyed glancing
over unpublished manuscripts, when he had any that
were interesting enough to be sent to her.

"I'll remember your kind offer, Lady Charlotte,"
said the publisher, readily. "Your opinion is often
worth its weight in gold to me." And he meant what
he said; for Lady Charlotte possessed the critical
faculty in perfection. Evidently he had kept his word.
He had himself written to say that a manuscript had
been submitted to him which interested him very
greatly, and on which he ventured to ask for Lady
Charlotte's judgment. She threw the note aside care-
lessly. "That will keep," she said.

The next letter gave her a momentary feeling of
pleasure: it was from Justin Thorold. But the pleasure very soon died away. He wrote from the Enga-
dine, saying that he meant to come home to Hurst for
the winter, and should be back almost as soon as his
letter.

"I have not heard from you for so long that I know
nothing of what has happened lately," he said. "You
will let me hope, dear Lady Charlotte, that all is well
between you and your niece, and that she is once more

in her proper place at Westhills. Write to me, I beg of you, and tell me this. Perhaps then I may be able to form a hope of winning back the one whom you know I love above all others."

Lady Charlotte crushed the thin sheet into a ball, which she sent to the other side of the hearth-rug. "It is sickening," she said to herself. "How these men persecute me about those two girls! I wish I were in my grave; then they could marry whom they like, the lot of them. What has Dorian sent me? I'll see: perhaps it is something amusing; something to help me to forget this wretched weather."

She drew the brown-paper packet towards her. It was beautifully folded as all publishers' parcels are: the string was neatly fastened by the smallest and tightest of knots: the address was a model of artistic caligraphy. "How does Dorian get all his clerks to write alike, I wonder," said Lady Charlotte, peering at it. "He must send them to a writing-master, first, I think. It's a beautiful hand."

She cut the string and threw the pieces recklessly into the fire; then she unfolded the wrappings, brown paper, gray paper, blue paper, with a final layer of white. The manuscript was not type-written, a fact at which she frowned. Then she bent her brows again, but with a different expression.

"Whose writing is this?" she said. "I seem to know the hand."

It was a small, fine hand, very legible, with every letter beautifully made. Lady Charlotte turned to the

first page, but there was no name.   The book was said
to be by "Veritas."

Then a change came over Lady Charlotte's face.   It
turned suddenly to stone.   She recognized the handwriting: she knew who had written this book, which
chance had given over into her hands.   It was by Arthur Ellison, the man whom she hated more than any
other in the world.

CHAPTER XVI.

A POLITICIAN OF THE OLD SCHOOL.

What grim chance had given Arthur Ellison into Lady Charlotte's hands? "Oh, that mine enemy had written a book" is a very ancient aspiration: but it is not often that it is so far gratified as in this case, when not only had he written a book but had delivered it over to the very person who was likely to look on it unfavorably. Of course, Lady Charlotte could condemn the book only in Mr. Dorian's eyes: Ellison would naturally take it to some other publisher if Mr. Dorian refused it, and the book would be published in spite of any adverse criticism from Lady Charlotte. But she could harass the young author with Dorian's refusal; and she knew very well that to be refused by a great publisher often depresses a writer unduly. It was within her power even to make him feel the lash of her criticism, by requesting Mr. Dorian to forward to the young author a copy of the "opinion" with which she had favored him. It was usually considered a compliment to make this request—a tribute to the young author's merits—but Lady Charlotte felt that she could make him wince very considerably while approaching him in complimentary garb. She smiled a little over the idea: she gloated over the lucky chance that had placed Arthur Ellison's work in her hands.

14

Lady Charlotte was one of a great number of distinguished literary people who act, in semi-official character, as "tasters" to great publishing houses. A book of unusual merit, on a subject which interested her, if sent to Mr. Dorian's office, was pretty certain to find its way into her hands. She would condescend to give her opinion on books of only a certain class, for she was not a professional "reader," bound to look at anything that came before her, but an expert on particular subjects and a good critic of their especial merits. Therefore she did not read novels for Mr. Dorian, or poetry, or essays; but she would read some books of travel, and memoirs relating to that part of the last century which she considered especially her own property. It had always been an understood thing that books of this kind alone should be sent to Lady Charlotte when she was "reading" for Mr. Dorian. Of late, as we have said, she had not troubled herself with his manuscripts, because she had had a quarrel with him; but now that they had made it up, and she had offered to do some work for him, she supposed that he would continue to send her books of the same character. But what could Arthur Ellison have written that would come under that head? Travel in the East? Impossible: he was not rich enough to travel. Biography? "What did *he* know?" Lady Charlotte said contemptuously. Art?—another of her favorite subjects —well, very possibly, he might think he could write about Art. In that case it would be her business to show him, sharply and unmistakably, his own ignorance.

But, still holding the half-opened manuscript in her hand, Lady Charlotte went through a few moments of conscience-stricken doubt. She thought it one of the worst of crimes to turn private knowledge of a man to public account: she had never once allowed a personal dislike knowingly to influence her in judging of a man's work. In one or two instances, where she had been asked to give an opinion of a book by a man whom she detested, she had at once sent back the manuscript to Mr. Dorian with a curt note of explanation. "Can't do this. Hate the man too much to be fair," she had written once. And this was a case in point. She was not at all capable of being "fair" to Arthur Ellison. She ought to send the book back unread. She knew before turning a page that she was prepared to find it without wit or wisdom or value of any kind.

But she was not prepared to forego her advantages. She rather wondered that the book had been sent to her at all. Perhaps there was some special reason for that. Everyone knew that Arthur Ellison had offended Lady Charlotte Byng, had made love to Lisa, and cruelly jilted her when she had given up her family for him. Ah, but of course his name was not on the title-page. It had probably never crossed Mr. Dorian's mind that she would recognize the author's handwriting, characteristic though it was; and he had wished to find out her real opinion of the book, when not seen through the distorting medium of personal dislike. Yes, she would read it; and—after all—she would try to be fair. But it was not possible that Arthur Ellison should have written anything that she could like.

What was it all about? She lifted the first page again and looked at the title. "A Politician of the Old School"—pray, what did he know about politicians, or about the "Old School," of which he wrote so glibly? Lady Charlotte's lip curled. She prided herself upon knowing a good deal about both. She said to herself that he had probably imagined his facts and invented his opinions. As to dates—but there was also a date upon his title-page. "1790-1830"—it was the period which she had studied most minutely, the period corresponding to that time when Lord Belfield was in power, and Lady Muncaster was becoming celebrated as the beauty in the fashionable world. The date of Lady Charlotte's own birth was 1842. What had Arthur Ellison to say about those dates?

Her eye traveled rapidly over a page or two. Then her color rose and her breath quickened. A suspicion of the truth dawned upon her. Before long it was certainty. Arthur Ellison, by some diabolical skill, had reconstructed the whole of Lord Belfield's private history, giving scandalous details of his early loves, still more scandalous accounts of the political "jobs" in which he had been engaged, most of the amusing stories which Lady Charlotte had intended to form the spice of her own memoirs of her grandfather, and some which she had intended to suppress. Where had he got the materials for these pages? She gasped with angry horror as she rapidly perused them. They were extracts from Lord Belfield's letters, given almost word for word. Worst of all, there were insinuations more damaging than actual statements; and it was perfectly certain that the whole book, when published, would make a profound stir in certain sections of the political and fashionable world. There would be very little left of Lord Belfield's reputation or that of some of his friends.

"No doubt, Dorian was delighted to get hold of it," mused Lady Charlotte, lifting her eyes for a moment from the beautifully written quarto sheets; "but how he came to send it to me passes my comprehension. Doesn't he know that I shall move heaven and earth to prevent its publication? I should think I could get an injunction as soon as the book is advertised. Perhaps Dorian counts on that to increase the sale, for no doubt the man would then publish it under another name, with the excision of certain passages, and I should be able to do nothing more. No, I must take other methods. But what was Dorian about?"

The question was to some extent answered by the arrival of a telegram at that moment from the publisher himself. Lady Charlotte read it with a smile of grim satisfaction on her face.

"Wrong parcel sent you by clerk's mistake. Kindly return it without delay; right manuscript to follow.
                                        "Dorian."

"I am very sorry for the clerk," thought she; "but I am not going to surrender what I have gained by his mistake. He'll be dismissed for carelessness, I suppose. I'll find him out and do something for him. And now for Mr. Dorian. He will understand what I mean—Lord knows whether he won't be here himself by next train if I don't choke him off."

She wrote her telegram, which consisted of few words only. "Too late. Shall be with you to-morrow. Charlotte Byng."

"And now I'll finish reading it," she said to herself. "For the sooner it's done the better." She turned eagerly to the book again: she had not yet read the last two or three chapters. It was one of these that roused her wrath more decisively than perhaps any of the others. The author had reproduced the letter written by Lady Muncaster to her father when she heard the report that the first Lady Belfield was yet living. This part of the book was managed—Lady Charlottle acknowledged it—with great skill. As a whole the volume purported to be the work of an intimate acquaintance—one can hardly say a friend—of the Belfields; but no hint of age or sex was given by the writer, who might have been a contemporary of Lady Muncaster, or a young connection of the family, to whose sacrilegious mind nothing was more sacred than to Beranger's noted sapeur. It did not purport to be a connected history of the time, or a memoir of the statesman, or even the record of a family. It was a pot-pourri of anecdotes, conversations, fragments of letters, old newspaper paragraphs, worth nothing from a literary point of view, but very amusing and very readable. Only

Lady Charlotte could estimate how far the value of her own book would be discounted by a publication of this kind; for she alone knew that almost every incident of importance, every interesting phrase and witty bon-mot, was written in the pages before her, for the amusement of the world—ten years or so before the proper time.

But in the last chapter, there was an attempt at connected narrative. Here the author changed his style a little and did not give names. But as he preserved initials, it was very easy to identify the persons meant. The Earl of B—— was naturally Lord Belfield; Lady M—— stood plain for the Marchioness of Muncaster: there were unmistakable references to Lady C—— B——. This was naturally the most objectionable portion of the book, as the author of it could dare to say in this manner things which he would never have ventured to utter when speaking of persons by their full names; and Lady Charlotte writhed under the conviction that although all the world would believe what was said or hinted of her family, she could never obtain redress; for no one could prove that the author had meant it to apply to them.

Here, then, under the disguise of initials, he recounted the history of "Some Old Marriages." The first one was the marriage of Lord Belfield with Miss Anketel and her subsequent elopement; his second marriage, the birth of a daughter, his wife's death, and the report of the first Countess' reappearance; and then, worst of all, to Lady Charlotte's mind, the letter of Lady Muncaster to her father, detailing the scandal that she had heard, and calling on him to refute it.

At this point, Lady Charlotte hastily turned over two or three pages as if searching for something; but what she sought was not to be found. The author, however, made a comment which stung his reader to the quick. "The answer to this letter," he said, "is not, I believe, to be found among the B—— papers, and in the absence of any denial on Lord B——'s part—a denial which would surely have been most carefully preserved, if it existed." Then the writer went on to compassionate Lady Muncaster's position, with a husband who scorned her for the accident of her birth; but added, with a touch of acrimony, that her daughters had nevertheless done well in the world, since one had died early, leaving an only child, and the other had married a man who possessed the estimable virtues of wealth and obedience to his wife. "It seems perhaps fortunate," the writer concluded, with something of a smirk, "that the number of Lord B——'s descendants in the direct line was so limited; for one and all were distinguished for some eccentricity in their love affairs: even the youngest and fairest of the line had lately chosen to leave her guardian's house because her affections refused to take the precise direction indicated by those in authority over her. The young lady in question is now said to be solacing herself by philanthropy: slumming perhaps being more to her taste than continued residence with a lady 'whose

foible is omniscience' and whose chief object in life
to trample underfoot all the inferior persons who do
not come of such distinguished lineage as herself."

"I wonder if I shall 'kill' this young man?" said
Lady Charlotte, quite calmly, as she laid the book
down at last, and rang for lights. "It seems to me
the fate that he ought to expect at our hands. We
should have done it without compunction in any
century but this. But of course he trusts to his
anonymity. Does Dorian know who it is? I must
go up and see him about this."

She stood still, with her hands behind her, looking
at Andrews as he placed the lamp on the table, closed
the shutters and drew the curtains. A little earlier
she would have rejoiced to see the gray skies shut
out, but now the weather was entirely forgotten.
When Andrews had retired she opened the old cabinet, which she now kept locked much more carefully
than in former days, and instituted a very careful
search among her papers, now and then carrying one
to the table and comparing it with certain pages of
the manuscript. The result often surprised her.
"How can he have done it?" she asked herself, with
knitted brows. "He was scarcely ever alone in the
room for more than half an hour at a time: I, or Howard, or some one, was constantly in and out. And
if he had neglected the work I gave him while he
copied out these letters and memoranda, I should
certainly have found him out. His work was always
well done, I remember. He must have got a skeleton

key, and copied the papers at night, or when we were in the garden."

A sudden thought struck her, and she rang the bell for Andrews.

"Andrews," said his mistress, "are these windows always fastened securely before you go to bed at night?"

"Certainly, my lady."

"I do not mean simply latched: do you bolt and bar the shutters so that no burglar could get in? There are valuable things in this room, remember."

"The bolts and bars are always seen to every night, my lady. Always by myself. I leave it to nobody," said Andrews, with a touch of respectful offense in his tones.

"You have never omitted that practice?" said Charlotte, fixing him with her imperious eye in a way that would have made a less immaculate person than Andrews uncomfortable. But he answered, with a stiffness born of rectitude:

"Except when I have been away for an 'oliday, my lady, or in town with the family, I have never failed to bolt these shutters myself for five and twenty year."

Lady Charlotte could go no further. She said, "Very well, Andrews: you are right to be careful," and gave him a nod of dismissal.

"I hope your ladyship has not missed anything," said Andrews solemnly.

"No, I think not, thank you, Andrews," said his mistress, who could be very gracious to her servants when she chose. But the graciousness did not impose upon Andrews, who left the room perfectly convinced that there was something wrong.

Lady Charlotte turned once more to the cabinet, and continued her search. There was one paper missing, certainly. One paper, which she remembered now she had not seen for many months—not indeed since Arthur Ellison left the house—the one paper which would be important to her if she were forced to make some public repudiation of the aspersions thrown upon her father's fame. It was that letter to his daughter, Lady Muncaster, in answer to the inquiries as to the legality of her mother's marriage; and it contained a denial of the story, the refutal of the slander, which Arthur Ellison had declared in his book to be authentic. Was it possible that he had stolen this one paper, and then suppressed it, in order to paint Lord Belfield in the blackest colors, and to stain the honor of a family who had, once at any rate, been kind to him?

It was with a curiously colorless face that Lady Charlotte at last shut up the cabinet, with full assurance that the paper she sought was not there. She had always thought ill of Arthur since he left Westhills, but she was scarcely prepared for this revelation of his treachery. "It must have been going on all the time he was in the house," she said to herself as she glanced once more at his neatly-written pages, and acknowledged their almost daemonic cleverness: "The materials for this book were not collected in an hour. And this was the man that Lisa loved!"

She had forgotten to dress for dinner, and when the gong was sounded she went straight into the dining-room, without a word of apology for her morning-dress. Mr. Byng looked at her in wonderment, not unmingled with a little fear. Lady Charlotte liked to dress as a great lady at dinner-time: she would don velvet and diamonds for the pleasure of the thing, even when she was alone with her husband; and something must be seriously wrong with her, he thought, if she could forget the dressing-bell.

He had a shock when dinner was over, nevertheless. Instead of sitting quietly over the dessert, his wife got up, moved restlessly to the fireplace, and stood looking at the fire for a little while. "I am going up to London to-morrow," she said at last.

"I hope the weather will be finer," said Mr. Byng politely.

"Yes," she said mechanically. Then she crossed the room towards the door, but paused beside his chair. "You don't mind being left so much alone, do you, Howard?" she said, putting one hand upon his shoulder. It was this action, these words, that gave Mr. Byng such a shock. She had never seemed to care whether he had been alone or not—and distinctly he did not like it—and she had not rested her hand on his shoulder in that way for years and years!

"No, no, I don't mind—but, Charlotte, Charlotte, my love, are you ill? Is anything the matter? I don't understand," said Mr. Byng, scrambling to his feet, with limbs that actually trembled under him with agitation.

She uttered a short laugh, and took her hand away. "Nothing's the matter," she said, "only I was thinking—what fools we were, Howard, when we were married first—a good many years ago."

"My dear—my dear," stammered Mr. Byng, utterly disconcerted by this remark, "I was not a fool in one respect—in—loving you." And he put one hand on hers.

"Weren't you?" she said, in a softened voice. "Poor Howard, I should have thought you were of a different opinion by this time. Well, we're all alone: we may as well make the best of each other, may we not?"

"You've had bad news of Lisa!" said her husband, staring at her, and unconsciously tightening his grasp of her hand. She dragged it loose at once, and flung from him impatiently.

"It is always Lisa with you," she said bitterly. "You never think of your wife."

It was a very untrue accusation, and she felt that it was so, almost before she had shut the door behind her and left him to finish his dessert by himself. Mr. Byng, sitting dismally in front of the decanters, meditated much on the nature of women that evening, but made no actual effort to come to a clearer understanding of the one with whom he had to deal. He was a slow man, and when he had next morning made up his mind to pay his wife the attention of bringing her the best orchid-bloom that he could find, she had already started for London, and he was forced to postpone his amiable intention.

Lady Charlotte did not go first to her publisher's. She went to Mr. Furnival's office and deposited a flat brown-paper parcel with him, telling him that to no one but herself was he to surrender it. Having seen it deposited in the safe, and having obtained from him a certain address, she went straight to Mr. Dorian's office.

The publisher did not usually come to his office so early in the morning, but on this occasion he was seated in his chair of state and displayed some perturbation of feeling when Lady Charlotte entered.

"I am afraid, Lady Charlotte, that we've made a mistake about that manuscript," he said to her, when he had shaken hands and thought what a handsome woman she was, and made a remark about the state of the atmosphere.

"I'm afraid you have," said she, rather grimly.

"It was confided to me in the strictest confidence," he said, "and if I had known the nature of the manuscript, I should never even have glanced at it. It will be returned to the author at once. I am only sorry that such an unfortunate mistake should have been made—that the book should have been sent to you, of all people, was most disastrous—most disastrous."

"Then you don't mean to publish it?" said Lady Charlotte bluntly.

"Impossible—in its present state," said Mr. Dorian, with a courtly air. "It is almost scandalous—it contains details which I think must be malicious inventions; and I would not for the world do anything to wound the feelings of a client like yourself—a client, and, I hope, a friend——"

"If you don't publish it, some one else will, I suppose," said his client and friend, without much respect for Mr. Dorian's civilities.

Mr. Dorian started slightly. "You do not—desire —exactly to have it published?" he said, in a blandly inexpressive tone.

"A good deal of it is contained in my grandfather's memoir, and will no doubt have to be made public in time," said Lady Charlotte, fencing in her turn. "If I could meet the author of this book, I might be able to come to some arrangement with him."

"Arrangement!"

"Yes, as to what was to be published, and what left out. I want his name, Mr. Dorian, if you please."

She had carefully kept all excitement out of her voice. She wanted to trap him into giving the author's name, under the impression that she meant to treat the matter in a friendly spirit. But Mr. Dorian was not to be beguiled.

"I am very sorry, but it is quite impossible for me to give you the name without the author's consent," he said. "The book was shown me in the strictest confidence—it is by the most unlucky of mistakes that your ladyship has seen a page of it—and although I am not going to publish it—oh, certainly not!—I cannot betray a professional secret."

"Oh, very well," said Lady Charlotte, rising from her chair. "I am pleased to hear that you don't mean to undertake the publication, Mr. Dorian. It would have severed our connection at once if you had done so. As to the author's name, I asked as a matter of form: but I know it perfectly well. It is Arthur Ellison; and I am going to him now."

CHAPTER XVII.

LADY CHARLOTTE'S CONDITIONS.

Arthur Ellison had been fairly prosperous of late. But with his prosperity he had developed also a kind of carefulness, not characteristic of his later days; the eye to the main chance, which he had always possessed, having become quicker and keener with use. Hence, he had not removed into fashionable apartments, even when he had money in hand: he contented himself with comfortable rooms in rather a remote part of Kensington, and did not try to make any show, except among his friends at the club or the restaurant that he frequented. His second-floor sitting-room and bedroom, opening out of one another, were all that he required for the present; and the fact that his sitting-room overlooked a rather noisy thoroughfare, was, in his opinion, an advantage, for it gave him something to look at when he was in the mood for idleness. And after all, the room was comfortable, and even luxurious, with its soft lounges and deep arm-chairs, and the pictures on the walls were after his own heart, for he had replaced the lodging-house chromos by photogravures of Watts' and Burne-Jones' pictures, by autotypes of the old masters. These pictures and a few books in excellent bindings were, he used to say, his one extravagance. It was possible that he had more than one, but he

only owned to the pictures and the books—such re-
fined, even praiseworthy, tastes for a rising young
journalist and literary man.

He had had a chequered career since he left Westhills. The prospective engagement of marriage to
Miss Dorian had fallen through, rather through Arthur's own carelessness than from any unwillingness
on the lady's part. Sooth to say, he had begun to
think that he could do better for himself than marry
Fanny Dorian. There must have been some great
attractions about him—to women, at least; for he was
always petted and made much of by them, whitherso-
ever he went. And at this time, he was thinking,
not without satisfaction, of a certain Miss Crespigny,
a handsome girl with three thousand a year, and no
relations to speak of, who was quite ready to marry
him whenever he should throw the handkerchief. She
was a Creole, with a dangerously volcanic tempera-
ment; but Arthur was prepared to accept all risks
for the sake of three thousand a year.

In the meantime he wanted money, for, although he
was willing to accept his wife's thousands, he did not
wish to be dependent upon her altogether. If he
could achieve fame—or, at least, notoriety—as well,
he felt that he should be able to meet Miss Crespigny
on tolerably equal terms. So he had set to work on
his recollections and his notes of Lord Belfield's memoirs, and he had, by means of an excellent memory
and some invention, produced a book which would
most assuredly set London talking, if ever it saw the
light.

Mr. Dorian had not been quite frank with Lady Charlotte when he told her that he would not publish the book that Arthur had sent to him. If the manuscript had not so unluckily fallen into her hands, he would have been only too happy to publish it—with the omission, perhaps, of a few details which had struck him as indiscreet. He had not, however, announced his final acceptance of the book to Arthur, and this left him free to tell Lady Charlotte, with an air of virtuous repudiation, that he did not intend to publish it at all.

Arthur was hopeful. He meant to ask for a royalty on each copy, and he believed that it would sell like wildfire, and that he would make a fortune. The secret of his identity he meant to have very strictly kept—for a time. When the storm was over—for he knew that there would be a storm—he thought he might venture to let it be known in the literary world that he was the author of "that celebrated book—A Politician of the Old School," and he could then risk the danger of Lady Charlotte's denunciations, or the threat of a thrashing from Justin Thorold, or any of the other possibilities hanging over his head. Of prosecution he had no fear. He had done nothing that could bring him within reach of the law. Lady Charlotte's papers, with one exception, were intact. He had only made use of what his memory and his note-book had brought away.

He reflected pleasantly on his prospects, as he stood before his window one morning, and looked out on the busy street. There was not much change on him since the day when he had left Westhills, or refused to marry Lisa Daubeny. The slight, almost boyish figure was as alert as ever, the brilliant eyes were as blue as a bit of the northern seas; but there was an indefinable hardening of all the delicate features, and some tired lines at the corners of the eyes and mouth, which gave a less agreeable expression to his appearance than in days of old. But there was more hardihood, more assurance in his manner, and he had taken on the so-called "polish" of a man of the world, which by some people was admired and by others thought utterly detestable.

Lady Charlotte was of the latter class. When she walked straight into the sitting-room that morning she felt more contempt than pity for the fair young fellow in his quilted silk dressing-gown, his gorgeous smoking-cap and embroidered slippers, who stood at the window with a cigarette in his mouth and a yellow-backed novel in one hand. He was such a bubble, such a trivial thing, such a straw to bend and break, that he scarcely deserved the pains which she would have to take to crush him. And Arthur, turning round from the window, and meeting those scornful eyes of hers quite suddenly, faltered and turned pale, as if he knew that his hour of doom had come.

"Oh, I beg your pardon," he said, recovering his self-possession but speaking with white lips, "I did not expect a lady. If you'll excuse me, I will put on my coat and be back directly."

He made a step in the direction of his bedroom, but Lady Charlotte calmly planted herself in his way.

"Excuse me," she said. "I would rather you did not leave this room for a few minutes. You might wish to go out by the other door, and I have a particular reason for desiring to speak with you first. This door, I have already locked, and you will oblige me by not going out by the other."

Arthur was petrified by astonishment and terror. He thought that Lady Charlotte was about to call him to account for his behavior to Lisa—after all these months! The thing that really happened never occurred to him. He did not know that Lady Charlotte had renewed her old relations with Mr. Dorian, and he was quite sure that Dorian would never take her into his confidence regarding the publication of the "Politician." He could only regard her with shrinking aversion—for he was not brave, and cast a furtive glance in the direction of the bell-rope. Lady Charlotte's indignant moods were so incomprehensible to him, that he looked upon her sometimes as no better than a raving lunatic.

"I—I don't understand what you can have to say to me, Lady Charlotte," he stammered out.

"You will understand quite well in a minute or two," said his guest, with composure. "We need not protract our interview. No doubt you will be as glad to see the last of me, as I of you."

"Your ladyship was always complimentary," said Arthur, with irony which showed that he was recovering himself.

Lady Charlotte ignored the remark. She sat down at the center-table, with her back to the bedroom door, so that he could not make use of that exit, placed a little brown leather bag on the table before her, and deliberately took off her gloves. "I have come on business," she said, "and I shall be glad if you will give me your attention for a minute or two. You may not be aware that I have resumed my old acquaintance with Mr. Dorian."

Arthur changed color, and moved restlessly from one foot to the other. He was standing at the other side of the table, and it suddenly occurred to him that he looked like a little boy in front of a stern preceptress, and felt that Lady Charlotte wanted to make him ridiculous. He put his hand on the back of a light cane chair and swung it round.

"I am pleased to hear it," he said politely.

"I have long been in the habit," Lady Charlotte continued in a peculiar monotone, as of a person that had previously rehearsed the speech more than once, "of reading and giving my opinion on manuscripts which Mr. Dorian has submitted to me. He wrote me a note yesterday asking me to look at a manuscript which had recently been sent to him; and the manuscript came by post at the same time."

There was surely no need for her to ask Arthur whether her hearer understood. Every vestige of color had fled from his face, and his knees were manifestly shaking under him. He seated himself and covered his mouth with one hand: a significant gesture in Lady Charlotte's eyes.

"Unfortunately," she said slowly, "unfortunately, that is, for Mr. Dorian. whom the mistake has made annoyed, the clerk made a blunder about the parcels of manuscript; and the one submitted to me was not the harmless volume of travels in the East which it should have been—but a work of a very different character—anything but harmless in intention, Mr. Ellison: a book bearing the title of 'A Politician of the Old School'—you recognize it, I perceive?"

There was a dead pause. Then Arthur, with a sensation as if all the blood in his body were surging to his face, took his hand from his mouth and answered hardily:

"I never heard of it in my life."

"You lie!" flashed out Lady Charlotte immediately, with fire in her eyes, "you lie, and you know you do. You wrote it yourself—every word of it."

"Pardon me, you have not the slightest right to make any such statement. I presume Mr. Dorian cannot have mentioned my name in the matter, indeed, why should he? The similarity of subject has possibly led you to fancy that I wrote it, but——"

"Similarity of subject? I did not mention the subject. You betray yourself, you see."

Arthur bit his lips. "I meant—one knows the subject on which your ladyship's mind is fixed," he said, trying hard for self-possession.

"Am I so limited?" said Lady Charlotte with irony. Then, in graver tone: "It is useless to deny facts, Mr. Ellison. Do you think I do not know your handwriting? I know every turn of it to my cost. I have folios of it at home, which the manuscript you sent to Dorian's reproduces line by line. The testimony of an expert would not be needed. The handwriting is quite unmistakable."

Arthur started up, and swore. He was too angry, and too desperate to restrain himself. Lady Charlotte smiled; for the ejaculation had told her that she had practically gained the day.

"I have come here," she said, "to hear you acknowledge it, and I shall not leave this room until you have done so."

"I don't see what good you will get from that, Lady Charlotte. It is not much good waiting for me to acknowledge what I have not done. I know nothing of your manuscript."

"In that case," said Lady Charlotte, "I will see that it is destroyed. If you disown it, I am sure that no one else will care to claim it."

Arthur's eyelid twitched: the muscles of his face worked for a moment. Then he decided to alter his position, for it was quite evident that Lady Charlotte was not to be dislodged from hers. He tried to laugh, but the laugh was something of a failure.

"One is always permitted to disown one's own books: it is a thing allowable in literature," he said, with a pretense of ease. "Your ladyship's penetration has not failed you on this occasion. May I ask —what then?"

"You acknowledge that you wrote that book—of which you stole every word of the materials?"

"Stole—'Convey, the wise it call'—is a hard word, Lady Charlotte. I have as much right as anyone else to collect historical reminiscences and publish them.

Lord Belfield was a public man: even his own family have no right to suppress the details of his career."

"I think you are aware, however," said Lady Charlotte, with dangerous smoothness, "that by a clause
in Lord Belfield's will he prohibits the publication of
these details until the year 1900?"   .

"No," said the young man, coolly, "you must excuse me if I say that he does not. He forbids the
publication of his journals and private letters. If
you have looked at all carefully at my little attempt,
you must have seen that in no case is a letter quoted
entirely, or the journal reproduced word for word.
My memory is good, but it was not good enough for
that; and perhaps this was fortunate for me, and
has prevented me from infringing on the rights of
Lord Belfield's executors."

"I noticed that your cleverness had kept you tolerably on the safe side," said Lady Charlotte dryly, "but
I am not so sure as you seem to be that I could not
prevent the publication of the book by legal methods.
However, I am not going to do that."

Arthur could not forbear a little bow and smile.
"I am much obliged to you," he said. And indeed the
color had returned to his lips. He thought the worst
was over, and it had not been so bad as might have
been expected. "My manuscript then is safe in Mr.
Dorian's hands?" he inquired casually. "It is not
with you, I see."

"Not at present," said Lady Charlotte. "Mr. Furnival, my lawyer, has got it at this moment. But you

need not be alarmed: it will be returned to you quite safely—I will see that it is sent."

"Many thanks. It might even go back to Mr. Dorian's," said Arthur tentatively. He could not as yet make out why Lady Charlotte had come, or what she meant to do. The interview was almost too amicable for security.

"Oh, no, it is no use sending it to Dorian's," said his visitor, "or to any other publisher. It is not a book that is going to be published, Mr. Ellison."

Arthur shrugged his shoulders. "I really do not see who can prevent it," he said, almost insolently.

"I can." The words were rapped out strongly and sharply, like pistol-shots. "I can—and will. I have come here for that purpose. I am going to prevent you."

"I should like to know how," said the author, sneering. "You see, I have my materials ready to my hand, Lady Charlotte. Even if I were to destroy this manuscript, it would be perfectly easy for me to produce another. I do not quite see how you are going to put the shackles which you are so fond of employing, on my pen and on my brain.

"Nevertheless, that is just what I am going to do," said Lady Charlotte. She opened her brown leather bag, and took out a paper or two, which she laid before her on the table. Arthur eyed them furtively. Was she going to offer him a bribe?"

"I warn you, Lady Charlotte," he said, putting on an air of bravado, "that I will not take money for the suppression of truth."

"Wait till I offer you money," she answered dryly.
"I have no intention of doing it at present.   Now, Mr.
Ellison, the matter stands thus.   You came into my
house, giving me your word that you would not betray the contents of any papers you might happen
to see.   I trusted you—foolishly, as it seems—and
gave you every opportunity of handling my grandfather's papers and other valuable documents.   It appears that you copied or took notes in a most dishonorable manner of all you read; and that you have
turned it to your own ends by writing a book about
my family—a book that is a tissue of lies and misrep-
resentations from end to end.   Also, you have, I believe, willfully suppressed one letter, which I suppose
you stole from my desk, the letter from Lord Belfield
which entirely refutes the calumny about his second
marriage.   You have that letter now in your possession, and I shall ask you presently to hand it over
to me."

Arthur shrugged his shoulders.   "I am sorry that
I shall not be able to gratify you," he said.

"We will see presently.   Well, Mr. Ellison, I am
going to send that base and treacherous production
of yours back to you; but not until you have complied with certain conditions of mine."

"Conditions!   I shall comply with no conditions——"

He looked round the room uneasily, seeking for a
way of escape.   It began to occur to him that
flight was his safest course when he was engaged in
a contest with Lady Charlotte Byng.   But there was

no way of getting out of the room except by subjugating his opponent physically, for she literally barred the way to his bedroom, and the other door was locked. If he had never before cursed his want of thews and sinews, he cursed it now. He would have been powerless in Lady Charlotte's vigorous hands. She saw the look and smiled. For the first time, he began to feel really afraid of her: a pang of curiously unreasoning fear shot through him, as he saw that cold and almost cruel smile. She did not look like the woman that he had known. He had seen her hot, angry, vehement, excited; but she was cold as ice and hard as a stone.

"I have here," she said, indicating the papers before her, "made a rough draft of a statement which I mean you to write and sign in my presence. I think it would be advisable for me to have some such statement in my possession, not necessarily to be made public, but for my own satisfaction. I want it all in your own handwriting—you have a beautifully clear hand, I know—so that there may be no question of your having signed the paper with the contents of which you were not sufficiently acquainted."

"I will sign no paper," said Arthur Ellison, drawing away from the table. But the look of anxiety in his eyes was increasing. They roamed from side to side like the eyes of a wild animal in a snare.

"You will state," said Lady Charlotte, without heeding his exclamations, "that you had access to my papers, and, contrary to your promise, you surreptitiously and treacherously took notes of their con-

tents; that you afterwards embodied what you had
read in a manuscript entitled 'A Politician of the Old
School,' and that you used every device in your power
to blacken Lord Belfield's character and to misrepre-
sent the events of his life."

"I'll be hanged if I do," said Arthur, starting up.
But Lady Charlotte went on.

"You will also state that you stole a letter from
Lord Belfield in which he disproves the accusations
of bad faith brought against him with respect to his
first wife's death and his second marriage. You may
remember that you insinuate in your book that that
letter was purposely withheld by his executors, and
that Lady Muncaster was illegitimate. You will
write down, on this paper, that you told a deliberate
lie, and that you humbly beg my pardon for it, and
for the other lies and slanders contained in your vile
and abominable book. You will hardly dare to publish it, when I have this paper in my possession, Mr.
Ellison."

"You accursed old witch, get out of my room!"
cried the young man in an access of helpless fury.
"Do you think I'll set my name to a paper of that
kind? Why, it would damn me for life. I—I—I'd
die first."

"You can choose," said Lady Charlotte calmly.
"You know me well enough to be aware that I never
threaten without meaning to perform, don't you?
Now, look here. It sounds melodramatic, but it isn't:
it's deadly earnest. You will do what I tell you, or
I shall shoot you dead. I have made up my mind."

And she displayed before his eyes a pretty shining silver-mounted toy which Arthur suddenly remembered to have seen in the library at Westhills and which, he had been told, Lady Charlotte could use with unerring skill. She used to practice at a mark on rainy afternoons.

With that revolver pointing straight in his face, and Lady Charlotte's finger on the trigger, there was nothing for Arthur to do but to cower away from her in his chair and to cry hoarsely, "For God's sake, wait!"

CHAPTER XVIII.

NEMESIS.

"I will wait," said Lady Charlotte, lowering her weapon, "but I shall not wait for very long. You may have a few minutes in which to discuss the matter further, if you like, and to make up your mind. You will write what I dictate, and sign the paper, or I shall shoot you like a dog. I have done it before, when I was traveling in Syria."

"But we are in England—a civilized country——"

"Some of us are none the more civilized for all that. An Arab who eats your salt is at least faithful to you for life: if not, you shoot him down remorselessly. An Englishman apparently thinks he can lie and thieve and slander as he pleases, and that there is no one to call him to account; but if he has to deal with me, he is mistaken."

"It is not loaded," said Arthur, trying to brave the matter out.

"Oh, yes, it is, and I am not such a fool as to threaten without meaning what I say. I have used it before. If a man proves himself worthless, his life had better end. He's dangerous to society."

"But—you forget—the law—the law will take vengeance on you."

"I am not afraid of the law," said Lady Charlotte coolly. "Do you think I lay my plans no better than that? Your landlady and her servants are down on the ground-floor: the noise of a shot will not alarm anybody very particularly. I shall go back to West-hills, and nobody will even question me on the subject. You will be supposed to have committed suicide."

"Are you a fiend?" cried the young man wildly. "Or only a mad woman? Oh, my God, what am I to do?"

He buried his face in his hands and began to sob hysterically. Lady Charlotte, with her hand on the revolver, watched him grimly, like remorseless fate.

"There is no help for you," she said at last, in a low but perfectly determined tone. "You are bound to do what I wish. And you may be thankful that I have given you a chance for your life. My grandfather would have shot you down without question or parley."

"He was a brute," said Arthur, with white lips and staring eyes.

"You have had time to consider," said Lady Charlotte dryly. "Have you made your decision yet?"

She slightly raised the pistol. He shrank back and put up one trembling hand between the weapon and his head.

"Give me the paper," he cried. "Sign! Good God, yes! I'll sign anything—anything; but for heaven's sake, put that thing away!"

"You are a coward in grain, Mr. Ellison," she said, as she quietly lowered her weapon, and pushed the paper toward him. "I should have been better prepared for this interview if I had brought a horsewhip instead of a revolver. You would lick the dust, I believe, sooner than let me flick you across the face."

"You—you have the advantage of me, with a weapon in your hand," said Arthur hoarsely. He was prepared to submit, but he could not deny himself a gibe. But Lady Charlotte was always ready with a repartee.

"You see, one does not approach honorable men with weapons: it is not necessary in their case," she said. Then, curtly, and with a terrible frown, she gave the order—"Write!"

The young man obeyed with slavish haste.

His hand trembled, so that he could scarcely guide his pen, and it was evident that his eyes were dim with fear. His handwriting was unlike itself: a fact of which Lady Charlotte took careful note. "Take time," she said. "Don't spoil your handwriting by overhaste, man. It is too beautiful to be spoilt—or forgotten."

"What am I to write? I don't know," said Arthur, dashing down his pen. "You make me accuse myself of things——"

"Of the things that you have done," said his visitor, implacably. "Go on: copy my words. They are legible enough, on the other paper. And you will give me back the letter written by my grandfather to my mother?"

Arthur groaned, and shaded his eyes with one hand, while he wrote, but he made no reply. In a few moments, he had reached the end of the document, and

16

was about to sign, when Lady Charlotte stayed his hand. "Wait a moment," she said. "I should like your signature witnessed, if you please. Who is in the house that can act as a witness? Your landlady?"

"I suppose so," said the young man, drearily.

"Ring the bell for her, then. And pull yourself together—don't look as if you had just been beaten. Only remember, there's no evasion possible, now that this paper is written, it has to be signed—or my warning holds good."

She put the revolver back into the bag, produced the key from her pocket, and unlocked the door, while Arthur, after ringing the bell, sank helplessly back into his chair without much attempt to regain an appearance of self-command. Lady Charlotte, standing at the table, glanced at him contemptuously, but did not speak until the landlady, summoned by the maid, made her appearance in the room. Lady Charlotte's black brows cleared as if by magic, and she turned a frank ingratiating smile upon the woman.

"We have ventured to trouble you," she said, "because Mr. Ellison has been drawing up an important document, which he wants to have witnessed. I will be one witness—here's my card; Mrs. Jevons, your name is, I believe—if you will kindly be the other."

"I hope it's nothing that will bring any trouble to anybody, my lady," said Mrs. Jevons, hesitating between respect for a title and concern at the misery plainly written on Arthur's face. Arthur was intensely miserable; for, after all, how callous soever you may be, it is no light thing to write yourself a liar and a traitor, and see your signature formally witnessed to the document, which is afterwards to remain in the possession of your bitterest enemy. Arthur Ellison had some reason to be wretched; and he did not care to disguise the fact.

"Not at all, Mrs. Jevons," said Lady Charlotte briskly. "It's the sort of thing that he will be more and more pleased to have done, the more he thinks of it. Now, Mr. Ellison, please: we are waiting to see your signature."

The touch of sharpness in her tone made Mrs. Jevons glance at her curiously. "A lady with a temper of her own, I doubt," she said to herself, and looked at her lodger with pity. "It's plain she's made him do something that he didn't want to do. Well, it's no business of mine, I'm sure, but I wonder what it's all about."

She could not see what was written on the paper, for it was folded over, so she watched Arthur discontentedly as he scrawled his name, and then wrote her own beneath Lady Charlotte's, and hoped that she had not committed herself to anything very terrible. "It must be all right when a great lady like that's at the bottom of it," she said to herself; and this conviction was strengthened as Lady Charlotte pressed a sovereign into her hand at the door. She went down-stairs with a joyful heart, and Lady Charlotte was left with her defeated enemy.

"Let me see," she said, taking up the paper, and she proceeded to read the document aloud, with clear and cutting emphasis, while Arthur sat and winced as at the touch of red-hot iron upon his naked flesh. He would willingly have killed her at that moment, if he could; he would have liked to choke her into silence with his hands. But if Lady Charlotte perceived his rage and pain, she was rather pleased than otherwise. "That is right," she said, when she had finished. "This paper brands you by your own confession as a liar and a thief, and it would utterly destroy your character in decent people's eyes if I made it public. You see that, do you not? Now, if you publish that book, or any book at all like it, dealing in any way with my family, Arthur Ellison, I shall immediately publish this paper. Do you understand?"

He made a sign of assent.

"And now suppose you give me Lord Belfield's letter," she said calmly.

He was utterly cowed. He turned to a little drawer in his bureau, and took out a sheaf of papers. From these he selected one, which he laid on the table before Lady Charlotte. She took it up, glanced through it and nodded.

"That is it. This letter will appear in its proper place when I publish Lord Belfield's memoirs. What are those other papers? Any of mine among them? Ah, surely I see——"

She had caught sight of Lisa's handwriting, and caught herself up suddenly, with a pause for self-command. "You will give me my niece's letters also, Mr. Ellison."

He dared not hesitate. He laid the packet before her and watched sullenly while she turned over its various items. There were three letters from Lisa which she selected and put aside.

"Have you any others from her? No? You are sure? You had no business to keep them—but then of course you do not understand matters of delicacy and good feeling. And now before I go, have the goodness to tell me why the engagement between you and my niece was broken off? Did she discover your unworthiness? I can imagine that; for with all her faults, Lisa knew right from wrong. Had she some reason to be disgusted with you?"

"I—I—it was I who—who—at least, I tried to make her understand that I was too poor to marry," said Arthur.

"You mean you broke it off? You refused to marry her?"

"I was too poor."

"You were a miserable cur," said Lady Charlotte. "The girl had thrown over everything for your sake, and you stopped to consider whether you would have to curtail your own luxuries, I suppose." Her eye ran impatiently over the expensive engravings and beautifully bound books with which the room was decorated. "You spoilt her life for the sake of your own cowardice and selfishness: I am quite sure of that."

"I thought she would go home again," Arthur muttered.

"Ah, yes, any way of getting rid of her was good enough for you. Upon my life, I'm sorry I have undertaken to keep that paper to myself, A man as base as you are deserves punishment."

"I'm no worse than other men," said her victim.

"Then I am very sorry for the human race. But, good heavens, you are as much beneath other men as a cockroach is beneath an archangel," said Lady Charlotte, dashing into hyperbole. "Why you have been allowed to cumber the earth so long is more than I can imagine. One thing I intend, which may curtail your powers of doing mischief, Mr. Arthur Ellison, I shall send a letter to the public papers and to all the principal London publishers, cautioning them against employing you in any capacity of trust."

"Good heavens, Lady Charlotte, you will ruin me!"

"And I wish to ruin you," she said, giving him a look of steel from under her curved dark brows. "I mean, if I can, at any rate, to prevent you from ever being received as an equal by respectable people. I mean to let it be known that you are a dishonorable scoundrel, whom no one can safely employ in matters that require trust and confidence."

"There is such a thing as a law of libel——"

Lady Charlotte laughed mockingly. "You would like to apply to the Court, would you not? You would like the whole story to come out? For I should not spare you then! Your conduct would be discussed at every breakfast-table in England."

Arthur buried his face in his hands. "I think you are a devil in human shape," he said bitterly. "You leave me no chance—no hope, you undertook to keep the matter secret, I understood, if I gave up publishing the book——"

"I undertook nothing absolutely. I promised nothing—except that as far as lies in my power, Mr. Arthur Ellison, I shall always try to make you suffer as much as I can."

There was a strange vindictiveness in her manner: a look of bitter enmity in her eyes. Young Ellison did not understand it: indeed, Lady Charlotte was half-surprised at the strength of the feeling which had been roused in herself. It seemed as though that old tenderness for Lisa, lately risen as it were from the dead, was spending all its vigor in an effort to avenge Lisa's wrongs. Lady Charlotte felt no pity for the miserable object to which Arthur's cowardice and misery had reduced him: she was only anxious at that moment to make him writhe under the lash of her scorn and the fear of its consequences.

"And now I will leave you," she said, taking up the bag into which her papers had been bestowed. "I hope I may never see your face again, Mr. Ellison, but I daresay you will often hear of me."

"But, Lady Charlotte—one moment—have some pity—for God's sake. Don't ruin me—don't expose me!" cried the young man, falling on his knees and catching at her dress as she turned to leave the room. He sobbed as he pulled at the folds of her satin gown. "I will do anything I can to make amends: I—I'll—I'll marry Lisa, if you like—!"

"You miserable hound! get up and don't snivel!" said Lady Charlotte, who was peculiarly unlikely to be moved (except to wrath) by the sight of a man's tears. "Marry Lisa indeed! I'll make your name a by-word in every house in England if I hear you speak of her again!"

She disengaged her dress from his grasp, and left the room, leaving him at full length upon the floor, sobbing like a child. She opened the front door, and stood for a moment on the steps, looking up and down the street until she could see a cab. "I hope I frightened him sufficiently," she said to herself, with a grim kind of humor, as she drove away. "He'll have a bad time of it, I fancy, for the next few days."

The next few hours were bad enough, if she had only known. The man dragged himself from the floor to his bed and lay there in a torpor of exhaustion, varied by cries of rage and anguish in which he made his teeth meet in his own flesh for very madness of over-wrought feeling. His fear of Lady Charlotte had increased to positive agony at last. He beheld himself everywhere pursued by her enmity, a tall dark figure meeting him at every turn, the tones of her accusing voice for ever in his ears. She would ruin him: she would hunt him down—even to the death. She would never forgive.

He believed every word that she had spoken. He saw no hyperbole, no exaggeration in any of her threats. He pictured her sitting at her desk in the library at Westhills, writing a letter to the Athenaeum perhaps, and another to the Times. He had seen similar letters, warning the public against "unscrupulous adventurers" who had tried to swindle the unwary. Was he to be classed with them? And he could do nothing: he could neither deny, nor remonstrate, nor prosecute for libel: he could but sit down quietly under any imputation she chose to cast upon him and eat out his heart in what would look like conscious guilt.

Of course, he knew that he was guilty. He knew that he had done what no honorable man would do. But surely he was excusable, if anybody ever was. He had always been clever, and he had had so few chances of getting on, it was absurd to suppose that he could reject any that came in his way. If he had been a rich man, it would have been different: it would have been easy to be virtuous, then! But now—if Lady Charlotte carried out half her threats—he was utterly ruined—ruined more completely than if he had failed in business, or lost his money in a bubble speculation. For, mixed with his desire of wealth for the luxuries that it would bring, or of success for the sake of a flattered vanity, there was some sort of aspiration after a better and more enduring kind of fame—that of the writer of beautiful verses, of lines that the world would not willingly let die.

From this field of achievement, he seemed to himself cut out. Publishers would no doubt print his books if they were really good: but he felt a sick shame at the idea of sitting down to elaborate sweet fancies, when so many of his readers would know him to be dishonored, base and vile. Better go to the backwoods and earn his living by the sweat of his brow!

But here again he shrank from the thought of toil and peril, hunger and cold. He wanted his life to be softly lapped about in folds, as it were, of velvet: he cared for no harder manual labor than that involved by handling a pen. He thought with passionate regret of the marriage he might have made, if his name had been unsoiled; but he knew the West-Indian heiress too well to suppose that she would let her thousands pass into his hands, if he were branded with the name of an adventurer. The prospect of a wealthy marriage had vanished, probably for ever, from his view.

His fear of Lady Charlotte was like a possession. He set no limits to her power. She was rich and influential and unmerciful: she would crush him, as one crushes a noxious insect. If only he could get away from her, surely he might begin again—he might win his way to fame and fortune yet!

The excitement of the day was telling upon him and making him feverish. His thoughts began to be vague and confused: his head was aching violently. He had turned from food all day with loathing, and now it was evening and growing dark. His door was locked: he had a nervous fear lest Lady Charlotte should come back, and he would not even admit his landlady, who came once to his room with a cup of tea, and once with a parcel, which she said had just been brought for him from a Mr. Furnival's. This announcement roused him a little, and when she had gone downstairs, he crept out upon the landing and brought the parcel into his room. Yes, it was the manuscript, still in Mr. Dorian's wrapper, addressed to Lady Charlotte. How he cursed Dorian and Dorian's clerk in his own mind!

He unfastened the wrapper with hot, trembling fingers; then, without trusting himself to glance even at the words he had written, he tore the neatly-written pages across and across, and then thrust the fragments into the grate, where a few red embers were still aglow. The edges of the paper grew black, then brown, then broke into a light flame, which spread from sheet to sheet until all was destroyed. Ellison held the burning papers down with a poker, so that the flames should not mount too high and turned them about until every page was blackened and illegible. Then he went to his private drawer and took out the note-books from which the book had been compiled. These also he piled upon the heap—first tearing them across, so that they should burn more easily. Soon all that remained of his labors was a little pile of ashes, at which he stood staring stupidly for a little while, with a childish desire that Lady Charlotte and Lisa could know what he had done. Of Esther he had long left off thinking; but at that moment he wished that she were near him, and that he might do as he had done before so many times in his bright and eager boyhood—make her his confidante, his confessor, as regarded all that went wrong in his impulse-ridden life.

He sat down and even wrote a word or two. "Dear Esther"—he began, and paused. What had he to say? How could he, even to her, confess the treachery of which he had been guilty to her friends? He left the sheet on his desk, without writing another word, and went back to his room. His head was aching horribly and his skin was feverish. The old resource against sleeplessness was standing near. He seized the fluted blue bottle and poured out his accustomed dose. Did his hand shake, and had he poured out more than enough to ensure him a good night's rest?

"It does not matter to anybody if I never wake again," was his last thought, before he sank into the utter tranquillity of unconsciousness.

CHAPTER XIX.

A MESSAGE OF MERCY.

Lady Charlotte went home that afternoon, after short interviews with Mr. Furnival and Mr. Dorian, and rather amazed her husband by the serenity and peaceableness of her demeanor. True she was grave, and sometimes he thought that she looked troubled; but she was very amiable to him, and accompanied him in a tour round the conservatories before dinner in the evening. He wondered where she had been and what she had been doing; but he could not raise his courage sufficiently to ask, even when she played piquet with him in the evening—a great concession on her part.

Next morning, however, things did not go so smoothly. Lady Charlotte found something wrong in the stables, and, as the head groom expressed it, "stormed all over the place." It was a relief to her to express in this way a growing sense of dissatisfaction with herself and with everybody else. And she was still angry when she thought of Arthur Ellison. The remembrance of things that he had said repeatedly brought a gloom to her face that morning. But she seemed resolved against stopping to think of anything but the occupation of the moment. After upsetting the grooms and stable-men by a scolding which it must be owned that they deserved, she or-

dered her horse and rode over to Hurst, where she
carefully inquired when Mr. Thorold was coming
back, and what preparations were being made for his
reception. Then she lunched at a farmhouse, and conferred with the farmer about his land, and then, riding
home again, she reached Westhills a little after four,
and was told that some one had come from London
to see her on business.

"What sort of business?" said Lady Charlotte,
thinking of Dorian and his clerks.

"She did not say, my lady," answered the man, who
was new to his place. Andrews had managed to
hurt his foot and was confined to his room.

"She!—Where is she?"

"In the little book-room, my lady. She said she had
come from London, and must wait to see you, and I
think she is one of those ladies that come to you from
the poor when you're in town, my lady."

"Oh, one of the Little Sisters," muttered Lady
Charlotte, half-disposed to rebuke the man for his
loquacity; but she turned aside to the book-room,
which was a smaller and plainer library, near the main
entrance to the hall, feeling meanwhile in a small
breast-pocket for the sovereign-purse which she carried about with her. She always gave gold to the
Little Sisters of the Poor when they came to her
house in London.

But on pushing open the door, which was slightly
ajar, she saw that she had been misinformed. It was
not one of St. Vincent de Paul's black-veiled Sisters
that waited for her, although she did not altogether

wonder at the servant's mistake. For there was a seeming similarity in the garb: the visitor's dress was black, and she wore a long black veil affixed to a plain black straw bonnet, with white strings, framing the face. It was when she turned her face, that Lady Charlotte forgot all about the dress; for it was Lisa's face!

There was a moment's pause, during which the aunt and niece looked straight into each other's eyes without a word. It was a crucial moment. Lady Charlotte was very much inclined to turn and walk out of the room again, but something in the sight of Lisa's white cheek and quivering mouth, and in the sweetness of her glistening eyes, attracted her. Her own features contracted with a nervous spasm. Then they turned to stone. She was the first to speak.

"I hardly expected this—this honor," she said, shutting the door carefully behind her, and looking at Lisa with hostile eyes. She might grieve over Lisa's defection in private, she might even fight her battles for her in public; but she could not yet bring herself to soften her voice to her, or give her a tender word. But Lisa did not expect it: she had come for that.

"Oh, Aunt Charlotte," she said, holding out her two white slender hands, "let me speak to you for a moment. I have come here only for one thing: to tell you how deeply I repent my ungrateful and undutiful conduct to you, and to beg you to forgive me. I know—I see now how badly I behaved," said Lisa, with the tears upon her cheeks, and her sweet eyes shining like rain-washed flowers in the sunshine, "and

I could not rest in peace until I had asked your forgiveness."

There was a curious change in Lady Charlotte's face. It did not exactly soften. But the lines of it seemed to relax. She stood perfectly motionless, looking into Lisa's face. Suddenly she moved her hand and touched the girl's dress.

"What does this mean?" she asked, almost fiercely. "You are not a—Sister—a nun?"

"Oh no,—I could not become one so soon," said Lisa tranquilly. "I may be a Sister of Charity one day, but not now. I will tell you all about that by and by, if you will let me. Just now, I only want one thing—your forgiveness."

She came nearer and laid her hands on her aunt's arms. She was surprised to feel that Lady Charlotte was trembling violently. Suddenly the elder woman's sternness and coldness, which had been half-assumed, wholly broke down. She took Lisa into her arms and held her there, while the slow difficult sobs surged up in her throat and made her incapable of utterance. But she kissed the soft lips that met hers, and Lisa's readier tears mingled with rare drops that quenched the fire in Lady Charlotte's proud eyes. It was Lisa who presently drew her aunt to a chair, where she sat for a time in silence, with Lisa on her knees before her and the two faces very close together. Lady Charlotte found it very difficult to recover her self-control when once she had lost it. And it was some time before Lisa could find words in which to put her story.

At last she began to murmur short broken senten-
ces in Lady Charlotte's ear, to which Lady Charlotte
listened with an odd feeling that this was not Lisa who
was speaking, but some other person whom she had
never known. Perhaps it was Lisa that she had never
known.

"I thought you were unjust to me at first .   .   .
I thought I had the right to live my own life—in my
own way. I acknowledged no control—not even
yours, although I owed you so much .   .   .
When *he* came, he spoke to me in what seemed a new
way—he spoke of poetry and love and art; and I
listened, thinking it beautiful when he said that love
superseded all law, that love was, in one's own particular sense, a fulfilling of the law. It seemed to me
that nothing else was so beautiful as that idea; and
I could not bear that worldly prudence should stand
between us and our love.".

"My poor child! You know by this time how little worthy he was of such a love," Lady Charlotte
found words to say.

"Oh yes, I know," Lisa answered sadly. "I found
it out when—when I went to him, expecting him to
be so glad to see me, so ready to protect me against
all the world. You know how he failed me—how I
suffered for my mistake."

Lady Charlotte pressed her closer, but did not
speak.

"But I wished to lead my own life still. I did not
see that all my suffering came from that initial mistake of thinking that my love, my fancies must super-

17

sede even the laws of right and wrong. I thought nothing of any allegiance to any higher power. I thought my own self my first concern. That was why I would not own that I was wrong—because I believed that I had the ordering of my own life in my own hands and might do as I chose."

Lady Charlotte held her breath. It darted through her mind that Lisa was only expressing in words what had been the law of her own life. For what had she, Charlotte Byng, ever cared, except the maintenance of a foremost place in the world and the glorification of her own family?

"I thought I would gain experience for myself," Lisa went on, "so I began to work among the poor. People seemed to think that visiting the poor makes you better. It only taught me my own intolerable need: it taught me that if my ideas of life had been true, every one of these poor people had better be dead. And then I met women who went in and out among them, tending them, comforting them, telling them that their troubles did not come by chance but by the hand of God; that the beauty of life lay in submission to God's will, and that our lives were not our own to do as we like with; but meant to be offered up to God. That is what I learned; and it seemed to me as if the world were made new."

"A saint may feel like that," said Lady Charlotte abruptly: "not an ordinary woman of flesh and blood like me."

"I think I am an ordinary woman of flesh and blood," said Lisa, with a soft happy laugh,—how long it was since Lady Charlotte had heard her laugh like that!—"and I believe my will is almost as strong as yours, Aunt Charlotte—"

"Quite as strong, my dear!"

"And yet I have found the highest wisdom and the greatest happiness in—submission."

"You mean to have no will of your own then, for the future?"

"Oh yes, indeed, I do! It is not broken, but it is learning how to bend—that is all."

"Lisa, Lisa, this is all very well, but do you mean to tell me that you are going to give up an independent life of your own—enter a Sisterhood, or some such institution, and spend the rest of your days among gossiping women and wretched ungrateful poor?"

"I hope we shall not gossip," said Lisa sweetly, "and I don't think my poor people will be ungrateful. But I am a long way off from the consummation you speak of with such dislike, dear Aunt Charlotte. I am only a probationer at St. Stephen's—," mentioning the headquarters of a celebrated English Sisterhood, devoted to mission-work among the very poor—, "and it will take me seven years to go through the varying degrees of probation. So there will be plenty of time for me to change my mind."

"I am very glad to hear it," said Lady Charlotte. Then she held her niece's face from her for a moment and looked at it intently. "You are pale and thin," she said, "but I think you look happier than when I saw you last. Oh, Lisa, how could you leave us?"

"Will you not forgive me, Aunt Charlotte?"

"Of course, I do, child; but—won't you come back to us again?"

Lisa shook her head silently.

"Ah, that is just where it is. You are as obstinate as ever, Lisa."

"I hope—I hope not. But you have a right to command," said Lisa, hiding her face. "I said to myself that I would do anything to make amends. I had found my vocation, I thought; but if you tell me to give it up, I will."

"No," said Lady Charlotte, with her old decisive energy. "That wouldn't be fair. I have lost you through my own hardness, my own anger with you when you left Brook Street. I have no right to ask you anything; besides, I know too well that you would not be as happy with me as you are now. If ever you want to come home, Lisa, remember that it is always open to you; but if not—for God's sake, go on your own way, do your own work, and be happy."

Lisa thanked her with a kiss, and for a few minutes they held each other's hands in silence.

"And Esther? How is Esther?" Lady Charlotte asked at length. Lisa knew that the question meant concession—to a certain extent.

"She is well. She is working very hard, and sometimes looking tired and sad."

"She would be sorry to lose your companionship."

"Yes, poor Esther! She is very much alone in the world. I wish you would see something of her."

"I?" said Lady Charlotte, recoiling. "When I think of all the harm she brought upon us—"

"Not consciously—not knowingly. No one could be more sorry than she has been. She wished me to say so to you: she dared not approach you herself."

"She would dare still less if she knew what that man has been doing!" cried Lady Charlotte, carried further than she meant to go by the force of her passion. Lisa turned a little pale, but looked up quickly and bravely.

"What has he been doing?" she said. "Tell me."

And Lady Charlotte told her, in hurried but scathing words, laying full stress on the baseness of his conduct, the cruelty of his insinuations, the treachery to herself of which he had been guilty. "I can never be glad enough that the book was sent to me to read," she said. "Of course it was one of the most extraordinary of coincidences; but it happened in the simplest way. Dorian telephoned to his clerk in the next room, 'Send MS. No. 23,941 to Lady Charlotte Byng.' The clerk took down the order and handed it to his subordinate, who read the last figure as a nought instead of a one, and therefore sent me the manuscript immediately preceding the one that I ought to have received."

"What did you do, Aunt Charlotte?"

"I made Mr. Ellison abandon the idea. He has given me a written confession of his villainy, and he knows that if he publishes that book, I shall put his confession into print and give it to the world as well. That will effectually deter him, I think."

"I wonder you were able—," Lisa began, hesitatingly; and she did not like the ring of her aunt's laughter, as Lady Charlotte replied:

"Able! I stood over him with a pistol, and threatened to shoot him if he refused to write what I dictated. And I would have done it, too!"

The look of grim determination on the dark handsome face was one which Lisa had seen before. She knew its force, and shuddered at the thought of what might have been.

"He yielded like a coward, as he is," said her aunt contemptuously. "He cried like a child—he groveled on the ground—he begged me not to expose him before the world. Here, read his confession: you see I have not let him spare himself."

Lisa drew a long breath: her eyes filled with tears as she looked at the scrawled shameful words.

"He has had his punishment—in this," she said, slowly.

"I left him in doubt as to whether I would not publish it still. He had behaved so scandalously that I thought it good for him to suffer a little more. I gave him to understand that I should at any rate write to the papers and warn other people against him."

"But you do not mean to do so, Aunt Charlotte?"

"Well—no, it would be a little too bad, perhaps. But I let him think I would do it; and I left him on the floor—in an agony of fear."

"Oh, Aunt Charlotte, it was cruel! I cannot bear it! You must relieve him from that fear: it is enough to weigh a man down to hell!"

"You don't care for him now, do you?" demanded
Lady Charlotte, sharply and suspiciously.

"No, not at all in that way. But I am sorry for him.
I know there was—once—some good in his nature:
I am sure of that. The worst way to treat him would
be to turn every one's hand against him—to make
him feel himself an outcast, a criminal. Oh, Aunt
Charlotte, be merciful! You have made him humble
himself to the dust before you. Now let him go
free."

"Do you plead for him, Lisa, after the way he in-
sulted and injured you?"

"All the more because of that. I could not bear to
think that my wrongs, such as they were, had sunk
him deeper. It would be a bitter grief to me. Have
pity on him, Aunt Charlotte—as we trust that God
will have pity upon us!"

"Child, what do you want me to do?" said Lady
Charlotte, not unmoved by this appeal made to her
while she still felt the warmth of Lisa's affection about
her heart. "I punished him, I think; and he deserved
it; but now—a little fear will do him no harm, and
I can't consent to give up this paper, even to you."

"Why not?" said Lisa calmly. "The good of it has
been accomplished, if ever there was good. As you
say, he has been punished, and I am sure that he has
suffered. Let him burn the manuscript and any other
papers of the kind in your presence, and then do you
in turn destroy this paper, and give him another
chance."

"I will never go near him again."

"Let me do-it," said Lisa quietly. "I will write to him, or see him, and let him know that we forgive his wrong-doing. Dearest Aunt Charlotte, how can we ask for forgiveness, if we do not forgive the trespasses of those who sin against us?"

"My dear child," said Lady Charlotte, with great gentleness, "I promise you I will never use this paper, unless he obliges me to do it by publishing libels on our family. For all our sakes, I must reserve that power in my hands. But I'll do nothing else against him—he is safe as far as I am concerned. If it would make you any happier, you can let him know I am not" —with a tender smile—"afraid of your seeing him now."

It was as much as Lisa could expect, and she submitted to a change of subject, and to being taken into the drawing-room where Mr. Byng nearly dropped his favorite orchid at the very sight of her.

They made much of her: they petted and caressed her, but they could not keep her long. She had promised to be back in London by seven o'clock, and she had to leave them very soon in order to keep her word. But she said that she should come to them again very soon, and stay for a long, long holiday.

In the Sisterhood to which she was attached, she was allowed a good deal of freedom; and no one even asked whither she was bound when she set out soon after breakfast next morning for a certain house in Kensington. She had set her heart upon going to Arthur Ellison herself, and carrying him the message of mercy that her Aunt had given to her. She pleased herself with the thought of his relief; and she felt a great desire to tell him of her happiness in her new life, and her utter forgetfulness of the past.

Judging by what she knew of his character, she felt sure that he must have suffered an agony of shame and terror, when Lady Charlotte threatened to make his conduct known; and her very knowledge of his weakness made her more inclined to pity—such pity as an angel might feel for the woes and sins of men.

She reached the house, and was struck by a little air of confusion about it. Some ragged children hovered near. A policeman stood at the area-gate: two or three rough-looking men were lingering in the hall, and the front-door stood wide open. Lisa approached timidly, and, seeing a woman who looked like a landlady, asked if she could speak to Mr. Ellison.

"Lord love you, Sister! Don't you know?" said Mrs. Jevons effusively. "Why it's been in all the papers, yesterday and to-day; but of course, you Sisters don't read newspapers, do you? Poor Mr. Ellison! As nice a gentleman as ever lived—but too much given to sleeping-drafts—took an overdose of chloral night before last, Sister, and the jury's bringing of it as 'Death by misadventure.'"

Lady Charlotte's message of mercy had come too late.

CHAPTER XX.

NEW DEPARTURES.

It has been truly said that greatest virtues sometimes have their root in faults; and that noble deeds
and saintly lives may spring out of the memory of a
secret unsuspected sin.

Lady Charlotte Byng had not perhaps the makings
of a saint in her; but she was a woman of nobler impulses than her undisciplined temper would have led
one to suspect; and the news of Arthur Ellison's
death gave her a very great shock. "God forgive
me!" she had said when first she heard of it, "did I
drive him to that?" And for many days she wore the
air of one who grieved sorely, and it was only through
Lisa's words of hope and comfort that she won her
way back to peace. She was a gentler, more pliable
woman for the rest of her life, through the memory
of the man, erring though he was, whom she thought
that she had driven to his death.

Lisa, however, never credited the rumor that he had
committed suicide. It was found that his·heart was
weak, and that a comparatively small overdose of
chloral might have produced fatal effects. He had
been in the habit of taking it for many months and it
was easy to imagine that he had unintentionally swal-
lowed more than he intended to take. There was the
letter just begun upon his desk—"Dear Esther" at

its head—to show that he had meant to write a letter to his cousin. On the other hand Mrs. Jevons declared that he had seemed greatly distressed ever since the visit of Lady Charlotte Byng, and there was some talk of calling her as a witness, but to Lady Charlotte's great relief it was not deemed necessary that she should appear.

Mr. Dorian had his own ideas concerning Arthur Ellison's death however, and as he severed his connection with the publishing trade shortly afterwards he had no hesitation in stating his belief that Lady Charlotte had goaded him to suicide.

The heap of ashes in the grate which showed that he had been burning papers excited a good deal of interest; and one of the jurymen advanced a theory that the young man had written a novel which the publishers had rejected, and that he had therefore taken his own life in a moment of depression. This theory was very generally accepted. Even Esther never knew the truth. Arthur's confession was consigned to the flames by Lady Charlotte as soon as she heard of his death; and she bound Mr. Byng and Lisa by solemn promises never to reveal the manner in which he had · abused his trust.

Lady Charlotte was not a woman to do anything by halves.

One day when Esther had been working hard and was feeling unusually dispirited she came home to find Lisa's aunt in full possession of her little sitting room. The shabby room seemed transfigured by her presence. Lady Charlotte might mourn for her misdoings in her heart, but her attire was as gorgeous as ever. An Indian cashmere glowed on the back of Esther's rocking chair: a satin cloak lined with silver fox had been thrown upon the table; and Lady Charlotte's velvet skirts trailed in all their splendor over the chintz covered sofa, while the feathers in her bonnet nodded with more majestic effect than if she had worn a crown. Esther in her black frock and crape trimmed hat, with the tired foot and the wearily grieving face, crept slowly upstairs to her room and stood amazed at the sight she saw. Looking at her Lady Charlotte was rather thankful to feel that at any rate she did not know the story of her cousin Arthur's last day on earth. But probably she remembered all his long conflict with the Byng family, and was distressed by the sight of Lady Charlotte. Even Lady Charlotte herself acknowledged that this would be very rational.

She got up and came over to the door where Esther still stood, holding out her hands in a very kindly manner. "My dear," she said, "I've come to ask you to forgive me."

Esther could only gasp out "Lady Charlotte!" and say no more.

"You may well be astonished," said Lady Charlotte, kissing her with decision. "I've not asked anybody's pardon for more years than I quite like to count. But Lisa has brought me to a better mind, my dear, by asking mine. I feel as if I owed an apology to everyone in the world after that."

But seeing that Esther still could not speak, she adopted a softer tone.

"And my dear," she said, "I want to tell you that I am very sorry for your cousin's death." She found some difficulty in going on, and cleared her throat rather loudly, but seeing Esther's eyes fixed upon her as if in doubt, she made a valiant effort to overcome her pride. "I think I was perhaps hard upon him once or twice. There's no knowing; many a man mends as he grows older, and I was sorry to hear that he was dead." It was poor comfort but it was all she had to give.

"You saw him that last day," said Esther, rather hoarsely. "He was in trouble, they said—"

"Only about the rejection of a manuscript by Mr. Dorian, my dear. I can assure you of that. I called to see him on a business matter, and we discussed the book a little. That was all."

"He may not have been very good, very worthy," said Esther with a little sob, "but he was the only relation I had in the world, and now—now—"

"Now you are all alone. But you needn't be always alone," said Lady Charlotte, drawing her to the sofa and making her sit down beside her. "You will marry."

"No," said Esther, shortly and decisively.

"My dear, Justin Thorold has come home."

Esther said nothing but colored to the roots of her hair.

"And he's as mad after you as ever," quoth Lady Charlotte.

Esther made a movement as if to go, but Lady Charlotte detained her.

"He is very lonely and miserable in that old house of Hurst, and I believe he'll lose his career completely, unless some good woman gets hold of him and makes him settle down and do his work. Esther, I have come here to ask if you will be that woman. Do you remember you said once that you would not marry him unless I asked you to do it, or something of that sort? Well now I ask you, and I beg your pardon, my dear, for all the unkind things I said to you, although I think you laid yourself open to them, you know, by being such a little fool as to let your cousin lead you into any sort of deception. Well, well, we've done with that now have we not? I always liked you, Esther, and was sorry when we fell out. But now that Justin has come home what do you say?"

"Can I answer anybody but Mr. Thorold himself?" asked Esther.

"That's answer enough to my thinking. We women understand each other. He shall have his opportunity, and I hope you won't keep him waiting, my dear. Kiss me, and say that you bear no malice."

"I am very glad to be friends with you, Lady Charlotte."

"Yes, and Esther"—Lady Charlotte's voice quivered a little, as Esther had never heard it quiver before, "you will not find me, I hope, so hard to deal with as I have been in days gone by. You know you will have to put up with a good bit of my company if you come to Hurst, and as Westhills will be Justin's one day, you will be forced to spend part of your time there with me. I want to tell you that I think I am not quite the same. I have had a lesson—a hard lesson, and I shall perhaps be the better for it by and by. I want you to be to me, Esther, all that I ever hoped of Lisa, when she was a child at my knee and we had not begun to chafe one another. Perhaps I shall make a better kinswoman to you and to your children than I did to her."

"Lisa loves you," said Esther, impulsively putting her arm round the stately neck, "and I love you too."

"God bless you, my dear!" said Lady Charlotte, and there was a tear in her eye as she returned the kiss.

"Now," she added, "you've just time to change your dress, and be carried off to Brook Street before dinner. We've come up to London for a little while, you know. Run away and make haste; there are one or two people coming to dine, so we mustn't be late."

"But, Lady Charlotte, I have no dress that's suitable for a dinner party. Besides—I am not going out—"

"Nonsense, it's not a dinner party, and any dress will do. Make haste, my dear; I told James to call for me at half-past six, and I daresay he is waiting now."

Esther disappeared with some misgivings into her bed room, and came back in a thin black gauze over silk at which Lady Charlotte looked with critical dissatisfaction. "Oh, yes, it's good enough," she said, as Esther expressed a doubt of its suitability, "but it doesn't suit, you know. Black's not your color."

"But I am in mourning," said Esther.

Lady Charlotte stopped short. "I beg your pardon, dear," she said so humbly and quietly that Esther was amazed.

But by the time they reached the drawing-room at Brook Street Esther's cheeks were aglow with the old scarlet flame that used to make her beautiful, and the lack of color in her costume was remedied by the glow of her face and eyes. At first she saw nothing; the room was in a haze, but she heard Mr. Byng's voice speaking kindly to her, and she felt her hand shaken by two or three people in succession. And when at last she could look up, she saw that she had been placed in a low chair in an alcove, rather away from the little group that surrounded Lady Charlotte at the fireplace, and that Justin Thorold was standing close beside her, and bending down to speak.

"I am to take you in to dinner, if you will let me," he said. "But not yet—tell me just whether you object, whether you would rather Captain Gethen took you in? It has been left, I think, between him and me."

"I would rather not go in with Captain Gethen," she said, a little smile hovering about the corners of her lips.

"Then may I believe also that—some day—you will forgive me for my want of faith in you?"

Her voice was low, but it seemed to Esther as if Lady Charlotte were observing her, and as if her answer would be unavoidably distinct. Dinner was announced at that moment and Mr. Thorold offered her his arm; but his face wore so unmistakable a look of disappointment that she could not help murmuring as they crossed the hall together:

"I forgave you long ago."

His face changed completely, and for a moment he placed his hand over the fingers that lay so lightly upon the other arm. "You make me happy when you say so; will you not some day make me happier still?"

Surely there was never an odder time or place for a proposal of marriage; yet it was made and accepted in the course of that transit from drawing to dining room. And both Esther and Justin thought that they had never been at such a delightful dinner-party before; although on examination it was proved conclusively at a later date that neither of them knew who had been present, what they had eaten or drunk, or what anybody had talked about.

In due time Hurst was gladdened by the arrival of a mistress, and few persons who had the privilege of being received there by that brilliant and fascinating little lady would have recognized in her the care-worn, somber-hued teacher who had plodded homeward one wintry night to find Lady Charlotte awaiting her in her shabby sitting-room.

"I was a veritable fairy godmother, my dear," that lady sometimes says to her. "I transformed you into a fairy princess all at once, and I hope you are grateful to me."

But although she laughs and jests about the matter, Lady Charlotte's eyes have a trick of growing sober when she speaks of Esther's marriage and sometimes she sighs a little unawares. And Esther is sorry for her, believing in her heart that she is sad for want of Lisa, who nevertheless has most certainly found her vocation, and is far happier than she would have been in Lady Charlotte's company at Westhills. But Esther, tenderly as Lady Charlotte regards her, is not in all the secrets of the house. She would not be surprised indeed to hear that Lisa still murmurs instinctively at her prayers the name of the man she loved; but she would be amazed beyond expression if she were told that Lady Charlotte has mourned for no one in her life as she still mourns for Arthur Ellison.

THE END.